"You're going t...

But Lara couldn't bring herself to do that. Her glance fell to the little ball of fur, now upright and clinging to Cole's shirt like an infant. "Isn't there a kennel or something at the ranger station?"

"That's not the problem. I'm not going to be around for a few days, and he can't be left alone. He needs to be kept warm and fed, and he needs to get this—" Cole reached into his coat pocket and pulled out a small bottle "—so he doesn't get an infection."

Without thinking, Lara took the bottle. The cub's little ears were twitching. So was his nose. She didn't want it to be cute.

"Come on," Cole coaxed. "You women are supposed to have instincts about these things...."

"About baby-sitting bears? I don't think so."

Dear Reader,

Welcome to Silhouette **Special Edition**... welcome to romance. Each month, Silhouette **Special Edition** publishes six novels with you in mind—stories of love and life, tales that you can identify with—romance with that little "something special" added in.

This month, Silhouette **Special Edition** has some wonderful stories in store for you, including the finale of the poignant series SONNY'S GIRLS, *Longer Than...* by Erica Spindler. I hope you enjoy this tender tale! *Annie in the Morning* by Curtiss Ann Matlock is also waiting for you in September. This warm, gentle, emotional story is chock-full of characters that you may well be seeing in future books....

Rounding out September are winning tales by more of your favorite writers: Jo Ann Algermissen, Christine Flynn, Lisa Jackson and Jennifer Mikels! A good time will be had by all!

In each Silhouette **Special Edition** novel, we're dedicated to bringing you the romances that you dream about—the type of stories that delight as well as bring a tear to the eye. And that's what Silhouette **Special Edition** is all about—special books by special authors for special readers!

I hope you enjoy this book and all of the stories to come.

Sincerely,

Tara Gavin
Senior Editor

CHRISTINE FLYNN
The Healing Touch

Silhouette Special Edition

Published by Silhouette Books New York

America's Publisher of Contemporary Romance

To Doug Stockdale of the U.S. Forest Service,
Tongass National Forest,
with thanks for all the information

SILHOUETTE BOOKS
300 East 42nd St., New York, N.Y. 10017

THE HEALING TOUCH

ISBN: 0-373-09693-3

First Silhouette Books printing September 1991

Printed in the U.S.A.

Books by Christine Flynn

Silhouette Special Edition

Remember the Dreams #254
Silence the Shadows #465
Renegade #566
Walk upon the Wind #612
Out of the Mist #657
The Healing Touch #693

Silhouette Desire

When Snow Meets Fire #254
The Myth and the Magic #296
A Place to Belong #352
Meet Me at Midnight #377

Silhouette Romance

Stolen Promise #435
Courtney's Conspiracy #623

CHRISTINE FLYNN

is formerly from Oregon and currently resides in the Southwest with her husband, teenage daughter and two very spoiled dogs.

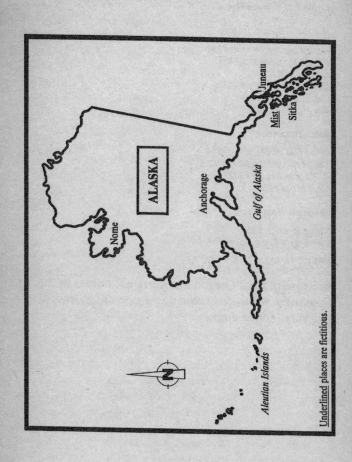

Underlined places are fictitious.

Prologue

The scream sounded human.

Lara Grant slammed on the pickup truck's brakes, sucking in her breath as her body lurched forward. An instant later, she'd bounced back in the seat, the truck at a full stop. Five long seconds passed before she dared breathe. When she did, all she could hear was the heavy beat of her heart.

Her hand shaking, she pushed her dark, wildly-curly hair from her face. Visibility was so poor that she'd barely been crawling along the muddy and rutted logging road. Even going as slow as she had, the sudden stop was jarring. She peered at the windshield. The wind-driven rain washed over the window, frustrating the efforts of her wipers. She couldn't see a thing.

The storm had come out of nowhere.

So had whatever it was that she'd hit.

Urgency countered dread as she fumbled with the seat belt. The unfamiliar clasp gave way on the third try and she slid from the cab of the pickup. Within seconds, her hair was plastered to her head. Water ran down her face, its chill a startling contrast to the heater blasting in the cab. Clutching her parka at her throat, she blinked against the torrential rain.

The forest surrounded her. Dark and dense, the towering trees further dimmed the storm-caused twilight. Patches of snow clung to the more sheltered areas, the scallop-edged drifts slowly diminishing as angry gray clouds opened with vengeance. Rain came in sheets, the wind intent on driving it straight through whatever stood in its path.

Propelled by muffled cries coming from behind her, Lara moved toward the bed of the truck. She hadn't seen what she'd hit. All she'd been able to see through the sudden deluge were glimpses of the narrow logging road parting the trees.

The sobs sounded like those of a child.

Her heart pounded faster, her frantic glance sweeping the tangled alder thickets underpinning the forest. Her chest seemed to constrict and a fog of panic restricted her breathing. The awful sensations bore down on her, too familiar to be ignored. She tried to fight past the encroaching fear; to concentrate on what she was looking for. The sensations only intensified, allowing subconscious to overcome will. Memories were suddenly there; terrifying reminders of another dark, rainy night. A night she'd spent eighteen months trying desperately to forget.

A rushing sound filled her ears. She tried not to hear it, but the sound grew more distinct, fed as it was by flashes of nightmare memory. She knew she was alone in a forest; that the deafening roar was only the wind. But that logic didn't keep her from hearing the dissonance of car wheels on rain-slicked pavement, or the incessant honk of horns as brakes squealed and twisting metal groaned. Covering her ears with her hands to block out noises she knew weren't really there, she met a moment of blessed silence before the only sound remaining was of a single horn, stuck and blaring as a siren screamed in the distance.

"No." The word was half sob, half whisper.

"No!" she repeated, louder this time, and the sound of her own voice brought her back as the thunder rolled overhead.

She opened her eyes, her lashes wet with raindrops. Slowly she lowered her hands to clutch her middle. There was no traffic. No ambulance. Only the gray-green forest and the steady beat of rain filling the puddles at her feet—and a pain-filled cry coming from somewhere in front of her.

The sound went straight to her heart.

Lara's eyes darted in the direction of the sound. Darkness was quickly gathering, making it even more difficult to distinguish what might be out among the shades of rainblurred green and brown. She continued on anyway, oblivious to the mud sucking at her tennis shoes as she frantically searched for the source of the cries. It was so hard to see; harder still to bear hearing the distress in the broken whimpers. There was nothing on either side of the road—except for a ball of brown and bedraggled fur laying in the thicket behind the truck. She didn't realize what it was until it moved.

The cub couldn't have weighed more than ten pounds. Looking more like the teddy bear she'd slept with until she was twelve than the grizzly it would become, the little animal tried to drag itself into the thicket. She hurried toward it, stopping short when she hunched down to touch the gleaming wet fur. The cub's foreleg hung at an awkward angle and the brown eyes that blinked back at her filled her with its pain.

It didn't occur to Lara to be relieved that the cries hadn't been those of a child. Her only thought was that she needed to get help. Help had come too late before.

Chapter One

The pounding didn't register at first. Cole MacInnes sat at his desk, his boot-clad feet propped on its scarred surface while he cleaned his rifle. The logs in the wood stove snapped and hissed, the sounds blending with the rain and the static on the CB's emergency channel. He'd left the channel open and the volume up. Just in case.

Evenings like this were a crapshoot. If the men working the lumbering operation along Little Dagger ridge had made it back to their camp before the storm hit, and if the fishermen could ride out the waves with parachutes they attached to their trawlers for these "joy rides," then the citizens of Mist might weather nature's latest temper tantrum without loss or injury. Williwaws, the sudden, violent storms that tormented coastal Alaska every spring, were a familiar threat to her residents. Getting caught in one was no picnic. Trying to help someone caught in one was no fun, either.

Satisfied that the barrel was well-oiled, Cole slid the stock of his rifle back in place with a solid click and tossed the cleaning equipment into a drawer of the low, gray metal file cabinets behind his desk. The cabinets housed the thick United States Forest Service studies and projects he tried to keep up with, and a copy of the regulations he tended to ignore. Right now he was in the middle of ignoring one of those required duties: the small mountain of paperwork teetering on the corner of his desk. The endless reports he was supposed to prepare on the thousands of acres in his section of the Alaskan panhandle was the one part of his job as a district ranger that he could do without. The rest, the relative solitude, the freedom, he wouldn't trade for his soul.

The pounding came again.

Cole cocked his head toward the cabin's door, trying to separate the sounds of the storm. As he did, he set his rifle on the cabinet and lowered his feet to the floor.

With the wind battering the walls and driving the rain in blasts against the shuttered windows, the dull thuds seemed like part of the storm. Almost. The three short raps he heard now had a distinct quality about them. A banging tree branch wouldn't sound so urgent.

He crossed the room in three strides, jerking the door open as soon as his hand hit the handle.

Cole ignored the chill and the rain the wind brought in. A woman stared up at him, looking cold and frightened and reminding him vaguely of a nearly drowned muskrat. Her dark hair was plastered to her head and her slender shoulders were hunched over a green plaid blanket. Eyes the color of a summer sky and clouded with fear beseeched him.

"Please," he heard her plea, her voice muted by the roar of the wind. "I hit it. I didn't mean to. It's bleeding and I can't stop it. And its leg..." Her glance jerked from the middle of Cole's flannel shirt to the top of his head a foot above hers, then fell anxiously to the bundle in her arms. "It ran in front of the truck. The storm came up so fast." She shook her head, looking as if she were desperately searching for the words she needed to make him understand. "All of a sudden . . . I just couldn't see."

A hearty gust of wind blew the rain over his boots and wetted the plank floor. As her last words had been spoken, Cole's hand closed around her upper arm, its slenderness evident to him even through her quilted parka. Now, he pulled her inside.

The storm was closed out with the bang of the door.

Beneath his hand he felt her jump. Whether at the slam of the latch or his abruptness, he wasn't sure. It didn't matter. He released his grip on her arm, more concerned at the moment with what she held than with her. "What did you hit?"

Very quietly she said, "A little bear."

A frown slashing his dark features, he stepped closer and lifted a corner of the blanket.

The cub's eyes were open, its nose twitching at the new smells. The response wasn't nearly as strong as it should have been. When Cole pulled the blanket back farther, exposing its injuries, he could see why.

"Can you do something for it? I didn't know where else to go. I've only been in Mist for a couple of days, but I'd heard there was a veterinarian here at the Ranger station."

Cole figured she must have been talking to Rosie. Rosie exaggerated everything. This time she'd overblown his credentials.

"I'm not a vet, but we don't have time to worry about that." Cautiously, so not to startle it, he raised his big hand toward the tiny cub and pushed back more of the blanket. The fabric was saturated, and not only with water. "Looks like he's lost a lot of blood. How long ago did this happen?"

"I don't know exactly. Ten or fifteen minutes, I guess." She drew a trembling breath. "Can you help it?"

Cole looked from the cub to the odd desperation in the woman's eyes. He did what he could when he found a wounded animal or when one was brought to him, but his methods were mostly an unorthodox combination of old native remedies learned from a Tlinget elder and a lifetime of sewing on his own buttons. He didn't bother to explain that now. The cub looked like it was in shock. The woman holding it didn't look much better.

She was obviously shaken, and her face—a face far more delicate than he'd become accustomed to seeing—was as pale as a snowbank.

She must belong to Bud's summer crew, he thought, wondering if her initiation to the wilderness might not be a little more than she'd been prepared to handle. It was certainly more than she was dressed for. Wearing canvas sneakers, new denims and an impractical and now bloodstained white parka, she had *cheechako* written all over her. He'd seen them show up in less practical outfits, but he'd never known one to do something as stupid as she'd just done. Obviously she hadn't paid attention to her orientation.

He decided not to mention her foolishness now. Other tasks needed tending first.

"Why don't you go dry out by the fire? There's coffee on the stove back there. If you want something stronger, there's a bottle of whiskey in the cabinet above the sink."

He nodded toward the short hall that led to his living quarters, then turned, thinking he'd take the cub. Another glance at her pale features made him change his mind. It also made him retract his offer. She looked confused, as if she'd been thinking of something else as he'd spoken and was now trying to understand what he'd said.

Alcohol, he thought, might not be a very good idea. From the looks of her, he'd better keep her where he could keep an eye on her. "On second thought, you'd better come with me."

The confusion vanished. "No. No, I can't." Suddenly looking anxious to be away from both him and the injured animal, she held the cub toward him. "Really. I have to...I need to go."

She clutched a key ring. Cole noticed it when the blanket fell away from her hand.

"No, you don't," he told her, ignoring her attempt to have him relieve her of the bundle. "Take the cub back to the kitchen. I've got to get a few things together to fix him up with. You can't leave right now, anyway."

Rather than waste time discussing it, he snagged the keys dangling from her fingers. The woman obviously knew nothing about Alaskan storms. "It's still blowing like hell out there. You said yourself that you couldn't see and I don't want to have to stitch you up, too, in case the next thing you hit is a tree. I don't think you'd want it, either. I've been told that my work isn't all that neat."

He wouldn't have blamed her if she'd been annoyed with his manner. But she didn't seem at all irritated. Not even mildly annoyed. When she met his eyes, he almost wished she would have been. He wasn't comfortable with what he saw lurking in there. The vaguely haunted look—and naked vulnerability.

His long shadow preceded him down the hall, his footsteps solid and heavy. Moments later, her less decisive ones followed.

A yellow Formica table with three chrome chairs sat in the middle of a small, functional kitchen. The Forest Service

provided the essentials and though there wasn't much beyond basic creature comforts, it was as much as Cole had
ever owned. Right now, he just wished the lighting were a
little better.

After spreading a clean towel on the table, he left the
woman to settle the cub on it while he gathered supplies
from the storage room. The ranger station was the closest
thing to a first-aid facility in the area and, though the supplies were intended for people, Cole had found that they
usually worked for the occasional injured animal, too.

He returned to find the woman standing by the table, her
hand on the cub's chest and her thoughts seeming miles
away. He handed her a towel.

"To dry your hair," he explained when she frowned at it.
"You might want to take your coat off, too. It's soaked."

"Thank you," was all she said and stepped back to set the
towel on the counter behind her. The faint rasp of her zipper as she undid her parka was joined a moment later by the
sound of her quickly drawn breath. The cub's blood had
soaked through the blanket. Seeing it on her jacket, she went
stock-still.

Cole swore to himself. She already looked as if she were
hanging on to her composure with nothing more than the
blind courage that had brought her this far. The sight of the
bright red blotch threatened to snap that tenuous hold.

"Are you all right?"

She wore a pink turtleneck sweater over a pair of jeans
that lovingly molded the sweetest little backside he'd ever
seen. Forcing his attention upward, he watched her slender
shoulders rise with her deeply drawn breath. Her quiet,
"I'm okay," sounded more like assurance for herself than
for him, but he chose to take her at her word. He could only
take care of one problem at a time. Given the choice, he'd
rather work on the animal.

Pushing a hypodermic needle through the rubber top of an ampoule, he filled a slender syringe with anesthetic. Even as he did, he was aware of the woman's movements as she hung her parka over the back of the nearest chair and sank onto its seat. She reached across the table and touched the cub's uninjured forepaw, stroking it with her finger.

"I didn't realize bears were ever this small. How old do you think it is?"

The animal's head fit in his palm. When it had been born, almost its entire body would have fit there. "I'd say about two months. They're about that when their mothers first take them from their den. This time of year we see lots of them this size."

She looked away when he injected the anesthetic, but she didn't let go of the cub's paw. Cole wondered if she even realized what she was doing: if she were trying to comfort the animal—or seeking comfort for herself.

Her head was bent. But not so much that he couldn't study her while he waited for the medication to take hold. The brilliant blue of her eyes was hidden for the moment by crescents of long silky lashes. Her nose was pert, her bones delicate and her mouth, sensual and full. Even looking as if she'd done battle with a tidal wave, she was an attractive woman. If pressed, he'd put her somewhere around thirty and hope he hadn't insulted her if she were actually younger. God knew he was no judge when it came to anything about women. But something about her eyes made her seem older than the college kids who came for the summer jobs. Nearing thirty-seven himself, he found that he became more aware of that age gap with every passing year.

She lifted her head, releasing a calming breath as he'd seen her do a few moments ago. With her free hand, she pushed back her damp and bedraggled hair—hair the color of mink and showing a heavy hint of curl now that the heat in the room was beginning to dry it—and looked up to meet his scrutiny. As she did, Cole noticed a scar above her left eyebrow. Pale and silvery against her fair skin, the scar angled toward her temple and up into her hairline.

Her eyes cautiously held his. She seemed to know what had drawn his attention. A little self-consciously, she fluffed her bangs to cover her forehead and looked back to their furry patient.

Cole's glance followed. Each blink of the tiny animal's eyes seemed slower than the one before. The last time its lids lowered, they stayed that way.

"Is he okay?" she asked.

"The anesthetic's working. Now that he's out, I can see how bad he is."

He didn't look at her again. He didn't need to to know that she hadn't found any reassurance in his words. What he did want to do was keep her talking while he worked on the cub. As long as she was talking, he'd know she hadn't passed out. "What's your name?"

"Lara. Grant," she added as an afterthought.

The name sounded vaguely familiar. "You're working for Bud at the ice house?"

"The ice house?"

The way she repeated the phrase made it sound as if she'd never heard of the place.

"Great" Cole muttered to himself, wondering if she had a concussion or something as he separated fur from flesh with hands far too big to handle such a delicate limb. Everyone knew where the ice house was. The cold storage facility dominated the end of what the citizenry called "Main Street" and Main Street consisted only of a board-walk and six buildings.

"Did you hit your head?"

"My head?" she repeated, sounding confused.

"Either you're not following what I'm asking, or you've got a bigger problem than this little guy. When you hit the cub," he clarified, "did you hurt yourself? Did your head hit the wheel or the window or anything?"

She said she hadn't, but as he tossed aside a soiled swab and reached for a bottle of vile-smelling orange liquid, he told her to look at him anyway so he could see her eyes. They looked clear enough, the pupils equal and reactive, and he glanced away before he got sidetracked by the little chips of turquoise visible in the lighter iris. Accompanied by her assurance that she was uninjured, he settled for thinking her distraction was because she was still shaken from the accident. With that decided, he went back to his task—and to considering something he'd noticed earlier.

She held the cub's paw as if it were a child's hand, cradling it gently in her slender fingers. Her nails had a bit of length to them and were a shiny, pale pink. Soft. Her hands looked incredibly soft. Not like those of the few women around here. Those women had working hands, feminine in their own way, he supposed, but far from delicate. If this Lara was working at the ice house, it was certain she wasn't packing fish. With the cold and the abrasive salt water, a worker's hands were red and raw after just one shift.

The thought was unbidden. Surely it was unwanted. But he couldn't prevent the thought of her soft fingers caressing his skin, her pale pink nails pushing through his chest hair.

He cleared his throat. "You're not the new cook out at the logging camp, are you?"

"I'm not much of a cook."

He took the oblique response to mean "no." He hadn't really thought the possibility likely. The woman couldn't have been more than a fraction over five feet three inches and with her slight frame, he was hard-pressed to picture her slinging around fifty-pound sacks of potatoes and wrestling hindquarters of venison. Jack Clark's men ate every meal as if it were their last and whoever cooked for them had to have the stamina, and the disposition, of a bull. The woman gently stroking the cub's paw hardly looked capable of handling thirty hungry men. On the other hand, with those incredible blue eyes, she could well have them eating out of her pretty little palm in no time.

Refusing to let his thoughts wander any further in that direction he focused on the cub's wounds. The animal's foreleg was broken and its shoulder dislocated. The good news was that, for all the blood, the cuts weren't as deep as he'd first feared.

"I'll stitch up the gash on his shoulder first. Then, I'm going to slide his shoulder back into the socket and set his foreleg. I need you to hold the splint while I do that, then hold his foreleg to his chest while I wrap the bandage around him. Can you handle that?"

She didn't look like she wanted to, but to her credit, she did it anyway. He worked quickly, wondering as he did if she wasn't grateful for the silence his concentration imposed. The lack of conversation allowed her to give full attention to her preoccupation; the thoughts that took the life from her eyes and made him sharply aware of her distress.

She should appreciate that silence while she could. He had plenty to say to her when they were through.

He didn't know what to say at the moment, though, to relieve her of the burden of responsibility she obviously felt for injuring the cub. So he said nothing and continued patching up the animal as best he could. The cub was his concern; not the woman. His only worry was that she might get sick or faint, which was a possibility when he realigned the cub's shoulder.

Since Lara didn't hit the floor when that happened Cole figured he could stop worrying about her. The pungent smell of wet bear and antiseptic hadn't gotten to her, either. He wished he could say as much for himself and the light and disturbing scent that clung to her. It reminded him of something innocent, yet slightly wild, and every time he breathed, his body got a little tighter. It seemed to take forever to get the bandage in place.

The cub was resting in a blanket-lined box when Cole came down the hall to find Lara standing by the wood stove. The heat had nearly dried her hair and the strands had shortened to an unruly, shoulder-length mass of mink-colored waves and ringlets. He saw her push her fingers through the riotous locks, her attention on the intricately woven blanket hanging above the file cabinets. Stylized symbols of birds and animals were woven of blue and white and black. She seemed as fascinated by the designs as he was with the soft part of her mouth.

Her head snapped up at his approach. "Will he be all right?"

"Depends on how much blood he lost. If he makes it through the night, he should be. Bears are tough."

He thought she must have been holding her breath as she'd waited for his response. He saw her slender shoulders lower a little, but his words weren't the encouragement she'd sought. The pain in her eyes remained, haunting and raw and reminding him of the fear he'd seen in the animal's eyes when it knew there was no escaping whatever held it captive.

She managed the faintest of smiles, as if she were aware of what she revealed and needed to apologize for not being able to hide it. She looked a little lost, and terribly uncertain of what she should do next.

Touched by that uncertainty Cole moved closer. Her strengths seemed to outweigh her weaknesses, but at the moment she didn't look strong at all. She looked as though she needed to be held.

He didn't realize how deeply that need had touched him until his hand settled on her shoulder. Beneath his fingers, he felt her muscles tense.

Immediately his hand fell, as much in reaction to her surprise and his own. The sudden surge of empathy made him uncomfortable. The need to touch her made him even more so. Offering comfort to a distressed woman was a skill way out of his league.

The woman was gracious enough to forgive him his ineptitude.

"Thank you for taking care of it," he heard her say, her eyes avoiding his. "I wouldn't have known what to do if you hadn't been here."

"What you should have done was left it where it was."

Her head came up. "But it might have died."

"It might have," he easily agreed. "But better it, than you."

"What?"

He calmly met her incomprehension. "Don't you realize what could have happened if that cub's mother had come after you?"

Apparently she didn't. She simply stared up at him, waiting.

"A grizzly's claws are like six-inch knife blades," he told her, wanting to impress her with the danger she'd put herself in. "Didn't it occur to you that there was probably a bigger bear out there somewhere?"

Her quiet, "No" was nothing if not honest. He found her guilelessness all the more frustrating.

"Lara," he went on. Patiently, he hoped. "Next to a polar bear, an Alaska brown is the biggest carnivore in the world. A male can take down a thousand-pound moose and haul it to its cache clamped in its jaws. The only thing nastier is a female when she thinks somebody's messing with her cub. If you'd come across our patient's sow, she'd have made hamburger out of you and served you up for lunch."

It wasn't what he said that made Lara blanch. His words were alarming, to be sure, and they managed to lift some of the protective numbness she'd felt during the past hour. But it was the lack of tolerance in his tone that finally punched through the fog of remembered pain.

It sounded very much as if he'd given this speech before.

"Not every bear will attack," he was telling her. "Sometimes, one will get gracious and let you back away after giving you time for a quick review of your life. But don't ever count on one being in a forgiving mood." His gray eyes pinned hers. "And don't *ever* approach a cub. Mama can come out of nowhere. Were you carrying anything? Halt or a gun?"

From her expression he knew she didn't fully understand his question. If she didn't understand the question, then the answer was "no." Over the years, his patience with people who blundered into the wilderness without understanding it had grown unflatteringly thin.

"If you're going to wander around here, you've got to have some way to protect yourself. Spray dog repellants work. That's what Halt is. But you've got to be closer than you'll probably care to get to use it. A gun's better, if you can use one. Whatever you carry, you've got to know how to behave in their space. Let them know you're there."

The best way to do that, he told her, was to make noise as you walked. Some folks carried a can of pebbles to rattle.

Others put a bell on their belt. And in case the noises didn't work, the majority carried a gun.

The weapon was a measure of last resort. Like him, most of the people around Mist knew that unless someone's idiocy caused aggravation, the animals tended to mind their own business. Cole had a deep-seated respect for the animals' constraint. He leaned toward keeping a certain distance from others himself.

He glanced at the rifle on the file cabinets. "Do you know how to use one of those?"

Lara's focus settled with hesitation on the object he'd indicated. She'd never held a gun in her life.

He didn't seem at all surprised by her quiet, "No."

"You might want to think about learning."

Some color had returned to her cheeks. Possibly, Cole thought, from the heat of the wood stove since she was standing so close to it. Or maybe it was because his little lecture was making her angry. From the spark in her eyes and the pinch of her mouth, he tended to think it was the latter.

She seemed to have some life to her after all.

"I imagine there's a lot I'll have to learn here, Mr. . . . ."

She let her voice trail off, waiting for him to supply the introduction he'd yet to offer.

"It's just Cole."

"Cole," she repeated, thinking the hard sound of the name quite suited him. "I won't take up any more of your time. May I have my car keys now?"

Cole hesitated, listening as he did to the pitch of the wind. It still surged in unpredictable bursts, hurtling rain against the cabin and making the trees moan at its fury.

His fingers closed around the key ring in his pocket. He wished he could let her leave; that he could be spared the obligation of offering her shelter. The thought wasn't rooted in selfishness; more in self-defense. The thought of holding her had yet to leave him. But when he thought of holding her now, it had nothing to do with comfort, and everything to do with the way her soft, seductive curves would fit against his body. Even though he had no intention of indulging that little fantasy, he didn't particularly appreciate being reminded of how long he'd been without a woman.

"I'll give them to you, but I'm afraid you're stuck here. It's too dark to see out there now, even without the rain. If it decides to, the wind can hit with a blast hard enough to lift you off the ground. You might as well make yourself comfortable."

The offer was grudging at best—which was exactly how Lara accepted it. He was right, of course. Even though she didn't have all that far to go, it wouldn't be very wise to leave in the middle of such a miserable storm.

Watching him watch her, aware that he wasn't overly pleased with her or her presence, she was hard-pressed to say anything other than, "Thanks."

Thus assured that she wasn't going to do anything else foolish tonight, he withdrew her keys from his pocket. He was sure she had removed them from the ignition out of habit. It was another sign of her unfamiliarity with the area.

"You didn't need to take them out of your truck. No one's going to steal it here. Not that we're exemplary citizens," he added, because men who lived in the wild tended to make their own rules. "It's just kind of hard to steal a truck in a place where the only road you've got dead ends in a forest."

Lesson number two, Lara thought, wondering if behind those cool gray eyes he was laughing at her. Before she could decide, something hit the side of the cabin. The sound, solid and loud, caused Lara to jump and Cole to scowl. The noise came again a couple of seconds later.

After a moment, Cole seemed to recognize the sound. Looking as if he were wrestling with the inevitable, he muttered an eye-widening profanity, then glanced at Lara as if he wished he'd remembered her presence before the words had slipped out. He didn't apologize, though. He merely looked a little more disgusted and turned on his heel.

Rain gear hung next to a tan, sherpa-style jacket by the door. Snatching a yellow slicker off its wooden peg, he jammed his arms into the sleeves, flipped up its hood and jerked open the door. Wind rushed in, fluttering the papers on the desk and bringing in the smell of wet earth and rain. The papers settled down as soon as he pulled the door shut behind him.

Lara stared after him, unable to imagine what had prompted his irritation and his exit. She heard him stomp down the wooden steps and jumped again when the sharp banging reverberated three times in quick succession.

Closing her eyes, she took a deep breath and willed herself to relax. Storms always made her jumpy. They had ever since she'd been a little girl and she'd seen lightning split a tree outside her bedroom window. The unsettling effect of the storm combined with what had happened with the cub was reason enough for her to feel edgy. Add to that the fact that she seemed to be stuck, however temporarily, with this Cole person and she had enough on her mind to make her forget she even knew what "calm" felt like.

Earlier, he'd said something about coffee. And whiskey. She wondered if the offer still stood and if he'd mind if she combined the two.

The door opened and Cole was inside before she even realized that the banging had stopped.

He hesitated when he saw her staring warily at him. "Loose shutter," he muttered and hung the slicker, still dripping, back on its peg. When he turned around, she was still watching.

She didn't seem to know what to do with herself. He'd told her to make herself comfortable. What in the hell else was he supposed to do? He was lousy at this sort of thing.

"Look, you want a drink or something?"

Not when he put it that way. "No. Thank you."

"Well, I do," he muttered and decided to make it a double.

Chapter Two

Cole's long strides carried him with impatience down the short hall. Lara watched him go, wishing that she hadn't been so quick to turn down his offer of a drink. She'd wanted one, but her pride had gotten in the way. Though she could be as stubborn as sin once she made up her mind—a trait that had been pointed out often enough before she'd left California—it wasn't like her to be contrary. Obviously something about the man brought out a hidden perverse streak. That was not exactly the kind of thing she'd come here to discover about herself.

Too agitated to sit, too tired to pace, Lara settled for hugging her arms around herself and faced the unusual weaving hanging above the utilitarian file cabinets. From the kitchen, she heard the sounds of a cabinet door closing, the click of a glass against a hard surface, water running. She tried to concentrate on the sounds and on the room she was in. There wasn't much to distract her, small and basically

bare as the room was. But she'd become very good at focusing on the immediate. It was how she'd made it through
some very long, difficult months and how she now kept her
mind from wandering back to a time that no longer existed. To a life that no longer was.

Even now the tactic was working, calming the inner
trembling the memories had brought. But concentrating on
her present circumstances was disconcerting in its own way.
Pushed to the forefront of her thoughts were those of the
stranger she could hear moving around in the other room.

He was an imposing man: tall, broad shouldered, lean
hipped. The kind of man her incorrigible friend Samantha
would have called "Grade A Prime." Since Lara had been
interested in only one man for most of her life, she had never
quite developed Sam's appreciative eye. She'd met Steve
Grant her sophomore year in high school and married him
two days after college graduation. But she did suppose that
Cole was attractive—in a raw and rugged sort of way. He
was certainly a powerful-looking man. Yet, beneath the
power, hidden from most, she felt sure, was gentleness.
She'd seen it in the way he'd handled the cub. She'd felt it
in the unexpected touch of his hand to her shoulder. That
gentleness intrigued her. Not because it drew her; though,
if pressed, she would have to admit it was one of his more
redeeming qualities. It intrigued her because he didn't look
entirely comfortable with it. She had the feeling he wasn't
gentle often.

He'd cared for the cub. Yet he'd told her she should have
left the animal to fend for itself.

She shook her head at the thought. He was, she supposed, a little like the unique and oddly fascinating blanket
on the wall. Intricate, unusual, and something she clearly
didn't understand.

The thud of his boots announced his return. "The cub's doing okay."

"Okay?" she repeated, wanting to know exactly what that meant.

"He's holding his own. No better, no worse."

Relieved for that much, she quietly thanked him for telling her. Another thing she had noticed about Cole was that he didn't pull any punches. False assurances weren't his style.

When he said nothing else, just stood there holding his drink while the silence grew awkward, she motioned to the weaving. "What is that?"

Idly he swirled the amber contents in his glass. He seemed to prefer his liquor neat. "A Chilkat blanket."

That told her absolutely nothing. He must have realized that. A moment later, he added, "Native women make them. They're considered a symbol of wealth and status among the Tlingets."

"The Tlingets?"

"They're one of the native tribes in the Tongass."

He took a sip of whiskey, watching her over the rim of the glass.

Still feeling too shaky to deal with his scrutiny, Lara glanced back to the blanket. At least she didn't have to ask what the Tongass was. The enormous Tongass National Forest encompassed all but what little private and native land was left in Southeast Alaska. Tongass was synonymous with *Southeast*, which was what the people who lived there called their home. At least she knew that much about the place.

Curiosity pushed past her reticence. "Are you Tlinget?"

Wondering what ancestry his features might betray, she glanced back at him. His hair was thick and dark, a color closer to black than brown, and his skin was weathered from the elements. A certain nobility underlined the angles and planes of his face. A face too rugged to be called handsome; too arresting to be thought otherwise. Strength and purpose were revealed in his hard features. And his thoughts, like whatever secrets he held, were almost constantly concealed by his enigmatic gray eyes.

Those thoughts were never more mysterious than they were now. Challenge tightened his jaw, making his stillness all the more formidable. Lara had no idea why the challenge was there.

"I don't know. It's possible."

"You mean one of your relatives might have been?"

"You could put it that way."

"I don't understand."

For about three seconds, he stood looking at her as if she were as dense as a stone. He spent another couple of seconds considering whether or not he wanted to bother enlightening her. For some reason he couldn't begin to explain, he decided he wanted her to know.

"I have no idea what my father was," he finally said. "Or who. I doubt that my mother even knew." A good portion of whiskey disappeared in one swallow. "I don't know who her relatives were, either. She didn't seem to have any. At least none the welfare people could find when she took off. So like I said, it's possible."

The edge had left his tone, replaced with indulgence. As remarkable as that was to Lara, considering what he'd revealed, even more so was what he hadn't quite said. His mother had abandoned him. He'd tossed the telling phrase off as if it were of no consequence, and maybe it wasn't to him now, but Lara couldn't help thinking how devastating it must have been at the time.

It was difficult to picture the imposing man in front of her as a child. Still, she couldn't help wondering what he had been like then, and how old he was when his mother had left. She didn't ask, though. She'd had no idea her innocent interest would edge into something so personal. What she wanted to do was apologize for intruding, but a warning had flashed in Cole's eyes. He'd accepted the circumstances under which he'd been born and raised. He didn't try to hide them. He certainly didn't want anyone to apologize for blundering onto them.

She was embarrassed. Cole didn't know why the phenomenon intrigued him, but as he watched her eyes shy from his, he found himself wishing he hadn't baited her as he had.

"I guess the blanket isn't an heirloom, then," she said, sounding uncomfortable with the silence. "Still, it seems like something rather special."

Actually it *was* an heirloom; something usually passed down from father to son. "It was a gift," he told her, feeling he should offer that much. After all, she didn't know she was stepping on sensitive borders. "From a friend."

"I've never seen anything like it. It's beautiful."

She'd thanked him for what little he'd allowed with a soft smile. That smile, gentle as it was, carried the impact of a charging moose. Meeting her haunted blue eyes, Cole felt his gut twist.

Physical distance suddenly seemed mandatory. Doing something with his hands sounded like a good idea, too.

He picked up a green folder from the other side of the desk, effectively adding six feet of space between them. "You never did say what you were doing in Mist."

Cole really didn't care what she was doing here. He just wanted to change the subject. It was her interest in that blanket that had first made him so defensive. It usually took a lot to make him feel that way. But her questions made him feel exposed, far more so than telling her of his less-than-illustrious parentage. The blanket had once belonged to Jud Walker, the Tlinget elder who'd been the closest to family Cole had ever really known. He never talked about Jud. Not anymore.

"I bought the store."

Cole's eyes narrowed as they swept the length of her slender frame. Now, he knew why her name had sounded so familiar.

"I thought the Stanleys said the new owner wasn't taking over until the end of the month."

The Stanleys were the couple who'd sold Lara the Mist Mall, a good-humored appellation for what was only an old-fashioned general store with attached living quarters. The clapboard building, including the part Lara now lived in, had less square footage than the modest home she'd sold only weeks ago. Harry and Iris Stanley had moved to Tucson for Mrs. Stanley's health as soon as the deal had closed, leaving one of the local women, Sally Cassidy, to tend the place until Lara arrived.

"I was able to tie things up quicker than I'd first thought. I got here yesterday."

Cole noticed that she was using the singular. The Stanleys had said that the new owner was a young widow. The "merry widow" was actually what she'd been called for speculation purposes by those frequenting Rosie's Bar—which included just about everyone in town. Having met her, Cole would give her "young." "Merry" didn't seem too likely, but then he supposed that he had caught her on a bad night.

"Harry said you're from California."

"San Diego," she supplied, wondering why Cole had made the statement sound like an accusation.

"You ever been to Southeast before?"

"No, I haven't. Why?"

"Just wondered. I had a feeling you were a *cheechako.*"

"A *cheechako?*" she repeated, knowing from the way he'd said it that the word wasn't a compliment.

"It's kind of like a greenhorn. Someone who hasn't put in their first year in Alaska."

"What made you think that? Because I didn't know about bears?"

His glance slid the length of her frame. Assessing, dismissing. "Among other things."

Cole finished off his drink and set his glass on the edge of the desk. A wood box sat beneath the paned window by the stove. Taking two quartered logs from it, he kicked up the latch on the metal door with his boot and bent to add the fuel to the glowing coals.

It didn't matter to him that she intended to be a permanent part of the community, though how long she'd last remained to be seen. All he cared about was that she was alone. He didn't like that. He'd have felt a lot better about her presence in Mist if she'd been someone's responsibility. If she'd belonged to Bud's crew, or if she'd been the logging camp's new cook, there would be people to watch out for her. At least, there would be someone around to explain what she'd need to know to get along.

As much as it bothered him that she'd be stumbling around on her own and winding up in God only knew what kind of trouble, it disturbed him more that he let it bother him at all. In some respects, he felt about her pretty much the same as he did the cub. It was in need of protection, but it was also an imposition. He didn't begrudge the cub its need. The woman, though, was another matter entirely.

Sap sizzled as flame licked over the logs. Closing the door with a clank, he brushed his hands off on his jeans and wondered what he was supposed to do with her now. He could hear her behind him, moving around in the small room as if trying to figure out what to do with herself.

Cole appreciated the feeling.

The rain showed no sign of abating and he wasn't going to stand out here making small talk until it did. He got a cot and a sleeping bag from the storage room, which used up a couple of minutes, then took a spare pillow from his bed. He was halfway down the hall with the pillow when he thought it might be a good idea to change the pillowcase for her. She should consider herself lucky that he'd done laundry yesterday and had a clean one to put on it. Not that he thought she'd say anything if he hadn't had one. He didn't know why, but she didn't strike him as a woman who complained much.

After he'd collected the bedding, he unfolded the cot. "It's warmer out here than it is in back," he told her. "But if it cools down too much for you, shove another log in the stove. The bathroom's the first door on your right."

She thanked him for his trouble, for setting up the cot for her and again, for taking care of the cub. He told her it was nothing and stood for a moment watching her fidget with the neck of her sweater. To keep the silence from getting longer, Cole decided to go to bed.

It was well beyond midnight when he found himself standing in the darkened hallway. He'd gone to check on the cub, which he'd set in its box in the hallway so it would stay warm. The box wasn't where he'd put it. He'd left the kitchen sink light on, its faint illumination spilling down the hall. In that pool of light he saw that Lara had moved the box near to her.

Cole moved closer, the beat of his heart louder to him than the soft sounds his bare feet made on the cold floor. Lara lay on her side with one arm beneath her head and curled in a ball so tight she took up only half the length of the cot. Her hair formed a dark puddle of tangled curls against the white pillowcase. He moved closer, his eyes drawn to the clean lines of her profile—the small, straight nose, her full, sleep-softened mouth. The dark crescent of her lashes curved against her cheek and though the light was too faint to see the scar above the arch of her eyebrow, he knew it was there. There wasn't much, he realized, that he hadn't noticed about her.

If she hadn't moved the cub, he wouldn't have needed to come so close to her. It seemed like a violation of sorts, invading someone's space while they were sleeping and defenseless against prying eyes. But he didn't intend to pry and he needed to assure himself that the animal was still doing all right.

As quietly as he could, he hunkered down beside the box, pushing back the edge of the blanket she had drawn over the little bear. Its eyes were open and it blinked at the intrusion, still too weak to move much. After a halfhearted sniff at Cole's fingers, it tucked its nose under the edge of the warm blanket and closed its eyes again.

"Is he okay?"

The question came softly. It was little more than a whisper really, but Cole's head snapped up as if she'd shouted it.

She'd risen to her elbow. Pushing back the fall of corkscrew curls from her eyes, she looked from Cole to the cub and back again. "He seemed all right awhile ago."

Her voice was hushed. In deference to the dark, he matched her tone. "He's fine now, too. Why did you move him?"

She sat up slowly, pulling the sleeping bag around her because the fire had burned low. "Do you think I might have hurt him by doing that?"

Squatting as he was beside the cot, one hand on the box, the other dangling across his knee, Cole was at eye level with her. Even in the dim light he could see her concern.

For one unguarded moment he questioned what it would be like to have someone feel that much concern for him. Real concern. The kind that didn't expect anything back for showing it. "I'm sure you were careful. I just wondered why you had. I told you I'd check on him tonight."

"I was afraid he might be lonely."

The rain continued to fall. Its sound was softer now that the wind had died down. The rhythm soothed as it beat against the roof, cloaking the dimly lit space in intimacy. The late hour, the rain, the quiet, all conspired to short-circuit his common sense. He should get up and go back to his room.

Her scent reached toward him, subtle, soft, dangerous. She'd thought it might be lonely. Incredible.

"Were you?"

"Was I what?"

"Lonely."

She didn't acknowledge the question. Though her expression was hidden mostly in shadow, he saw the denial form. But she couldn't utter the lie any more easily than she could admit what he suspected—that she did feel alone. He thought it might be worse for her tonight. Out of her depth with all that had happened, that sense of isolation could easily be magnified.

Cole understood the need for denial. Admitting loneliness only made it harder to bear. She'd had a rough time of it tonight and he hadn't made it any easier for her. It could be pretty frightening to be in a strange place where there was no one around who gave a damn. Though it had been years since he'd experienced that fear, no one knew it better than Cole.

"Do you want me to stay out here while you go back to sleep?"

The offer seemed to surprise her. It surprised him, too, but once it was out he couldn't very well retract it. What he found even more disconcerting was that he didn't really want to.

The sleeping bag slipped from her shoulders. He reached out, pulling it back up over her sweater. She was sleeping in her clothes. He'd spent many a night like that himself.

"I'll put another log on," he told her, thinking it simpler for both of them if he had an excuse to remain.

Lara's simple "Thank you" seemed inadequate to her. But it was all she could think to say as he cupped his hands over his knees and pushed himself upright. His solid presence seemed to lift the shadows that had followed her into sleep. She wasn't anxious for their return.

The muffled sounds of a metal door opening, of a poker carefully nudging at coals were comforting somehow. She laid her head back on the pillow and curled her knees into her chest.

Earlier that evening she would have thought it impossible to relax enough to sleep with him in the room. Yet she had no trouble drifting off into the dreamless slumber that comes from feeling protected, secure. She hadn't known that feeling in well over a year; hadn't even appreciated it until its absence made feeling secure impossible. She felt it now, though, in those few precious moments of consciousness before sleep claimed her. And in those moments it occurred to her, vaguely, how odd it was that a man who clearly regarded her as an imposition should offer her such a reprieve.

The gift was fleeting. The sense of security that lulled her to sleep was about as substantial as wood smoke when Lara awoke to the sound of static the next morning. Cole was at the radio behind the desk, alternately speaking into a hand-held mike and frowning in concentration at the words coming through the crackle. To Lara's unattuned ear the transmission was far from decipherable. Cole didn't seem to be having a problem understanding whoever was on the other end, though.

His back was to her and remained that way as she folded up the sleeping bag and placed the pillow neatly on top of it on the cot. Cole had moved the cub. It now sat in a wire cage on the desk, amusing itself with a water dish it had upended.

Cole hadn't noticed. He was too busy writing on the pad by the radio and asking the owner of the static-laced voice to repeat whatever it was that he'd said.

"What kind of rope? Over," she heard him say as, running a hand through her sleep-tangled hair, she hesitantly edged into his view.

She wanted to leave. With the storm gone, the pale gray light of an overcast morning coming through the unshuttered windows, she had no reason to stay a moment more. The cub looked to be doing just fine and she felt awkward enough having imposed as she had. She felt downright embarrassed that he'd been up long enough to shower, dress and open the shutters while she'd slept like a hibernating bear.

She couldn't remember the last time she'd slept that soundly.

She cleared her throat. Occupied as he was, he didn't seem to hear her.

It appeared that she'd have to wait. Tugging her sweater over her hips, she moved toward the desk. She couldn't go without thanking him for what he'd done—especially now that she could see the cub was doing so well. She wanted to thank him, too, for letting her stay.

When he finally deigned to make eye contact, he put his hand over the mike. "This is going to take awhile."

"Oh." Prompted by his silence she added, "Well, I'll uh . . . see you later then."

The lift of his chin was all the acknowledgment she got. The crackle of the radio had already reabsorbed his attention.

She hadn't thanked him. But when he glanced at her a moment later as if displeased that she was still there, she decided not to bother him with her gratitude. She lifted her hand to say goodbye. He did the same while telling whoever he was talking with that there was no way he could get there before the end of the week. Yes. Damn it. He was sure. Over.

Wondering if her presence was responsible for his lovely mood or if he always woke up in such a charming frame of mind, she hurried down the wooden steps to her truck. She was inside with the keys poised at the ignition when she thought she heard him call her name. She waited, listening intently, but no sound came from the neat brown cabin with the U.S. Forest Service shield by its front door. All she heard were the whisper of wind in the trees and the riotous squawk of birds greeting the misty morning.

The unfamiliarity of her surroundings suddenly hit her. Along with it came an awful emptiness; the same dull void she awoke with every morning. Oddly, it hadn't been there when she'd awoken awhile ago. She felt it now, though, along with a vague sense of panic. She was scared. Frightened by the enormity of the decision she'd made. She'd actually done it. She'd left everything she'd ever known behind and moved to Alaska.

It had taken a lot of courage to do that.

"Or a total lack of brains," she muttered and turned the key.

"Lara. Wait a minute!" Cole hollered again toward the closed door just as he heard her gun the truck's engine. "Damn it," he muttered, then hurriedly spoke into the mike. "Hang on a minute, would you, Asa? Over."

"Wha'd ya say? Over."

"I said," Cole began and repeated himself. By then Lara was backing onto the crushed-gravel road.

He decided he might as well let her go and finish his call. He had to stop by the store later anyway.

Shortly after ten o'clock Lara having showered, changed and fortified herself with hot chocolate, was standing by her stockroom's near-empty shelves. It had become clear in a hurry that the Stanleys had omitted a few pertinent details when the sale had been finalized. They'd been honest enough about most of the repairs the place needed; torn screens that would eventually replace the storm windows, and the need for a new roof within a year or so. They'd grossly understated the need for paint, however, and they hadn't mentioned at all that the stock was so low. It wasn't that Lara had no experience with upkeep or merchandising. Not exactly. Seven years of teaching grade school provided no useful background on that score, but the home she and Steve had shared for those years had required its share of maintenance, so she knew how to use a hammer and a paintbrush. And though she wasn't so sure that her high-school job of bagging groceries at her uncle's supermarket necessarily qualified her to run her own store, she figured she could manage. As small as the place was, she shouldn't have any real trouble.

She would overlook the fact that she'd held that same thought when she'd left yesterday to check out the only road in town.

"Here they are."

Sally Cassidy, the young mother who'd tended the store after the Stanleys left, had arrived within minutes of Lara's flipping the Closed sign to Open on the door window. She held out a stack of old invoices, which hadn't been with the account books as Mrs. Stanley had told Lara they would be. Sally, who seemed familiar with the old woman's eccentricities, had finally located them.

"They were in the back of the catalog drawer with the order forms. Iris had a tendency to get confused," Sally explained. "What's next?"

Clipboard in hand, Lara rubbed the middle of her forehead. As much as she appreciated Sally's assistance, the woman was threatening to give her a headache. Lara was sure the threat wasn't deliberate. The young woman, visibly pregnant with her third child—a girl this time, she was sure—seemed starved for female company. Sally was nice enough and she was proving an enormous help in answering questions Lara had about the stock she needed to order. She was just very chatty. Lara didn't really mind that, though, as long as she didn't talk about her baby.

Lara hadn't said that to Sally, of course. She just hadn't had any comment when the woman had given her a blessedly brief rundown on how awkward her girth was beginning to feel. It seemed that no matter how hard Lara tried, she couldn't get past the longing she felt when she saw a pregnant woman. After eighteen months, she thought she should be getting used to the idea that she'd never have children of her own.

She was discovering that some dreams took longer to die than others.

By the sheer force of will, Lara pushed the errant thoughts aside. Sally's talkative nature did have its benefits. Concentrating on her convoluted conversation made it impossible to think of anything else.

The woman was a veritable fountain of information about the town's sixty-eight, mostly male, residents. The problem there was in keeping up with her meanderings. Sally leaped from one subject to another with the skill of a seasoned trapeze artist.

Sally settled herself on a closed barrel. The end of her pale blond ponytail hung over her shoulder and she swung her rubber-booted feet as she spoke. Before she'd gone in search of the invoices, she'd been talking about Bud, the guy who ran the ice house where Gus Cassidy, her father-in-law, took the fish he caught for storage before the cannery plane from Juneau picked them up. Before that, Gus, the proud owner of three fishing boats with a crew of eighteen, not including her husband, had been the topic. Now, she held forth about one of Gus's men, a young fisherman who, according to her, would gamble the shirt off his back if he could find a taker.

"Wait till you meet Chuck. He'll want to flip you for whatever he comes in here to buy. Anything from a week's worth of groceries to a can of snuff. Heads he pays for it, tails he doesn't. Don't you let him con you, though. He had a two-headed coin for a while. He may still have for all I know." She shook her head, crinkling her freckled nose. "Rosie probably took it, though. She makes him give her half of his paycheck every payday, so he doesn't bet it all away. He didn't like it at first, but now first thing he does before even ordering a drink is hand it over. It was actually Cole's idea. He asked Rosie to do it because he was tired of pulling Chuck out of fights after he'd lose everything in a poker game. It's not like Chuck's the only one who likes to gamble," she added in an offhand sort of way. "Most of the men do. There's always a card game over at Rosie's and they've always got a pool of some kind going. Right now, the bet is to see how long *you'll* last."

The only food item of any quantity in the storage room was spinach. Lara promptly lost count of the cans with Sally's blithely delivered statement.

"I've only been here for two days and people are already betting on when I'll leave?"

"Oh, it's nothing personal. We do it with everybody. Well, I don't," she amended. "I'm terrible at guessing anything, and usually the guys wait until the folks actually show up before putting their money down. But when they heard you were young and a widow, they anted up on the spot." Curiosity danced in her soft brown eyes. "Are you really looking for a husband? That's the other thing their money is on. This is the perfect place to find one, you know." Her look of utter innocence made the logic seem inescapable. "What with all the single men working for my father-in-law and the logging camp only a mile away and most of those boys being footloose, Cole figured that's why someone like you would come here."

At Cole's name, Lara felt the muscles in her shoulders stiffen.

"You've mentioned Cole a lot," she observed in her most casual tone. "Is he always so quick with his opinions? The man doesn't even know me."

"You said you met him last night."

Lara met Sally's frown, certain by now that the woman expected details. One of the first things she'd asked was if Lara had met any of her neighbors. Lara mentioned the guy at the marina, Rosie next door and Cole. She hadn't, however, said a thing about having spent the night on his cot.

"I did meet him. What I meant is that he doesn't know anything *about* me."

That wasn't quite true. But he certainly didn't know enough to second-guess her reason for coming to Mist.

From the front of the store came the tinkle of a bell.

"There's the front door." Sally slipped off the barrel as gracefully as her seven-month pregnancy would allow. "I'll get it. Then, I've got to go check on my boys. You'd better finish up your order before the mail plane gets here or you won't have anything left to sell. Don't forget the white gas. You're almost out."

Irritation with Cole's presumption gave way to more immediate concerns. "White gas?"

"We use it for lamps and stoves. You'll be needing it for campers, too. Cole opens up the campsites next month and we get lots of hunters and fishermen through here. And kerosene. Oh, and gloves. A couple of guys were in from the logging site a few days ago and bought the last three pair. Seems they've been picking up more jaggers than usual."

"What kind of gloves?" Lara asked. Canvas? Leather? Rubberized? And what was a jagger? Some kind of insect? But Sally was already gone.

Sagging against a stack of boxed canned goods, Lara glanced through the storage room doorway to her very own country-style store. There were so many things she didn't know, so much that was different.

And that, she reminded herself, was precisely why she was here.

Immediately she straightened, refusing to indulge discouragement. With a decisive jerk, she tugged the baggy hem of her new black-and-blue flannel shirt over the seat of her not-so-new faded jeans. It was by coming to this place that was so completely the opposite of everything she'd known that she would start over and build a new life for herself. Her family thought she'd gone off the deep end. Her best friend had even offered to pay for therapy. But Lara knew what all of them refused to see: that she wasn't giving up anything that hadn't already been taken from her. She'd never be able to forget what she no longer had if she re-

mained surrounded by the memories of everything she and
Steve had shared. Memories of all the dreams that had died
with him. Southeast Alaska was as different from San Diego
as she was from the woman she'd once been. She had accepted the changes in herself. Or she was trying to, anyway.
She wished the people she cared about would try, too.

A muffled conversation drifted toward her. Sally ex-
claimed over something in cooing tones. A deep, disturb-
ingly familiar voice responded.

Cole was here. Cole MacInnes. Lara had learned his name
from Sally.

"Is she around?" Lara heard him ask. "I need to see
her."

She moved from the doorway, the soft soles of her ath-
letic shoes muffling her steps on the plank board floor. He
stood with Sally near the front windows, by the empty
magazine rack. His dark hair was windblown; his skin ruddy
from the cold. He'd turned up the collar of his sherpa
jacket, but he hadn't buttoned it. The rough suede hung
open over a flannel shirt and jeans that strained against his
powerful thighs. As Lara drew closer, she couldn't help but
think that he was a man who looked to be very much a part
of the immense, untamed wilderness on the other side of the
front door.

He turned slightly, facing her. As he did, Lara could see
what Sally was getting all soppy over. The cub. Cole had it
tucked under his arm like a football, the wide white bandage stark against his downy brown fur.

Caught unprepared, Lara looked from the cub and hesitantly met Cole's eyes.

For a few fleeting moments last night, she'd leaned on
him. That was something she hadn't let herself do before—
allowed herself to give in to the weariness. The lapse had
lasted only until she'd fallen asleep. But those precious mo-

ments had been long enough for her to realize how badly she'd needed the comfort his presence had offered. He'd known it, too. Without the words. It was not a comfortable need to have admitted to a total stranger.

It was impossible to discern his thoughts. Gray and unrevealing, his eyes held hers until she was forced to look away. She felt no more at ease when her focus shifted to the cub.

She wished he hadn't brought the animal here. She really wished he hadn't come here at all.

Resigned to the fact that he had, she concentrated on Sally. The woman was blissfully occupied with the cub. It's golden-brown eyes were wide open and alert as it blinked up at the ceiling. It seemed to like the security of being tucked against Cole's side.

"Hard to believe they grow up to be so nasty, isn't it?" Sally said to no one in particular. She touched the damp and shiny nose. "What happened to it?"

"Did battle with a fender," Cole replied and said nothing more.

Lara's eyes flew to his.

Sally muttered, "Oh, dear."

Cole, still watching Lara, simply shrugged as if to say *why go into details?* then frowned impatiently at Sally. She was now chucking the animal under the chin.

The cub turned away. Thus rebuffed, Sally reined herself in and smiled brightly at Lara.

"Well, listen. Cole wants to see you and I've got to run. No telling what kind of damage the boys have done with their dad's tools. They found directions on how to make a solar cooker in an outdoor magazine and were determined to build one for me. Haven't had the heart to tell them the thing won't work with our liquid sunshine. Who knows, though, we might see the real thing yet in another month or two.''

She cut down the aisle displaying paper and cleaning products and was halfway back up it, blue-and-white box in hand, when she added, ''I'm taking a box of laundry soap. Put it on my account, okay, Lara? I'll be back to help in a while. Bye, Cole.''

Lara didn't have a chance to tell her that she really didn't have to hurry back. The tinkle of the bell met the groan of arthritic hinges and the door banged shut behind her.

The sound hadn't had a chance to settle to silence when Lara's head snapped back toward the man standing six feet away.

''Do you really think I came here to find a husband?''

As surprised as he was by her feisty challenge, he wasn't going to deny his position. He knew what he thought and Cole believed in calling things as he saw them. This morning, though, he had to admit that he was seeing *her* a little differently than he had last night.

The vulnerability he'd seen before had vanished—replaced by challenge that put a spark of defiance in her eyes and brought her whole face to life. The delicacy was still there; haunting in its own way. But it was the hint of steel beneath the softness that intrigued him.

''I'll admit the thought occurred to me.''

The succinct statement wasn't very satisfying. She wasn't sure what she wanted to hear from him. More of a defense, possibly. All he did was stand there calmly watching her, which made her feel foolish for bringing the subject up in the first place.

''Well, I'm not,'' she informed him and really could have kicked herself. Her response reminded her of a whiny reply one of her former third-graders might have given. ''All I'm looking for here is a change," she quickly added, hoping to gracefully ease her foot out of her mouth. "Nothing else."

"Glad we got that cleared up. Look, I'm running a little late. Do you have any baby bottles?"

It was irritating to have him so cavalierly change the subject. However, since the matter was better dropped, she traded irritation for wariness and glanced toward the cub. She had a very uncomfortable feeling about the two of them.

"I think I saw some somewhere. I'll have to look." She'd taken three steps when she stopped. She didn't want to feel the concern that made her ask, but she couldn't put it off any longer. "Is it okay?"

"He'll be fine. Right now, he's hungry."

Lara hadn't yet familiarized herself with the location of all her merchandise. The store sold everything from soup to socks and what it didn't stock, Lara could, supposedly, order. A kayak dangling a red Sale tag hung over the front door; snow shoes were stacked along a back wall by knee-high rubber boots known as Tongass tennis shoes. A couple of kerosene lanterns and green camp stoves shared a shelf with a half dozen blue-and-white speckled cooking pots and cast-iron frying pans.

She found two bottles next to a package of diapers. From the dust on the wrappers, it appeared that baby items hadn't been in demand for a while.

"I've only got little ones. This holds—" she held one up to check the tick marks on the glass "—four ounces. Is that okay?"

"It'll work. You'll just have to fill it a couple of times a feeding if he wants more."

She lowered the bottle, meeting his unbelievably bland expression. He was waiting for her to react to the little bombshell he'd so subtly dropped. The perverse streak she'd discovered only yesterday surfaced again. She wouldn't give him the satisfaction.

When she let several, unblinking seconds go by, he finally said, "You're going to have to keep him."

She couldn't do that. "Why?"

This time, it was Cole who let the silence speak for him. As her eyes lowered, she was thankful for the good grace that had kept him from saying the words. She was responsible for the animal being hurt.

Her glance fell to the little ball of fur now upright and clinging to Cole's shirt like an infant. "Isn't there a kennel or something at the ranger station?"

"All I've got at the station is the cage he was in this morning. But that's not the problem. I'm not going to be around for a couple of days and he can't be left alone. He needs to be kept warm and fed and he needs to get this—" he reached into his coat pocket and pulled out a small bottle "—so he doesn't get an infection."

Without thinking, she took the bottle.

The cub's little ears were twitching. So was his nose.

She didn't want it to be cute. "I don't know anything about bears."

"It couldn't be any harder than taking care of baby."

That was not the right thing to say. She took a step back.

"Come on," Cole coaxed. "You women are supposed to have instincts about these things."

"About baby-sitting bears? I don't think so," she returned, deliberately misinterpreting his absurd statement. She was busy denying her maternal instincts, not deliberately cultivating them. "Besides, I think I'm allergic to cubs."

"If you don't know anything about them, how would you know if you're allergic?"

"Look, I don't know if I am or not. I just know that I'm not that good with animals." She really wasn't. In fact, she was proving quite detrimental to their health. "I kept my third-grade students' hamsters over Christmas break because no one else would take them and they both died of pneumonia. My friend's cat disliked me so much that it spent the entire week of Sam's vacation meowing from under my couch." She wouldn't mention that what the miserable creature had done under the couch had necessitated recarpeting the room before the house could be sold and burning what had been a perfectly good piece of furniture. "Maybe Sally would watch it."

He didn't look particularly sympathetic. At least, she assumed it was lack of appreciation for her inability to cope with animals that caused his frown. She couldn't imagine what else she'd said that would make him look at her as if she had two heads.

"I don't want it around her boys. They'll want to play with him and the less human contact he has, the better."

She reached out, her eyes guarded as she stroked the soft paw. The poor little thing didn't belong here. It belonged in its own familiar surroundings. It belonged with its mother.

Realizing what she was doing, she jerked her hand away.

"He's not going to hurt you."

Cole's tone was strangely quiet, his expression watchful. She hadn't feared that the animated teddy bear would hurt her. But she wasn't too keen on handling it, either. It had been different last night when she'd held it. Then, she'd had no choice.

It didn't look as though she had one now, either.

She reached out, and hesitated. The cub still snuggled in the crook of Cole's arm, its claws, impressive even for its tiny size, splayed against the front of his jacket as if fearing its protector might let it go. "Here," Cole said, and eased the animal out so she could take it.

Her fingers had barely secured around the cub's chest when she found her hands trapped beneath Cole's.

"Got him?"

She nodded, forcing herself not to pull back too quickly. A moment later, stepping back, she winced. In its attempt to find something solid to cling to, the bear had scrambled up her shirt. His little claws, sharp like an infant's fingernails, scraped the side of her neck.

Her fingers folded around the tiny paw. She'd barely pulled it away when she felt Cole's hand on her shoulder. An instant later, he pushed her thick curls from her collar.

He had calluses on his fingers. She felt them when he drew the tips along the faint scratch. His touch was light, far gentler than it had any right to be—and it carried an indefinable jolt.

Blue eyes locked on gray.

She didn't move. She didn't breathe. Neither choice was conscious. Something dark and elemental shifted in his gaze. Something as compelling as it was dangerous. Common sense told her to look away. A need, denied for so long she'd thought it dead, wouldn't let her. It seemed necessary that she absorb his quiet intensity; that she let it flow through her and awaken what lay dormant in her soul.

The pad of his thumb softly grazed the hollow of her throat, the faint friction eliciting sensations as alarming as her thoughts.

As if questioning his own reaction, Cole's lashes narrowed. A heartbeat later, he lowered his hand.

The flooring creaked when he stepped back, the loose board sounding as rusty as his voice after he'd cleared his throat. "You'll need to watch his claws."

The curls he'd pushed aside bounced back with her barely perceptible nod.

"I brought the cage for him. It's out in my truck."

He turned away. As he did, Lara thought she saw his jaw tighten. She couldn't be sure. About all she felt certain of was that something about Cole MacInnes required that she respond to him. Demanded it on more levels than she cared to consider. The feeling was frightening and enlivening and, sweet heaven, it had been so long.

She knew something else, too. One indisputable fact she couldn't overlook. She was only now gaining control of her life. Cole definitely threatened that sense of control—and that was more frightening still.

Chapter Three

The cold air, damp with mist and smelling of the sea, felt good against Lara's heated face. Clutching bear and bottle, she waited by the door, holding it open while Cole headed toward his truck. He'd parked at the end of the five-foot wide boardwalk that connected Mist's four businesses and two of its houses to the marina and boat dock. The marina itself was built on pilings.

There were no streets here. The only road was a narrow, crushed-rock surface running straight back into the forest and branching like a tree itself to the logging sites. The forest, thick with Sitka spruce and Western hemlock, pushed right up to the back doors of the little arc of buildings. The inlet, opening to the sea a mile out, stretched in front of them. This morning the water was calm, its gentle lap muted in the quiet gray fog. Last night, wind-driven waves had washed bits of seaweed right up to the buildings' front doors.

At the end of the boardwalk, she saw Cole lift a cage—the same wood-frame and wire-mesh one she'd seen on his desk—from the bed of his truck. Carrying it like a suitcase, he came back toward her, his boots making muffled thuds on the wet and weathered planks. That heavy, rhythmic sound seemed rather ominous.

She held the door wider, allowing him plenty of room to pass before following him in. Making a mental note to find some oil to lubricate the squeaky hinge when she pulled the door shut, she led him through another door at the back of the store.

The back half of the grayed and gabled building made up her living quarters. Though far from luxurious, her new home was much more comfortable than she'd anticipated. She'd only seen pictures of the place before she'd bought it; grainy snapshots supplied by the Stanleys after she'd responded to their ad in the real-estate section of the *L.A. Times*. But she hadn't been disappointed when she'd arrived and seen the real thing. She'd wanted something different from what she'd always known. If anything met that qualification, this oversize cabin-in-the-woods was it. The spacious house she'd sold in San Diego had been open and airy and light. This place had wood-paneled walls, paned windows with shutters to close out storms and, upstairs, two of the tiniest bedrooms she'd ever seen. It also had a wonderful stone fireplace that took up the entire end wall of the living area and gave the place a cozy, welcoming feel that more than made up for the lack of reliable electricity. Her generator was a gas powered contraption out by her very own wood pile.

Sidestepping a box of books, she pointed across the bare wood floor to the far corner of the room. "You can put it over there."

Cole didn't skirt the box as she had. He simply stepped over it, taking in the whole of the room as he did. A love seat faced the fireplace. A small basket holding matches and a shiny brass hurricane lamp with an unused wick sat neatly on a pine coffee table in front of it. Crisp chintz curtains, beige like the sofa and smelling of soap and starch, framed the windows. On the sill of one of those windows was a small vase filled with dried yellow buds.

"When did you say you got here?"

"The day before yesterday."

"You've been busy."

The observation sounded offhand, but to Cole her place looked more like a home after forty-eight hours than his did after years. Maybe it was the curtains that did it. Or the pictures of wildflowers she had grouped on one wall. Whatever produced the effect, it seemed warmer, more inviting than did his cabin. But a closer look revealed an unexpected oddity. She didn't have much, but what there was all looked new. The oatmeal-colored love seat was spotless. A tag still dangled from the brass lamp on the otherwise empty end table. And the yellow throw pillow on the love seat was still covered with plastic.

He could only assume that the rest of her possessions, the more worn and personal kinds of things the room was missing, were still in transit.

Lara hadn't been aware of his inventory. Her attention was on the cub. It kept sniffing at her neck, its soft nose tickling her skin.

"I hate not being settled," she told him, turning her head away from the cub. "Unpacking was the first thing I did. Except for books. I need a bookcase."

"Well, the rest of your stuff shouldn't be too far behind. Getting shipments takes a little longer up here than what you're probably used to. But your things will catch up with you eventually.''

"Oh, everything's here. I didn't think I'd need much," she explained, seeing him frown at the relative bareness of the room. She'd sold or given away most of what she and Steve had owned, buying only what she'd felt necessary to begin her new life. The wilderness life-style was too unfamiliar to really know what she needed just yet. But she had known she didn't need the huge family-room sofa or big-screen TV. "One of the reasons I bought a truck was so I could get everything in it. I just loaded it up and drove it on to the ferry when I got to Seattle." She would have told him, too, that she realized now that she didn't need a truck since there was nowhere to go, but she was interrupted by the cub's attempt to crawl up her shirt.

The cub seemed determined to get to her small gold stud earring. His tongue, pink and rough, lapped at the underside of her ear. Lara stretched her neck away, starting to smile at the tickling sensation, then caught herself when she caught a whiff of his musky fur. Before she drew another breath, she tucked the little beast's head against her breast, holding it there with her other hand.

That accomplished, she looked up to see Cole watching her intently. The cub's mission seemed to amuse him. A hint of a smile rested in his eyes. The smile didn't make it to his mouth, but even that small softening made him seem more approachable somehow—and that almost made her forget what they'd been talking about.

Cole reminded her. "You drove yourself from San Diego?"

She nodded, remembering just how long that trip had been. She and Sam had been on the road for five days. Both were now proficient at changing flats. "A friend of mine came as far as Seattle with me. She caught a plane from there and I caught the ferry to here." The scent of musk, not nearly as appealing as the bottled variety, drifted past her nostrils again. Her nose wrinkled as she frowned at the furry head. "Can I give him a bath?"

The quality of Cole's scowl underwent a subtle shift as he glanced at the cub snuggled against the gentle swell of her breast. Lara was a curious woman. He'd never made the trip himself, but a drive up the entire West Coast of the lower states followed by a two-day ferry trip up the coast of Canada and into Southeast was not a journey for the timid.

He wasn't considering that now, however. The animal's squirming had pulled the placket of her shirt aside, exposing a glimpse of porcelain pale skin and icy white lace bra.

Drawing a deep breath, he raised his eyes. "Why?"

"Because he smells."

"He smells like a bear."

The look she shot him was amazingly tolerant.

Cole could still see that tantalizing strip of skin and lace.

His jaw clenched. What in the hell was the matter with him? A little cleavage and he was hardening up like a sixteen-year-old.

"You don't bathe a wild animal." He sounded disgusted. Maybe she'd think it was because of her stupid question. "All you need to do is feed him, take him outside once in a while and give him that antibiotic three times a day. Keep that bandage dry, too. I'll be back in a couple of days to check on him."

Cole was across the room before Lara's irritation could work its way to the surface. He'd made it sound as if her question were ridiculous; as if she'd asked to powder and perfume the defenseless little creature. All she wanted to do was get rid of the bear smell. Which, now that she thought about it, probably wouldn't be the best thing to do for an animal that had to go back into the wild.

Lara hardly considered herself a genius, but she was a reasonably quick study. She was also honest enough to admit it when she didn't understand something. She'd acknowledged as much several times in the past two days—and to Cole himself last night after he'd been so kind as to point out her lack of knowledge about bears.

As he had implied last night, she did have a lot to learn. She knew that. She just didn't like the fact that *he* knew it. Ego had little to do with her reaction. His effect on her mental equilibrium definitely did. He made her defensive and she hated feeling that way. The man was opinionated, blunt and possessed an amazing capacity to annoy.

That he annoyed her deliberately was never more evident than when he reached the door. A smile, unexpected and wry, shifted into his eyes as they bounced from her to the cub in her arms and back again. She knew she did not look pleased to be stuck baby-sitting the local wildlife.

"Oh, yeah. One more thing, Lara. Welcome to Mist."

"Welcome to Mist."

Lara muttered the phrase to herself as she sat on the stoop of her back steps and faced the blue-green forest. The cub had already had one "accident" and she wasn't taking any more chances. She'd taken him outside once an hour since. Now on their third trip, she was waiting for the cub to answer the call of nature so she could take him back inside. He was more interested in playing in the tall grass edging up to the trees. Lying on his back about ten feet from her, he swatted at the winter-browned stalks, showing no interest at all in cooperating. So Lara watched, her chin in her palm and wondered why she let Cole get to her. It was safer than thinking about the stupid way her heart had jerked when he'd given her that cocky grin before he left.

"If it's the fate of the world you're contemplating, it must be in a sorrier state than I thought."

Lara's head snapped up. Forty feet away, on the back stoop of the building next door, stood Rosie O'Grady. The whiskey-voiced redhead had a cigarette in one hand and the other planted on the hip of her Western-cut jeans. At "forty-nine and holding," her green eyes held more cynicism than they had in her youth, but she could still play seductress if she wanted—providing there was anything around worth the effort, she'd told Lara in her usual outspoken way. More often, her expression held compassion and laughter; a combination of qualities perfectly suited to the proprietress of the community's bar and grill.

Lara had first met Rosie the afternoon she'd arrived in Mist. The assertive woman with the beehive hairdo had shown up at her back door with a cup of coffee strong enough to lift weights and a bottle of Irish whiskey to doctor it with; her own way of saying welcome. She'd only stayed for twenty minutes, long enough for an unpacking break. And long enough for Lara to realize that the community was not necessarily going to welcome her with open arms. Not that Rosie wasn't pleasant. She was. But it had been clear that Rosie was reserving her judgment of Lara; waiting, possibly like Cole, for her to prove herself. Lara could appreciate the reticence. As the newcomer, it was up to her to fit in.

A smile vanquished Lara's frown. Standing, she swatted at the seat of her jeans. It was now damp; just like everything else in Mist. She was beginning to learn nothing outside was ever dry. "Don't mind me, Rosie. I'm only killing a little time."

"You must be finished with your inventory then. Sally said you were sending a big order in with the mail plane today. I know everyone around here will be grateful when more supplies arrive. Lots of folks are running low on staples.''

With everything else on her mind, it hadn't occurred to Lara that people might actually be waiting for groceries. No one was starving. She was sure Sally would have mentioned that. But Lara had planned to paint the inside of the store and its shelves while her inventory was so low. It now appeared that she might want to alter that plan.

''I've had a couple of interruptions,'' she said, looking at the little bear but thinking of Sally who'd come back to show her the little pink caps and booties she was making. ''I'll have an order ready for the plane tomorrow.''

''The mail plane only comes on Tuesday and Friday.''

''Great,'' Lara muttered. She wished she'd known that. Not that knowing would have made a lot of difference. The way her day was going, she still couldn't have finished her list.

''Bud's got a phone over at the ice house. I'm sure he'd let you use it to call your order in, if you're willing to pay for the call. Or, I've got a radio in back.''

Lara remembered the static-filled sounds of the instrument she'd seen Cole using this morning. Her list was going to be *pages* long. ''Does the grocers' warehouse in Juneau have a radio?''

''Honey, about everybody in Alaska has a radio. Or access to one. It's how we communicate. It's also free entertainment. That's why you don't ever want to say anything over it that you don't mind all of Southeast knowing about.''

As Rosie took another drag from her cigarette, Lara's glance swung back toward the cub. Rather, toward where she'd last seen him. Eyes wide, she bolted to her feet. ''Where did he go?''

Rosie, wiping an ash from the white apron she wore over her blue shirt and jeans, frowned after Lara. "Where'd who go?"

"The cub. It's about this big—" she held her hands about a foot apart "—and it's got a white... Oh, jeeze."

She cut herself off and scrambled down the steps. Her head snapped from side to side, searching the shallow clearing in front of the trees. If the little bear had made its way to the trees she'd never find it in the dense undergrowth. "Where did it go?"

Just about the time the panic hit, she spotted the white bandage. The cub had run parallel to the row of buildings and now, seeming quite unhampered by its three-legged gait, charged for the woods. It had never occurred to her that, with his injury, he'd be able to move that fast.

She was scrambling toward him, wet to her knees from the grass when suddenly the cub tumbled sideways. An instant later, he righted himself and sat blinking at her approach. She was within ten feet when he stood up on his hind legs, looking very proud of himself for imitating her, then fell forward when he lost his balance.

She marched back to the porch, hugging the cub so it couldn't squirm and not, she assured herself because she was relieved that it wasn't lost. "I don't care what he said about taking you outside. It's diapers for you from now on."

Rosie had moved to her porch rail. Blowing out a puff of smoke, she shook her head as Lara passed her steps. "You're a better woman than I am, honey. You wouldn't catch me playing nursemaid to a grizzly."

"I'm not thrilled with the idea myself."

Rosie eyed the cub with distaste. Lara's glance followed. She refused to acknowledge how inquisitive the cub looked cocking its head from side to side as it studied her. He actually looked as if he were trying to figure out what he'd done.

"It's just until Cole can take him back." Which would be soon, she hoped.

"I'd heard he'd brought that thing to you." Speculation gleamed beneath the woman's carefully penciled eyebrows. "Mind my asking why?"

Mind my asking why he'd bring an injured animal to you to take care of instead of asking someone he knows?

Lara heard the unspoken words. A touch of challenge, possibly possessiveness, had tinted the woman's question.

"Because it's my fault the cub's hurt," she said, feeling as if she had trespassed on private territory. Acceptance wasn't going to come easily. "I ran into it during the storm yesterday. When you were over the other day, you mentioned that the ranger at the station was good with animals. So I took it there."

Rosie didn't look at Lara. Instead, she seemed vaguely preoccupied with an eagle flying overhead. "What did you think of our ranger?"

"He's impossible."

"He's a man." Rosie shrugged. "They're all that way. I've buried two husbands and had myself a fling or two enough to know that being impossible is as natural to them as growing face hair." The eagle circled out of sight. "What did you think of him aside from that?"

Lara opened her mouth, then closed it again. The question, she realized, was too complicated for her to answer easily. That in itself gave her pause.

To avoid Rosie's now watchful eyes, Lara concentrated on picking bits of grass from the cub's fur. "I don't think we got off on the best foot."

"That explains it," was the woman's enigmatic reply. "I was wondering why he didn't just give you this himself."

Coins jingled as she reached into the wide pocket of her apron and pulled out a slip of paper. She leaned over the rail, handing it down to Lara. "He came in late this morning to have me make him up some sandwiches and asked me to see that you got that. Said he forgot to leave it with you when he was in the store earlier. He won't need to pick the order up till the end of the week."

Balancing the cub on her hip, Lara unfolded the paper. "His grocery list," she surmised, wondering how many others she'd be getting before she could get her shelves stocked.

"More likely it's Asa's. If it were Cole's, he wouldn't be ordering oatmeal. I tried often enough to feed it to him for breakfast when he comes in here, but he won't touch the stuff."

The cub batted at the curls covering Lara's ear. Absently reaching for his paw to stop him, Lara stared down at the hastily scrawled list. The combination of items was decidedly odd. At least it would have been by San Diego standards. Listed below cornmeal, salt and sisal rope were bug repellant, powdered milk, and half-inch copper tubing. There were more items on the eclectic list. Some she was sure she didn't have, such as "detonators."

She glanced up. "Who's Asa?"

"Our local hermit."

"Interesting list."

"Interesting man. Won't let anyone near him but Cole."

"Why is that?"

Lara thought Rosie would explain why the man had become a recluse. Instead, she responded to his choice of confidant.

"I expect it's because they're so alike. Cole won't chase you off with a rifle like Asa will, but he does tend to prefer his solitude. Cole checks in on Asa about once a month.

Takes him his supplies. Makes sure he hasn't blown himself up. That sort of thing.

"Well, listen," she went on, dropping the stub of her cigarette into the coffee can she kept for that purpose on her back porch. "I know you've got things to do and if I don't get some chili or stew on to simmer, the menu's going to look mighty forlorn tonight. The boys at the logging camp are getting tired of fending for themselves with tuna sandwiches in the evenings, so most of them have been coming in to my place for something hot. Jack has a cook coming within the week, though. Don't mind the money I've been making, but can't say I care much for the extra work. I'd rather just pour drinks and visit with the boys."

She turned to go, hesitating when she reached the door. For a moment she appeared to consider whether or not she wanted to say anything else, then turned with her chin up. "There's no sense in you eating alone over there. Come on over anytime. Best place around to meet the rest of your neighbors."

Lara accepted Rosie's invitation. At least, that was what Cole overheard at the logging camp a couple of mornings later while warming his hands around a cup of Carolyn Clark's coffee. According to what the men at the long table behind him were saying, Lara had been into Rosie's twice now. The first time, she'd spent fifteen minutes on the radio to Juneau and had a cup of hot chocolate. Last night, she'd had a bowl of soup, then stayed long enough to visit with the marina owner and his wife, and turned down a couple of offers to dance. Both evenings, she'd left early and alone.

Cole didn't know why he was relieved to hear that.

Taking his coffee, he left the clank and clatter of the mess tent to stand outside.

Carolyn's coffee was even better than Rosie's. Her flapjacks, however, left something to be desired. Hungry men didn't complain, though. Drowning the heavy, doughlike disks in butter and syrup appeared to make them edible enough to fill the gap. Judging from some of the mumbled comments he'd heard, the cakes were heavy enough to fill the gap clear through to dinner.

Carolyn, Jack's wife, bookkeeper, inventory clerk and the mother of his two sons, was also filling in as cook—in the mornings anyway—until the new one arrived. Cole was sure everyone concerned would be grateful when the transition took place.

For himself, Cole was just grateful for the coffee. He hoped he hadn't hurt Carolyn's feelings when he'd declined breakfast.

"MacInnes. What brings you out my way?" Jack Clark, his beefy hands wrapped around a mug, too, joined Cole by a line of crummies, the buses that would shuttle the men from the camp to the site. The air was cold, their breath coming in little white puffs. "Do I have a problem?"

"No problem," Cole assured. "Not here anyway."

Cole's presence usually meant he'd been checking to see if the logging operation was being run according to its government contract specifications. What violations Cole had found on Jack's sites were always minor. Oversights really. And where he could, Cole helped correct problems himself. Cole didn't worry about Jack cutting beyond his boundaries or dragging felled timber through stream beds and destroying their banks. Jack ran a clean show. The majority of loggers nowadays did. Taking less than the best possible care of the forest would be more detrimental to them than to anyone else. The forest was the source of their livelihood, their home and their future.

It was Cole's home, too, the only place he'd ever really belonged. "I just stopped by on my way over to Corey Ridge."

Jack tucked one hand under the red suspenders holding up his cuffless pants and blew across his cup. Beneath his tin hat, his eyes were alert. "What's going on over there?"

"Not sure. I've spent the last couple of nights at the campground cutting back overgrowth and noticed that the stream is running awfully slow. Thought I'd go check it out."

"And you smelled coffee."

Cole grinned. "Your wife does know how to make it."

"I'd appreciate it if you'd tell her that. She's all down in the mouth since she got the mail a couple of days ago. Maybe a compliment would cheer her up."

Now that Jack realized the ranger's presence was nothing to be concerned about, he relaxed. Cole wasn't the kind of man who pried into another man's business, nor Jack the type to speak of personal matters. What was bothering his wife didn't just concern him, though. The other men with families were talking about it, too.

"The teacher she and Sally had lined up for next fall isn't coming. He decided Mist was just a little more remote than he'd like." He gave a derisive snort. "Took a job in Montana instead."

Cole's expression was philosophical. Of the eight school-age children in and around Mist, he knew them all by sight and most by name, but their education wasn't something he'd ever given much thought. "Mist has gotten along without a teacher before. What's wrong with keeping the kids on the state's correspondence program?"

"That's what I wanted to know. But it seems that with the kids getting older, some are getting to the point where they need help their folks can't give them. With the math and science especially. Hell, now Carolyn's talking about sending our boys to Anchorage. The last place I want my kids is in a boarding school.''

In Mist, families tended to keep their children occupied in and around their homes. Since Cole spent most of his time in his wilderness or at the station, he seldom encountered what to him were rather alien beings. He knew nothing about children. But he didn't have to know the children to feel the quick pang of regret for them. He was sure that the school Carolyn was contemplating was much different than those he'd been confined in, but he found the idea of sending a child away from his family abhorrent.

The rain started again. A soft drizzle that was so common neither man moved. Cole raised his cup. ''Why don't you have your wife talk to the woman who bought the store. She's lousy with animals, but she used to teach.''

Lara wasn't quite as bad with animals as she'd thought. The little bear had survived three full days in her care. She even told him he should feel grateful for that as the two of them sat in front of the fire in her living room while she tried to put together a light plug he'd pulled apart.

She couldn't believe she was talking to a bear. Fortunately, a knock on her back door saved her from having to contemplate the meaning of such behavior.

Thinking her caller might be Rosie, she tucked Bear, which she'd started calling the animal since that's what it was, back in his cage. Rosie didn't like the cub and Bear seemed to sense her animosity by making little growling noises that would no doubt be quite threatening when he grew up.

''You be quiet,'' she ordered and pulled open the door.

She'd barely stepped back when Cole came past her. He didn't wait to be invited in. He didn't even say hello before she turned to find him standing behind her. His only concession to civility was that he had the decency to drip on the throw rug instead of the floor.

It was raining. Still. In a place that got over a hundred inches of the stuff a year, Lara was beginning to learn that it had always just rained, was raining, or was about to rain. In some places people relied on a tan for color. Here, it was rust.

"Nice to see you, too." Closing the door, she leaned against it and forced her eyes up from the breadth of his solid chest. It had been three days since she'd seen him. She wished she could say it had been that long since she'd given him any thought. "Come in."

He didn't so much as blink at the dig. Grasping his Mountie-style hat by the brim, he pulled it off and ran his hand over the wet hair at his nape. "There's water pouring off your overhang. Your gutter must be clogged."

Lara cracked the door open again and peeked out. In the glow of the yellow porch light she could see a two-foot wide waterfall cascading off the eaves and splashing on the stoop planks. The deluge explained why he'd practically dived inside.

Being the basically forgiving sort, she offered him an apology of her own. She also added cleaning the gutter to her growing list of tasks and wondered when she could possibly get to it. Right after fixing the leak in her bedroom and before stocking the rest of the shelves, she decided, and moved painting the interior of the store farther down the list. At least, the store was cleaner than it had been. Painting her living quarters was last priority now; painting the outside of the building, little more than a distant hope. But she did still have everything under control.

She looked toward Cole.

More or less, she mentally amended and latched the door again.

"How's the cub?"

"Doing okay, I think."

She assumed that was all the information he required from her. Spotting a hook by the door, Cole shrugged out of his jacket, hung it there as if that were where he always put it and headed into the room. He had his hand clamped over the back of his neck. Beneath the heavy knit of his spruce-green sweater, she saw his shoulders rise and fall with a weary breath.

A fire crackled in the fireplace, a hint of wood smoke mingling with the scent of cooking spice. Lara had the curtains drawn and on the love seat, looking as if she'd been curled up under it at some point, was a patchwork quilt in watery shades of blue. A notepad and an account book lay between the folds.

Cole forced his eyes past the quilt, knowing that if he sat down he wouldn't get up until morning.

His glance moved on and he spotted the cage on the other side of the love seat. The cub sat inside it now, watching.

"Any problems with him?"

Lara told Cole she'd had none, certain he was interested only in the cub's health and not in the disruption the animal caused in her life. As they spoke, Cole hunkered down by the cage and opened the door. Bear stood up as he did.

"What in the hell . . . ?" Reaching inside, he lifted the little animal out. He was careful of the bandaged shoulder and foreleg, his big hands gentle. His expression lacked that trait completely. "What have you got on him?"

Tolerance met his disapproval. Obviously the man had never been around small children. "A diaper."

"What for?"

"Are you serious?"

"Yes, I'm serious," he said without the slightest hesitation. "You don't put these things on animals."

"It's a lot more practical than sitting outside in the dark waiting for him to...to do whatever he needs to do. And it's certainly easier than cleaning up after him."

For about ten seconds, Cole simply stared at her as he might some alien form of plant life. Proudly, he refrained from further comment. At least he did until he shifted Bear in his arms to see if its foreleg was still positioned properly beneath the bandage. When he turned the cub, Cole suddenly looked even more displeased. He lowered his head and sniffed the animal's neck.

Accusation laced his tone. "You gave him a bath."

"I didn't, either."

"Oh, come on. He doesn't smell anything like he did the other day. He smells like—"

Cole cut himself off. He'd started to say soap, but that wasn't quite right.

"Like what?" Lara wanted to know.

The cub smelled of wildflowers. And of something light and powdery. For some reason, he found it necessary to clear his throat before he spoke.

"Like you."

"That doesn't mean I bathed him. I haven't had him anywhere near water."

That being the case, there was only one other way the cub could have picked up that much of her scent. "Have you been holding him much?"

"I have to feed him."

The cub had slept with her last night, too, curled up under the comforter and behind her knees. But she didn't want to mention that. Bear hated the cage and she hated hearing him whimper. Bringing him to bed with her had nothing to do with the fact that she hadn't been able to sleep. Insomnia, after all, was nothing new to her. "I have to pick him up to change him," she added as if she'd been trying to think of other explanations.

Her reasons were logical. Yet, the way she avoided his eyes when she spoke made them sound suspicious. Either she wasn't telling him something, or she was getting defensive again. Whichever, he was too tired to figure it out. All he did was ask her to keep her contact with the cub to a minimum. If it became too accustomed to her, it wouldn't reacclimate when the time came to turn it loose. He also said it would be a good idea to move the cage out to her service porch. Since the area was enclosed, the animal would be out of the elements, but it wouldn't become spoiled by the warmer indoor temperatures.

Lara, telling him she understood, turned away. She didn't turn quickly enough. Cole had caught the oddly penitent glance she aimed toward the cub and wondered again at her odd ambivalence toward it. The thought had been fleeting, but when he'd left her the other day, he'd had the feeling that the real reason she hadn't wanted the animal around was that she feared she might get attached to it. The look in her eyes now, her concern as she surreptitiously watched him check the little animal over, told him she just might be getting attached to it anyway.

A few moments later, he had the animal tucked back in its cage. Hands on his knees, he wearily pushed himself back up. He could go now. Home to feed his hungry belly and then to sleep.

Cole was bone tired. He'd found the problem he'd set out after when he'd left Jack this morning and now there wasn't a muscle in his body that didn't ache. A tree had toppled over a nearly inaccessible spot on Corey Creek. The stream was an important spawning run for salmon and with all the debris the earlier storm had blown loose piling up behind the log, the stream had been reduced to a trickle. He'd spent ten hours cutting, hauling, hacking and climbing to clear it.

He'd thought all he'd want to do was go back to his cabin. As he turned to find Lara watching him, he found himself trying to remember why.

He no longer had a reason to stay. He *should* leave. But the idea of going back to his place right now had, in the space of seconds, lost its appeal. Maybe it had something to do with the warmth of her fire, or the delicious scents coming from her kitchen. They seemed to invite him to stay—even if she looked reluctant to extend the invitation herself.

Then he remembered. The excuse to remain a few minutes longer was only a few feet away, in his jacket.

"I brought you something to read. Here," he said, and turning his jacket around on the hook, pulled a booklet from its inside pocket. "Unless you have a religious objection to guns, I think you should learn how to use one."

Lara stared down at the booklet. It was a gun safety manual.

"I know the shoreline looks safe enough. But bears like to fish where the streams flow into the inlet. The route you've been taking in the mornings takes you over a mile from the nearest help."

She looked back at Cole, his large frame shadowing her. Fatigue etched itself in the lines fanning from his eyes. "How did you know that I walk in the mornings?"

"Gus saw you from his trawler as he was heading out."

"And he told you?"

"No. He mentioned it to Sally when he radioed in at their usual checkpoint."

You don't ever want to say anything over the radio that you don't mind all of Southeast knowing about. Rosie was right.

He saw her look back to the booklet. "You shouldn't pick up a gun until you know how to handle it safely. That's what the booklet will tell you. I'll teach you how to shoot myself."

Cole knew his offer surprised her. That was fine with him. When she was off guard she didn't argue and he didn't want to have to explain why he needed to do this. He was really only being practical. The woman was dangerous, if not to anyone else, certainly to herself. If he showed her how to protect herself, he wouldn't have to worry about someday having to bring her out of the woods in a body bag.

At least, that was what he told himself as he drew his fingers through his hair and waited for her to regroup.

Her quiet "Okay," was about the last thing he expected to hear.

It was also about the last thing Lara wanted to say. She didn't want to need his help, but she wasn't foolish enough to turn it down. She also didn't want to appear any more ungrateful than she already did.

"Would you..." She hesitated, her hand fluttering toward the kitchen. "Would you like a cup of coffee? It won't take long to make a pot."

That she'd waited so long to offer shamed her. Cole was helping her out by checking on Bear and he'd just offered to teach her a skill she apparently needed. It wasn't like her to ignore favors. And like it or not, she was in his debt. The least she could do was offer him coffee. The man looked beat.

"Yeah. I would," he said when what he should have done was say "no thanks" and dragged himself to the door. "Mind if I wash up first?"

He held up his hands and she pointed toward the bathroom. "First door on your right," she said and turned to the kitchen. It was too late to wonder why she really hadn't wanted to see him go.

Minutes later, the aroma of brewing coffee mingled with the smell of baking. Following the scent, Cole heard something slam shut, the sound like a stove door with an aggressive spring.

Leaning against the doorjamb he faced the neat little kitchen with its crisp white curtains framing the shuttered window above the sink. A row of white ceramic geese with orange beaks marched across the cracks in the yellow Formica counter. Lara had her back to him.

"My fresh fruit and produce came in this morning," she told him. "The bananas were all overripe, though, and I hated to see them go to waste. Now I've got enough banana bread to feed an army." She plopped the eighth loaf out onto the cooling rack. "Rosie said the woman at the logging camp could use some help, so I'll take them out to her in the morning." She flipped the potholders aside. "You wouldn't happen to know what time she serves the men breakfast would you?" Grabbing two mugs, red ones with white apple slices on them, she turned around.

"Six-thirty," Cole replied, and saw her go stock-still when she realized how closely he was watching her.

His gaze had been narrowed on her hips. Now his glance roamed upward, his imagination filling in the curves hidden beneath her long black sweater. She was slender, the dark color of the sweater and jeans she wore making her appear almost too thin. Yet, the word frail didn't apply to her. Despite the vulnerability that always seemed to lurk in her eyes, Cole was certain this woman wasn't as fragile as she looked. She was a survivor; like himself. Maybe that was what he recognized in her; that instinct that made a person keep fighting when the odds were stacked against him. He had the feeling, though, that with her the fight had nearly taken its toll.

It shouldn't matter, but it did. He should let it go, but he couldn't. She wasn't comfortable being alone. Not like he was; not the way a person would be if the choice to be alone were wholly voluntary.

"Why did you come here, Lara?"

Chapter Four

For a moment the only sounds to be heard were the drip of rain into the barrel outside the kitchen window and the click of mugs against the counter as Lara carefully set them down. She clearly hadn't expected Cole's question. Abruptly she plucked the pot from the stove. Pouring coffee bought her time to consider her response.

Cole followed her deliberate motions, willing to give her that time. Over the years, he had discovered that a person's reasons for coming to this last frontier tended to be intensely personal. Many came for adventure; most for the work, or the isolation, or in search of a simpler way of life. Some were running. Others, like him, seeking what they couldn't find anywhere else—a place to call home. He didn't think lack of roots was what motivated Lara, though. He suspected that she had that anchor: family and friends who cared about her.

No matter what reason brought a person here, only the tough, the brave, and the fiercely independent stayed. That was why even before Lara had arrived, Cole had bet old Gus Cassidy that a woman alone wouldn't stay beyond the first snowfall in October unless she found a man to marry her. But Lara had said she wasn't after a man. Whether or not that was the case, Cole was sure it wouldn't be long before every available male in the area came sniffing around. She had that air of vulnerable femininity about her that drew some men like bears to honey and made abject fools out of others. Cole was no fool.

But he was curious.

His silence finally prodded her to answer. She did so in a voice so soft he had to strain to hear her. "I told you before that I came because I wanted a change."

"From what?" His glance narrowed on her profile. "Are you hiding from something, Lara? Or someone?"

She set one of the mugs in front of him. Oddly, she seemed amused by his supposition. "I'm afraid my past isn't that colorful. Everyone I know, knows I'm here. That's hardly hiding."

A loaf of banana bread and a tub of butter were placed within his reach. Handing him a knife and plate, she motioned for him to help himself.

Waiting to see if she'd say anything else, he cut a hunk of bread from the loaf and slathered it with butter. He almost forgot what he was waiting for when he bit into the warm bread.

A half a minute passed before he spoke. When he did, he was contemplating the remaining bite. "I thought you said you weren't much of a cook. This is really good."

Her eyes, guarded seconds ago, lit first with surprise, then with pleasure. "Thank you," she said, liking that he enjoyed what he'd found at her table. "Help yourself to more. There's plenty."

He wasn't shy about taking her up on her offer. But then she was discovering that Cole wasn't shy about much of anything.

"You haven't answered my question," he reminded her and took another slice to go with his coffee.

His persistence didn't surprise her. That she felt vaguely defensive did. Not defensive the way her parents made her feel when they'd questioned her decision to move. *But everything you know is in California,* her mother had insisted. *Why in heaven's name do you want to leave everyone who cares about you and go live with strangers?* What Cole made her feel was far more disconcerting. He made her feel unsure of her well-considered rationale, as if he could see through her reasons to some motive she couldn't even define herself.

Lara sat down in the opposite chair and wrapped her hands around her mug. Maybe explaining to him would reinforce her reasoning. She didn't question why she found such reinforcement necessary.

"Mist appealed to me because it was so different from San Diego. I grew up with palm trees and beaches and freeways. I cut my teeth on a surfboard and spent every summer between my seventeenth and twenty-second birthday as a lifeguard. The closest I'd come to the woods was scout camp in the sixth grade. I thought it was time for mountains and forests."

"So what do you think of them?"

"Of the mountains and the forests?"

He nodded as the second half of another slice went the way of the first.

"They're . . . big," she decided, and made the mistake of thinking Cole might be diverted to a less personal topic.

"Big enough to get lost in," he said enigmatically. His eyes pinned hers over his mug. He took a sip, watching her through the curling wisp of steam. "You don't want to answer me, do you?"

The statement was as puzzling as the jolt caused by his quiet stare. Caught with her own mug halfway to her lips, she slowly lowered it to the table. "I don't know what you mean."

Cole was out of line. He knew that, yet he didn't really care. He wasn't sure what he wanted from her, but he did know he wanted more than superficial answers. He had no talent for games. He was lousy at small talk, worse yet at subtlety. In his world, a straight question deserved a straight answer. "I think you do. I asked why you're here. It's a pretty simple question."

He wanted the bottom line. She realized that when he refused to release his visual hold.

Her voice was steady even if her hands weren't. She tightened them around her mug so he wouldn't see their trembling. She had the uncanny feeling he knew they were shaking anyway. "I'm here," she said, reducing her decision to its simplest terms, "because there was nothing left for me in San Diego."

Any other person might have felt uncomfortable at having elicited such an admission. Not Cole. He simply tilted his head to one side to study her better. "You have no family there?"

His scrutiny, like his refuting statement, made her uneasy. "I do. My parents and my sister. And a mother-in-law who thinks I'm awful because I don't visit my husband's grave once a month as she does." Lara rubbed the finger where her wedding band had been. She'd only taken the ring off a couple of months ago. "They have their own lives. I needed to get on with mine."

"Does it matter what your mother-in-law thinks?"

Lara's hands stilled. The man didn't miss much. "Yes, it does. She's a very nice woman who needs someone to share her grief. I know she finds some kind of comfort in what she does, but going out there just made it harder for me. She couldn't understand that."

"How long has it been?"

"Since the accident?" she asked, scarcely aware that she hadn't mentioned how Steve had died.

Cole nodded.

"A little over eighteen months."

"What happened?"

"A truck blew a red light. We were just in the wrong place at the wrong time." The legs of her chair scraped against the linoleum as she stood, the sound harsh and grating. She didn't want to talk about this.

Cole watched her pick up her cup and set it back down again. Looking for something else to do, she took the coffeepot from the stove.

"We" she'd said. That meant she had been with him. Was that how she'd gotten the scar on her forehead? "I'm sorry," Cole said.

Lara turned to look back at him. He remained at the table, his dark eyes fixed on her pale features. She couldn't tell what the apology was for. Was he sorry about Steve? Or sorry that he didn't have the decency to pursue less intrusive conversation? She didn't need this. She should have let him leave.

Taking the lid from the pot, she poured the little remaining coffee down the sink. Dumping the coffee would keep her from delaying him with the offer of another cup. Washing the pot would give her something to do while he figured out it was time for him to go.

It was only a matter of seconds before she heard Cole's chair against the floor and his heavy footfall coming toward her. To her right she saw the sleeve of his sweater as he placed his mug on the counter by the sink. He'd stopped behind her, so close she could feel the heat of his large, solid body.

She'd felt her whole body stiffen at his approach. Now, knowing her defensiveness wasn't really his fault, she turned off the water, preparing to offer an apology of her own. He couldn't possibly have realized the combination of buttons he'd pushed.

Or so she thought.

"You shouldn't let her make you feel guilty just because you don't subscribe to her idea of how to mourn. No one but you knows how much you can take."

His voice was tight; as if he were speaking from an experience he wasn't prepared to share. Part of Lara wondered at his insight; part of her recoiled from it. But even as much as she wanted to let it go, she knew she needed to defend Steve's mother. It hadn't been easy for anyone.

"She only feels as she does because I wasn't able to go to the funeral. I was in the hospital with a broken leg... and some other problems," she decided to say, not willing to enumerate everything else that had gone so horribly wrong. "Anyway, Steve's mom thinks I'm denying his death by not going to the cemetery. I'm not denying it. I know he's gone."

Something shifted in Cole's eyes. Something that made it very hard for her to look away. It wasn't sympathy. She couldn't have handled that. It was more like respect. She couldn't begin to understand where it could have come from.

He lifted his hand and gently nudged aside part of the curls that tumbled over her forehead. With a touch as soft as a whisper, he drew his index finger from the apex of her left eyebrow to where the silvery scar disappeared into her hairline above her temple. "Was this one of those 'other problems'?"

"Yes," she said, almost swallowing the word.

The tender way he brushed her skin was far more threatening than anything he could have said. It seemed to say that he understood about loss and despair and the long struggle back. And while part of her greedily responded to that shared rapport, she almost hated him for making her remember those agonizing days when she'd needed Steve to hold her and grieve with her. But Steve wasn't there because he was part of why she was grieving and she'd had to try to heal alone.

"Can we not talk about this anymore, please?"

The look in her eyes begged Cole to leave her memories alone. He saw that silent plea and shrank from it. It hurt her to remember and he didn't want to cause her any more pain. Yet, as he lowered his hand and her bangs fell back to cover the scar, he couldn't help but wonder what else she had suffered, what other scars were even more well hidden.

A heavy silence stretched between them. He was so close, close enough to see the individual shades of blue in her eyes. Close enough to see the fine grain of her skin and the natural blush of her soft and lovely mouth. She was such a pretty woman.

Ah, Lara, he thought. What would you do if I touched you again?

He took a step back, not sure he trusted himself with that question. He'd already discovered more about her than he truly wanted to know. What he was discovering about himself was even more unsettling.

"I should go."

She had the good grace to hide her relief by turning to wipe her hands. "I appreciate you checking on Bear."

"Bear?"

"The cub."

"You call him 'Bear'?"

Her towel was threaded through the handle of the cabinet below the sink. When she faced him this time, she met his glance evenly. "What's wrong with that?"

"Not a thing." He didn't care what she chose to name the animal. His only concern was how relieved he was to see a hint of spiritedness in her eyes. He didn't want her to see how she affected him. He started for his jacket. "You can call him anything you want. Oh, by the way." Stopping himself short of the door, he took the jacket from the hook. "You mentioned that you wanted to take that bread out to Carolyn. Did she come by to see you today?"

"No. I haven't met her yet. Why?"

"When you see her, she might ask you about teaching next year. The teacher they had lined up isn't coming after all and I told Jack that Carolyn ought to talk to you about it. You said something the other day about your third-grade class, remember?"

"I wish you hadn't done that."

"Done what?"

"Told her I'm a teacher."

"You mean you're not one?"

"Not anymore. I'm retired."

He dismissed her statement by pushing his arms into his sleeves and shrugging his jacket up over his wide shoulders. "You're not old enough to be retired."

She handed him his hat. "Age has nothing to do with it."

"How old are you anyway?"

"Twenty-nine and don't try to change the subject."

She glared up at him, suspecting even as she did that the narrow-eyed expression that worked so well on eight-year-old males would have minimal effect on the grown-up version. When he didn't so much as blink, she inched her chin up.

"I didn't come here to teach, Cole. If I'd wanted that, I'd have stayed where I was." And if she'd stayed, she wouldn't have done anyone any good. Her students deserved better than what she'd been able to give them the past year.

She said nothing of that, though. She didn't want to explain any more to Cole of everything she was trying to put behind her—if he would just let her.

"I think you might at least listen to what she has to say." Cole's voice was firm, his expression much cooler than she'd seen it all evening. "We try to help each other out here, Lara."

He settled his hat on his head, shadowing his eyes with its brim, and reached for the door. "Read the book," he said, nodding toward the pamphlet she'd set on the counter. "I'll take you out with a rifle when the rain lets up."

With that, he was gone. She didn't doubt that he swore as he darted through the deluge on the other side of her door.

Lara swore, too. *We try to help each other out,* he'd said, and made her sound utterly selfish for not wanting to teach the children of Mist. He couldn't begin to understand what kind of a commitment teaching was; how much emotional and mental energy it took. Energy she just didn't seem to have anymore. And time. She had more to do now than she thought she'd ever accomplish.

Those were only excuses, but they served to work up a little anger at his presumption. Anger felt good. It felt real, and so much of what she'd felt lately was simply numbness. So she indulged her irritation at him. He wasn't being fair. She'd agonized over the decisions she'd made and she was not going to let some highly opinionated, mountain of a man with the subtlety of a Sherman tank undo the life she'd barely had a chance to start.

Lara had known it wouldn't be easy to make a new life for herself. She didn't, however, think it had to be as difficult as Cole was making it for her. It was bad enough that he'd saddled her with a bear cub that refused to believe it wasn't human. Now, he'd put her in the uncomfortable position of having to turn down the first request for help that anyone in Mist had made of her. Lara wasn't in the habit of saying no. If there was a way she could help someone out, invariably she found it. If anything, her unwillingness to refuse when asked to volunteer for some neighborhood committee or to take on friends' pets or children for a weekend had been a source of frustration for her husband. What Carolyn Clark wanted her to consider was impossible, though. Fortunately, Carolyn didn't ask.

The next morning when Lara took the cellophane-wrapped loaves of banana bread out to her at the camp, Carolyn Clark barely had time to say hello. Caught in the middle of serving up breakfast for forty hungry loggers, the rosy-cheeked woman with the deep dimples and short auburn hair could do little more than say how surprised she was at the gesture and how very grateful she was for the assist. Lara knew she was being a coward, but she didn't stick around for the coffee she was offered. She stayed only long enough to say she didn't want to get in the way, agree that they would see each other again soon and head back to the store to sand shelves. She doubted that the woman would have mentioned her teaching within minutes of first meeting her, but she hadn't wanted to take any chances.

Lara needn't have worried. No one said a word about it until over a week later, on a Saturday night Lara would remember for a very long time.

On Saturday night, life in Mist revolved around Rosie's Bar and Grill. Lara would have been content to stay home and go to bed early since, between customers, she'd spent most of the day attempting to stop up the leaks in her bedroom ceiling with caulk and priming the shelves she'd sanded. But Sally stopped by shortly after Lara had abandoned caulk for cooking pots to catch the drips, since it was still raining, and insisted that Lara show up at Rosie's for at least a little while. Just to get rid of the woman, Lara had agreed to go.

Sally was proving to be something of a chatty nuisance. It wasn't that Lara disliked her, she just didn't share the woman's affinity for gossip. She also wanted to fix the store up herself, so it would *feel* like hers, and politely refused Sally's numerous offers to help with the painting. A woman over seven months pregnant shouldn't be stretching with a paintbrush anyway and that was the reason Lara gave when she declined the offers of assistance. She was far from rude, though. As a result, Sally had put herself in charge of Lara's social life. Lara certainly didn't want to be thought of as antisocial, so if going to Rosie's on Saturday was some sort of inviolate custom, far be it from her to ignore it.

Aside from that, Rosie's was a rather interesting place. It had a bar at one end, a pool table at the other and a patch of black-and-white tiles reserved for dancing in between. Music for that purpose was provided by an old chrome jukebox stationed beneath a flashing Rainier beer sign. Snapshots were thumbtacked to the wall above the coffeepot, a cribbage board, checker boards and a Monopoly game were stacked on a shelf with bottles of liquor behind

the bar, and the back wall sported a dart board and medi-
ocre oil paintings a former resident and aspiring artist had
donated before deciding he had no real talent after all and
returned to his accounting job in Cleveland. Rosie had
smiled wistfully when she'd told Lara that she'd really been
sorry to see him go.

When Lara entered that night with Sally and Sally's husband, Tom—Big Tom, actually, to differentiate him from
Tommy, their nine-year-old—most of the twenty or so men
at the small square tables and leaning against the bar
glanced toward the door. Several of them lifted their drinks,
smiling amiably as the trio crossed the room to join Carolyn Clark at a table under a painting of a moose. Lara
smiled back, recognizing some of the men who'd come in to
buy gloves or cigarettes over the past couple of weeks and
waved to the burly Scandinavian logger who'd kindly explained that jaggers were little pieces of metal from the wire
logging cables, not insects as she'd once assumed.

For the most part, the men milling around were bunk-
house loggers, as Carolyn called those who lived in the
communal quarters the logging operation provided. Gus
Cassidy's trawler crews occupied the tables and the spaces
at the far end of the bar. That's where the television was—
its channel selector seemingly permanently stuck on the ca-
ble sports station that—weather permitting—Rosie picked
up with the satellite dish on her roof. The bets made between the loggers and the fishermen were occasionally responsible for fights that broke out after a few too many
beers. One of the men usually responsible for those little al-
tercations was here tonight, too, Lara noticed. Chuck Win-
chester, the lean, baby-faced fisherman who'd tried to get
her to go for double or nothing for his groceries last week
wasn't by the television. He was farther down the bar, sitting sullenly over his beer.

"What's wrong with Chuck?" Lara asked Carolyn as she sat down beside her at the scratched and scarred wooden table.

It was Sally who responded as Tom headed for the bar. "Cole bet him fifty bucks that he couldn't go a week without gambling."

"He's probably in withdrawal," Carolyn said and leaned back with a sigh to comment on how nice it was to do nothing for a change.

After working her tail off for the past two months, Carolyn informed the two women smiling at her that she was actually taking a whole day off. Jack, bless his heart, was overseeing the boys' supper and would be here soon—to spend their first "evening out" since she'd taken over the old cook's job. She was celebrating.

The reason for the celebration was the arrival of the new cook. He'd come in a couple of days ago and Carolyn was enjoying her reprieve immensely. Since Lara hadn't seen him yet, Carolyn surreptitiously pointed out the ex-navy hash slinger known as "Angel." Angel had the face of a bulldog, no neck and was as solid as a stump. He was currently at the bar giving Rosie a bad time about the seasoning in her chili. Rosie, who backed down from no one, was challenging him to match hers with a batch of his own.

Gus and old Walt, the retired miner who'd settled here about the same time as the glaciers, were taking bets on who'd come up with the better batch.

Her dimples showing, Carolyn lifted her drink to Lara. "Typical Saturday night in Mist. Think you can stand the excitement?"

"I'll try," Lara returned, and felt her smile falter when the door swung open. She had just started to relax. Now, she suddenly felt as tense as a spring.

Cole saw Lara turn, the smile on her face fading as their eyes met. Quickly she glanced away, only to look back again as if dismayed by her first reaction. She gave him a little smile. A reluctant one to be sure and he wondered if she was still upset with him for telling Jack that she was a teacher. If she smiled at him, she couldn't be too angry, he figured, and nodded back. It was a moment before he glanced from her though. She reminded him of a porcelain doll with her dark hair framing her pale face and her petal-pink sweater picking up the faintest hint of color in her cheeks. She looked soft and sexy and as he heard his name being called from down the bar, he realized she was the only person in the place he was interested in.

"Hey, Cole," Tom said, clutching a beer and two colas as he passed. "Come pull up a chair. You don't want to sit with these sorry cusses." He grinned at the guys behind him. "I'm over here with the women."

Since Jack hadn't yet arrived, Carolyn motioned to the chair between her and Lara, saying as she did that she was surprised to see him. Cole seldom came to Rosie's—unless he wanted something to eat or there was a fight to break up. He kept to himself in the evenings. As it was, Cole wasn't even sure why he was here, except that his cabin had seemed too quiet tonight and, with the rain, there hadn't been anywhere else to go.

He decided to ask Tom how the halibut were running, which sent Tom off onto a lament about how slow the fishing was right now and brought Bud from the ice house over to complain about how he was having to delay bringing in his summer packing crews because there weren't that many fish to pack. The men had about half of Cole's attention. The other half was on Lara. She'd turned sideways, listening politely and without comment as a separate conversation took place among the women. He had no idea what they were talking about, but knowing Carolyn it had something to do with the loggers' struggle against the misguided environmentalists—which explained why Sally kept drumming her fingers on the table. Sally wasn't at all political. But she did like to dance. Her fingers were tapping in time to the music and she kept sliding glances toward her husband.

There were currently two couples on the floor. The marina mechanic and his wife and a young couple Bud had hired, but hadn't been able to put to work. When the music changed to something slow Tom stopped trying to ignore his wife and hitched his head toward the floor. "Shall we?" he asked, and Sally grinned.

Sally, pregnant as she was, had long since passed the graceful stage. Tom didn't seem to mind a bit as he pulled his wife as close as his new offspring would allow.

Lara watched them go. Unlike Cole she didn't look away after the first few measures. And unlike Carolyn, who excused herself for a moment to go to the rest room, she seemed oddly interested in what the couple was doing. So Cole watched her, wondering what it was about Tom and his wife dancing together that made her look so sad.

"Do you want to do that?"

Her eyes jerked to his. "No," she said, far too quickly. "I . . . No. Thanks." She gave him a halfhearted smile, offering apology along with an excuse. "I'm not much of a dancer."

"Neither am I."

Her eyebrow arched at the admission.

"I just thought you might want to," he explained.

His thoughtfulness surprised her. It shouldn't have. To be fair, she knew he could be kind. She'd seen it before. With her. With Bear. She'd just become so guarded around him that she'd come to expect only his tough bluntness. In a way the kindness he'd just offered made up a little for other times when his manner had wounded, or angered. She would never understand him. Or herself for being so attracted to him. And she was. Far more than she cared to admit.

She should go home.

"I have the copper tubing your friend Asa wanted," she told him. "It came in yesterday."

"If this rain keeps up, I might not be able to get to him for a while."

A frown darted through her eyes. "Will he be all right for that long? I mean, Rosie said he's kind of old."

Her concern struck him. She didn't even know the man and she was clearly worried about him. "Old is a state of mind, according to Asa. It'll take more than spring showers to bring that old coot down. He's got his cabin and his antifreeze to keep him warm."

"His antifreeze?"

"His liquor. Mash. He's got a still up there. That's what the copper tubing is for. Lightning hit his old still and he's making a new one."

A delighted smile touched Lara's mouth. "He's a bootlegger?"

"I didn't say that."

She ignored the disclaimer. "Isn't that illegal?"

"Depends. He doesn't try to sell it, so I prefer to think of it as his form of subsistence living. He's not hurting anyone."

And you're the only friend he has, Lara remembered, recalling what Rosie had once said.

"He sounds very interesting."

"He is," Cole replied flatly. Then, not expecting it, he found himself reluctant to let the conversation end. Maybe it was because of her initial reaction to Asa's hobby; the delight he'd seen in her smile. Cole had the feeling that smiles such as that didn't come very often for her. Or maybe he didn't want to let the conversation go because he was afraid she would leave and he didn't want her to. Not yet. He wanted very badly to see that smile again.

That was why, leaning forward a little so he didn't have to compete with the music and shouts from the bar over the game, he wrapped his hands around his beer and told her about the eccentric old miner who had come looking for his fortune and found, instead, a dried-up claim and a ramshackle home in the wilderness.

Lara was fascinated. Not so much with Asa, though she sympathized with the man far more than she let on. She knew what it was like to have dreams die. Her fascination was with Cole. She was beginning to realize that he possessed an understanding of human nature that was far more accepting than most. According to him, Asa still worked his claim, and even if Cole didn't come right out and say so, it was clear to Lara that both Asa and Cole knew there was nothing in the mine worth the trouble. Asa had been working the site off and on for years, not accomplishing anything more than turning a mountain of rock inside out. His pride wouldn't let him admit defeat, though. And Cole, refusing to rob a down-and-out old hermit of his dignity, still kept him supplied with the parts he requested for his ancient equipment.

Beads of water had collected on the side of her glass. With the tip of her finger, she slowly traced through them. "Is there any possibility he'll find gold or whatever he's looking for? It's kind of sad to think he's spending his life looking for something that isn't there."

Cole shrugged. "He wouldn't know what to do if he ever did hit a vein. His life would change and he wouldn't know what to do with himself. He's happy doing what he does."

"You must be talking about Asa," said Carolyn, rejoining them.

Lara said they were and watched Cole tip back his beer and drain it. When he set the empty can down, Sally and Tom were taking their seats. Jack was right behind them.

Carolyn looked a little anxious as her husband pulled a chair into the group. "The boys okay?"

Jack, wearing his usual hickory shirt and cuffless pants, said they were fine. They were making popcorn with Sally and Tom's kids and the bigger boys were getting ready to watch a movie on the VCR while the little ones played Fish.

"Tim still upset?" Sally asked, seeming to know why Carolyn looked so concerned.

Tim was the Clarks' thirteen-year-old. "A little," Carolyn replied. "Ever since he saw the material I requested from that prep school in Anchorage, he's barely spoken to either of us."

Lara's hand slowly slid from her glass to her lap. For the next several minutes, while she sat contemplating the initials carved into the table, the two sets of parents talked around the subject that Lara had prayed wouldn't come up. She could appreciate that it would be difficult to get teachers in a place like this. She could also appreciate how difficult it was for some children to learn from their parents, and for some parents to teach. The outpost curriculum approved by the State sounded like a good one, based on what Lara heard in those few minutes, but she could understand why the parents might want a classroom situation for their children. She just didn't feel that there was anything she could contribute. And she hoped above all else that no one would ask so she wouldn't have to turn them down.

"I understand you taught, Lara," Jack said, and Lara felt her stomach clench. "What do you think about boarding schools?"

"I've never had any experience with them," she could honestly admit. "But I'm sure there are good ones."

She made the mistake of looking at Cole just then. He'd leaned back, watching, his arm draped over the back of the chair. The position emphasized the broadness of his chest, his lean hips and powerful thighs. He looked recklessly insolent, disarmingly casual and very, very male. He also seemed to be waiting for her to offer more.

What Lara was waiting for was a decent moment to make an exit.

Fortunately the conversation ended after a few rather generic questions about individual study programs and summer school. No one had even hinted that she might take the job, for which Lara was truly grateful, but the look Cole had given her when she'd failed to say she'd teach the kids so they wouldn't have to leave Mist, left her feeling as if she'd just let everyone down.

Lara could easily understand the parents' concerns. It was Cole's reasons for wanting her to take on the job that weren't quite so obvious. Yet, it was his reaction that she'd found the hardest on her nerves. She resented the position he'd put her in; what he seemed to expect from her. He was forcing her to confront issues she'd already agonized over, to justify again why it had been so necessary to leave a job she'd once loved. She simply couldn't let herself go back to what she'd left in San Diego, for the children's sake as well as her own.

Lara didn't know how to explain any of that, so she didn't even try. Cole had left the table anyway.

Cole headed for the bar, annoyed with himself for staying at the table as long as he had; annoyed with himself for coming in the first place. The Clarks and the Cassidys and the other parents would solve their problem, with or without Lara's help, and the matter of finding a teacher wasn't any of his concern. He also had no business caring what she did, one way or the other. It wasn't like him to get involved with this type of thing. Not that he *was* involved, he assured himself, since all he'd done was listen. His concerns were only for the land and how it was treated. That was his job. That was how he wanted it. And that was how it had always been.

Certain he had his priorities in line, he motioned to Rosie for another beer. With Chuck temporarily out of commission on the betting end of things, there probably wouldn't be any problems tonight. He couldn't help thinking, though, that a good fight would help to take his mind off of Lara. He might have convinced himself that he didn't care what she did, but he was still feeling as frustrated as hell—and he hadn't even touched her. The problem was that it took no effort at all to visualize his hand running over her small rib cage and up to cup those firm little breasts. As he'd watched her speak, he could almost feel that soft smile of hers curving beneath his mouth.

He jerked the stool out from the bar with a little more force than he intended. The burly, black-haired and bearded lumberman next to him gave him a frown then moved out of the way to give Cole more room. As big as the man was, Cole was bigger. Not that the Paul Bunyan-type was intimidated by that. He was just more interested in the fifty bucks he had riding on the basketball game.

Cole didn't even know who was playing. In the mirror behind the bar, he could see Lara looking at Sally as Sally pressed her husband's hand to her stomach. Husband and wife were laughing, as were the Clarks, but the smile on Lara's face was the oddest combination of sweetness and pain he'd ever seen.

To anyone else, it probably looked as though everyone at the table were enjoying themselves. Cole didn't think Lara was enjoying herself at all. From where he sat, it looked as if she couldn't wait to get out of there.

Within the minute she was standing, seeming very animated as she zipped her parka to her throat. A moment later, having said her goodbyes to those at the table, she waved at Rosie and headed for the door.

Cole had heard that she always left early and alone. As she pulled the door closed behind her, he wondered if she always left in such a hurry.

She was a strange woman. She seemed to want to fit in; was trying in many respects to do just that. Yet, she didn't seem to be developing a real friendship with any of the women. Certainly not Sally. There was something about the community's resident magpie that seemed to keep Lara at a distance. Her mouth probably, Cole thought, appreciating why Tom didn't mind spending so many days at sea. Lara didn't seem that friendly with Carolyn, either, though. Jack's wife said the first time she'd met her, Lara hadn't stuck around more than five minutes.

He glanced toward Rosie who popped the top off his beer and slid it down the counter. Knowing Rosie as he did, the older woman hadn't warmed enough to Lara to allow more than a surface friendliness. Rosie was a hard sell. But then, she'd seen a lot of people come and go through Mist over the years and she didn't waste time on the ones who wouldn't make it. She had an uncanny sense about that sort of thing.

Still, he wished Lara would develop a good friend or two. Then, he wouldn't have to worry about her himself. He wondered if she even realized how troubled she'd looked when she left.

As it was, Lara was trying very hard not to think about what had necessitated her rather hurried departure. She thought she'd done pretty well tonight, all things considered, but seeing Sally and Tom share their baby's movements had threatened too many emotions and calling it a night had suddenly seemed like a real good idea.

With Rosie's place only a few yards down the boardwalk, Lara had let herself in through the front of the darkened store. Now, she passed through the doorway leading into her living room. She'd left the kitchen light on when she'd gone next door, but she stopped at the threshold, unable to see. The room was pitch-black.

She took a step forward, feeling in front of her so she wouldn't knock anything over and opened the door to the service porch. Bear's little woofing noises greeted her. Having assured herself that he was all right, she made her way toward the kitchen door, feeling along the wall as she went. The dumb light bulb must have burned out. Three flicks of the light switch proved that assessment correct.

"Well, hell," she muttered now feeling along the wall that led to the stairwell.

She reached around the corner, groping for that switch. The light in the stairwell didn't work, either.

It occurred to her that the generator must have run out of gas, until she remembered that she'd filled it only yesterday. As she listened, she could hear its familiar chug. An instant later, something else registered. The paneling where her hand rested on the wall was wet. Odder still, she could feel a very moist, very cold draft coming down the stairwell.

It took a few seconds for her to realize what had happened. A few more for the reality of it to register.

"Oh, my God," she whispered into the darkness.

Her roof had caved in.

Chapter Five

Lara went back to Rosie's, not quite believing what common sense told her had happened, and stopped just inside the door. She hadn't made a conscious decision to ask Cole for help. He was simply the only person she thought to seek. Faced with the fact that it was presently raining in her bedroom, she didn't bother to analyze why.

He was obviously surprised to see that she'd come back. Had Lara bothered to look around, she'd have noticed that her reappearance raised the casual interest of a few of the other patrons, too. Several were wondering aloud what it was she'd forgotten that had brought her back in such a hurry. She noticed only Cole.

Separating himself from the bar and the men bellied up to it, he watched Lara come toward him.

"I think my roof's collapsed," she said and he could only wonder at how calmly she'd spoken.

For a fraction of a second, he saw the naked distress in her eyes; the expression that said "I can't believe this is happening." A moment later, she'd swallowed and quietly asked if he could come help her.

The request had a dozen able-bodied men pushing aside their drinks, sliding from their bar stools and heading for the door. Tom and Jack were among them. Carolyn, too. Sally started to follow, but when Lara saw her button her coat over her rounded tummy, she stopped her. With the power out, Sally might trip in the dark. Rosie agreed that Sally should stay and shoved a couple of emergency lanterns into Lara's hands. Lara had lanterns in her store, but Rosie apparently realized that she hadn't had time to remember them. She also told Lara that, in case she needed it, she had an extra bed she could use tonight. In the meantime, she and Sally would put on the coffee.

It seemed that in an emergency, everyone simply dropped what they were doing and did what needed to be done.

In Lara's case, what needed to be done couldn't all be taken care of in one night. The damage could have been worse, though. At least, that was the general consensus after the men had wandered around upstairs with their lanterns and someone had braved the rain to take a peek from a ladder leaned against the side of the building. The entire roof hadn't collapsed; only part of it over the back of the building. It was too dark to tell much more than that by flashlight. Inside, a ragged gap replaced the ceiling of her bedroom and part of an interior wall sagged like a bow. After long winters of heavy snow, of water-logged beams and trusses freezing and thawing, the weakened wood had finally given way.

Lara accepted that news with resignation. After all, the Stanleys had said the roof needed repair. As she followed the arcing lights across the ceiling and around the room, she thought it would have been nice to know that it had needed that repair immediately. It was hard to believe what she knew she was seeing.

The quality of the flashlights made everything appear black and white and gray. Somehow, her mind chose to be more impressed with the surrealism of awkwardly placed beams and dangling wires than with the actual destruction to her home. The feeling of rain on her face and the wind tugging her hair only added to the unreality.

After spending a full minute wondering where she should start, she gave up and went downstairs—as she was instructed to do by someone whose voice had carried enough authority to make her do so without questioning him.

It took over an hour to determine whether the structure was in danger of further collapse. Another hour to rig up support for a shaky-looking section. The men were finishing up a temporary cover for the ceiling when Lara heard Cole's voice drift down the stairwell.

"Damn lucky she wasn't in bed when it went."

The same thought had occurred to Lara.

The loud pop of the heavy staple gun precluded overhearing further comments. The noise continued for a moment, splitting the stillness every five seconds or so as it had for the last half hour. When it stopped this time, it didn't start up again. Instead, as Lara closed the door to the service porch where she'd gone to check on a peacefully sleeping Bear, she heard the gravelly murmur of male voices consulting as to the effectiveness of their efforts and the husky tones of Cole's voice as he called for her to come up.

She headed for the base of the stairs, flashlight in hand. Aiming the beam upward, she saw Cole and Tom at the top of the steps. Behind them danced the elongated shadows of the other men.

Before she could start up, the men started down, tools in hand.

"Hope that helps," Bud told her, adjusting his glasses as he emerged from the stairwell.

His foreman from the ice house simply muttered, "Ma'am," tipped the brim of his baseball cap and followed Bud out through the store. Tom was right behind them, brushing off her thanks as unnecessary, much as those who'd departed earlier had done.

"Just glad we were able to help," he told Lara, then added that he'd best be getting on home. Sally would be waiting up.

"Lara? Are you coming up or not?"

Tom hitched his thumb toward the stairs. "You'd better go see what we've done," he said and let himself out.

Lara pointed her light back up the narrow stairway. The beam bounced off a piece of lumber angled at the top. It hadn't been moved for fear that more of the roof might come down.

The bell over the store's front door sounded twice, indicating that Tom had let himself out. It seemed like only minutes ago that the place had been crawling with people. Carolyn and Rosie had come and gone, as had several of the others who'd been next door. Now, only Cole was here.

As Lara reached the landing and stepped over the beam partially blocking it, she saw him prop a roll of black plastic up against the end of the short hallway. There were two rooms up here, one directly across from the other. He turned when he heard her and motioned to the one on her right. Her bedroom.

With some reluctance, Lara went in.

The lighting was much better now than it had been earlier. A high-intensity lantern sat on her dresser, the mirror behind it doubling the illumination. The harsh light hid nothing. Where before she'd noticed only sections of damage, now she could see the whole picture.

It was not a pretty sight.

She felt Cole move behind her. The room was small. It seemed smaller still with him in it.

"You won't be able to sleep up here, but it's the best we can do for now. This should keep the worst of the rain out for a while."

She looked up from the light fixture shattered on the floor. There was a hole where it had once hung. The hole wasn't visible, though. Heavy black plastic had been stapled over most of the ceiling. Toward the center, where the plastic sagged, a hole the size of a quarter had been punched into it. Directly below, secured among the debris covering her bed, sat a bucket. The plastic patch wouldn't hold much weight by itself, but with the vent, the water could be directed into the container. Not that a little more water could possibly hurt. Practically everything in the room was soaking wet. One of the reasons her ceiling had been leaking so badly was that water had pooled under the roof.

Her attention shifted from the ceiling to the floor. A falling piece of lumber had knocked her hairbrush from the dresser. It lay next to a broken bottle of lotion. She picked the brush up, along with a saucer-size piece of ceiling.

"I really appreciate what everyone's done. I'm not sure I'd have even known where to begin." She hated that she'd felt that way. She'd always been so capable; always been the one who'd known what to do in a crisis. So often lately, she felt as if she did nothing but flounder.

She pushed her fingers through her bangs, taking a deep breath as she glanced around the room. The ceiling was all over the floor. The carpet, a faded remnant she'd already intended to replace, was soaking wet. Many of the things she'd had on the nightstand and dresser were either smashed, on the floor, or both.

She still didn't know where to start. "Lord, this place is a mess."

She knew Cole was watching her. She could feel his quiet scrutiny as she squatted by the dresser and picked up another piece of ceiling. Heaven only knew what his brooding scowl meant. He probably thought she was a disaster waiting to happen. First, Bear. Now, this. Whatever he was thinking, she couldn't let herself worry about it. She needed very badly to feel that she was doing something positive right now.

Her pile of broken plaster grew. "I'd wanted to redo this room. I just hadn't planned on adding a skylight." She glanced up, one hand on the dresser for balance. "Maybe that wouldn't be such a bad idea. This room was awfully dark. The store has catalogs for just about everything. Maybe I'll see if I can order one."

She didn't expect a response and she got none.

She set a soggy, lily-scented sachet on a corner of the dresser, stilling as her glance skimmed past her bed. The rust-colored water that had collected in the attic had ruined her new comforter. She'd bought the lace and white eyelet comforter because it reminded her of the one she'd had as a child. Life had been so simple then, so free of self-doubt and grown-up hurts.

She touched the delicate fabric. The dirty print of a man's boots, a logger's caulks from the looks of the stud marks, made a pattern across the bottom of the bed.

Her hand fell. A person could never go back. No one knew that better than she.

Cole must have seen where she was looking. A hint of apology, unnecessary as far as Lara was concerned, shadowed his voice. "Jack had to stand there to tie up a beam."

"It doesn't matter. It was ruined anyway."

The glint of silver caught her eye. A picture lay half hidden by the dust ruffle, kicked there possibly as the men had worked. Picking it up, she stood and slowly turned it over.

The silver-framed picture had been on her nightstand. Through the cracks in the glass, her husband looked back at her.

With the tip of her finger, she touched the center of the picture. If she'd left it packed, it wouldn't have gotten broken. Last night was the first time she'd taken it out since she'd been here—last night when she'd been unable to sleep and she'd lain thinking of the evening Cole had sat at her table, looking as if he were truly enjoying every bite he took of her banana bread. It had felt nice to have him be so comfortable at her table. Steve had always wolfed down his meals on the run.

She drew her finger away. She'd been so afraid she'd forget his face. As it was, she couldn't seem to recall it in any other expression than the one smiling up at her now. It frightened her a little to be losing that part of her memory of him. What frightened her more was how frequently she found herself thinking of the man watching her.

Her expression grew pensive, then softened. "Steve would never have been able to handle a mess like this," she said, lifting her glance to Cole. "He hated disorganization."

"I'm sure he'd have managed."

Cole wasn't at all sure of why he'd defended the man. Lara seemed to appreciate that he had, though, and gave him a little smile before she set the picture on the dresser.

She hadn't yet let go of the frame when Cole picked it back up.

For the briefest moment, his glance held hers, almost daring her to deny him the permission he hadn't bothered to seek. It was clear from the way she looked from him to the picture that she wasn't sure she trusted him with this part of herself. But she said nothing. She simply let her hand drop to her side and turned away, as if she knew he'd do as he pleased with or without her consent.

The glass was broken, but beneath it Cole could easily see the snapshot. The man in it had blond hair, smiling blue eyes and was what, he supposed, women would call handsome. He reminded Cole of the kind of guy an ad company would use to advertise suntan lotion. Or toothpaste. Mr. Clean-cut All-American. It was the woman the man had his arm around that had Cole's attention, though. Lara's hair was different; longer and smoother. Her smile, bright and easy. There was a carefree quality to her expression that Cole certainly hadn't seen before. An innocence now gone from her lovely features.

Cole had never known that kind of guilelessness. He felt as if he'd been born old. He was just sorry that she'd had to discover how really rotten life could be—even if he did find her maturity more compelling.

"What did he do? For a living, I mean?"

The chimes of her wind-up alarm clock made a dull tinkle as she set it back on her nightstand. "He was a teacher. We both taught at Sierra Vista Elementary." The nightstand drawer opened then closed again. "That picture was taken after our sixth-grade football team won the district pennant. He was the coach."

That explained the football Lara was holding in the picture.

Cole looked back to her. She was righting the lamp on her nightstand. Her attitude amazed him. She seemed so calm, so accepting of what had happened. All of it. The dead husband. The change of life-style. The fact that the roof had, quite literally, caved in. If he hadn't seen her practically lose it the night she'd first shown up on his doorstep,

nearly falling apart over a bleeding bear cub, he'd be inclined to think that nothing ever really got to her. But that
night, the hold she'd had on herself had been tenuous at
best. Still, somehow, she'd hung on. It was as if she knew
she couldn't let herself go. That if she did, she might not be
able to get it all back together.

His eyes narrowed on her slender shoulders. They were
hunched as she hugged her arms to herself and turned to see
what she should tackle next in the room. As he noticed her
hesitation, he wondered if what he'd perceived in her wasn't
acceptance, after all. Maybe it was something more like
numbness.

"Have you ever been married?"

Her question brought his head up and his brow down.
"Yeah," he muttered. "A long time ago." One last glance
at the picture, and he set it where she'd first attempted to.
"You know you really should get the carpet off the floor. As
wet as it is, it's going to warp the boards."

The change of subject hadn't been particularly subtle, but
when Cole didn't want to talk about something, he simply
didn't talk about it. Fortunately, the mention of warped
boards seemed to snag Lara's attention.

"You mean, now?"

"Leaving this carpet on overnight will about guarantee
that you'll have to replace the floor. If the finish in here is
as poor as it is in the hallway, those strips of hardwood are
as porous as a sponge."

Taking it up wasn't something she could easily do by herself. A wet carpet weighed a ton and even if she did manage
to roll it, he doubted that she could get it out. He could tell
from the way she was presently frowning at the floor and
looking from the door to the window, that she was trying to
do just that, though. He could also tell she was a little overwhelmed with the task. Before she could touch the carpet,

the furniture and a heavy section of broken beam had to be moved out.

She needed his help. For some reason he couldn't begin to explain, it made him feel good to know that. Just as it had made him feel good that she'd come straight to him when she'd come back into Rosie's.

"I guess we'd better get started," he told her and ignored her quizzical glance when he picked up the end of her dresser.

It didn't take long to clear the room. The pieces of broken plaster and boards were put into bags and carried out to the service porch and the furniture moved into the room across the hall. Since that room wasn't much bigger than a closet, they stood her bed on end and sandwiched it between the wall and her dresser. With the nightstand on top of that, she could get to her drawers. But she'd be sleeping on the sofa downstairs for a while.

She came to that conclusion as she stood in the harsh light of the lantern, listening to the wind whistle through her recently exposed eaves and the rain making ticking noises on the black plastic. At least it would be warmer down there. She could build a fire in the fireplace.

With that thought came a shiver as she rubbed her hands together and wished she could remember where she'd last seen her gloves. Even wearing a heavy sweater over a turtleneck and a shirt, she felt like a Popsicle. With the wiring damaged, they'd had to turn off the generator, which meant there was no heat. A separate generator handled the refrigerated case in the store, so she didn't have to worry about that. Not that refrigeration was a concern at the moment. With the elements contained by nothing more than the sheets of plastic, the temperature inside felt within a degree or two of the temperature outside. Somewhere around a nice, balmy thirty-six degrees.

"You want to rest for a minute?"

"No," she mumbled and knelt down again. All they had to do now was roll the carpet and they were finished. "Ready?"

"Whenever you are." Squatting at the opposite end of the twelve-foot-long carpet, he curled the soggy material over to start the roll. His brow furrowed when he glanced over at Lara. "What's the matter?"

Lara shook her head, mumbled, "Nothing," and with a determined effort, got the bulky carpet to cooperate. As cold as her hands were, handling the wet material only made them colder. That wasn't the worst of it, though. Kneeling on the hard floor caused a dull, nagging ache in her left leg. She tried to ignore it as she inched the roll forward.

The ache turned into a pain.

Best to think of something else.

"What was she like?"

"Who?"

"The woman you were married to."

The look Cole sent over his end of the carpet made it clear he was not receptive to this line of conversation. It had been all right to talk about what they were doing and what to do next. Then, it had been okay to talk about the expansion of the campgrounds Cole supervised because that was what had kept him away and she'd been curious to know what he'd been up to, in a neighborly sort of way. It had even been all right to disagree about whether or not she was spoiling Bear—a claim she denied, though Cole had thought otherwise when he'd seen the "den" she'd built in his cage out of logs and moss. But he clearly didn't want to talk about his ex-wife.

His eyes bore into hers, unblinking, unyielding. When Lara didn't look away, he turned back to his task. "She was like any other woman, I suppose. We'll need some rags or something to wipe the floor."

If he meant his comment to end the subject, he truly didn't understand Lara. Her determination was unshakable once she set her mind on something. Her task now was to ignore his tight-lipped evasion. What she'd told herself was only an attempt to get her mind off her leg was really a compelling need to discover what Cole was all about.

"I'll get some in a few minutes. Where did you meet her?"

He gave the carpet another shove. "At a fraternity party."

That stopped her. Absently rubbing her thigh, she stared at his chiseled profile. The man didn't give much, but what he did give only made him that much more puzzling.

"Are you going to tell me about it?"

He'd have preferred not to. She was sure of that. At least that was her initial impression.

It was also Cole's first inclination. What was there to tell? He'd been a fool, which was not something he felt inclined to share. He'd been attracted to a beautiful woman who'd roped him into one of the oldest cons in the book. When she'd gotten what she wanted, she'd walked away.

He was fully prepared to tell Lara that there wasn't anything to say. Somehow, though, the quiet sincerity in her expression as she waited for him to make up his mind seemed to reach past his reticence.

"I didn't belong to the fraternity." He wanted her to know that he was nothing like the man she'd been married to. He'd been lucky just to be a student. "I'd just crashed the party with another guy who didn't have anything else to do that night. And she was there."

She, Lara learned as they finished rolling the carpet, was a foreign student he called only Gina.

"I'd known her for about three months," Cole told her, tying the ends of the roll with rope so it wouldn't come undone, "when she turned up at my apartment and announced that she was pregnant. It wasn't like it wasn't a possibility and since she was scared to death of what her parents would do to her if they found out, she practically begged me to marry her. Seemed that where she came from, the shame an unwed mother brings to her family ruins the whole family's reputation. To make a long story short, I did." He tied a knot and gave the rope a sharp jerk. "It wasn't long after that when she told me the pregnancy had been a false alarm. Not that she'd ever truly thought she was pregnant to begin with," he muttered. "Somehow we lasted through graduation, which happened to be just long enough for her to acquire resident status. It took me that long to figure out what had happened. She'd wanted to marry me because her visa was going to expire and by marrying a U.S. citizen she wouldn't have to go home."

"Did you love her?"

"I don't even know what that word means." He gave a final yank on the rope. "Let's just drop it. Okay?"

Lara really didn't have a choice. She didn't know what to say anyway. Cole was already a formidable man. With his rugged features set like granite, his gray eyes as cold as an arctic sea, he was even more intimidating.

Though she found it infinitely sad that he didn't know what love was, Lara wasn't going to try to explain it to him. Being used in such a way deserved the resentment he no doubt felt. She couldn't fault him that. Something else bothered her about his bitterness, though. Earlier, when she'd asked what his wife had been like, he'd said she was just like any other woman.

She met the defense hardening his expression. Even through his coolness, she could see something that spoke of more and deeper hurts. Hurts she was sure he had no intention of revealing.

It became very necessary to break the echoing silence.

"May I ask you one more question?"

Sounding as if he knew she'd do it anyway, he muttered a flat, "What?"

"What did you graduate in?"

Incomprehension flashed through his eyes. Then, as he picked up the end of the carpet to test its weight, relief. "Forestry."

He was back to one-word responses. Lara sighed and rubbed her leg again. It hadn't been this bothersome in months. The combination of the cold and the pressure on her knees were obviously taking their toll.

"What's out this window?"

"The forest," she said, amazed that he'd have to ask. The forest was out every window.

His tone was indulgent. "I mean below it. Is there a porch or an overhang?"

She had to think for a second. "The rain barrel is down there. Kind of off to one side. Why?"

"We'll try to miss it. Come on."

"What are we going to do?"

They were going to dump the carpet out the window.

Lara wanted to hold up her end. Literally and figuratively. And she tried. The late hour, the cold, and the increasing ache in her leg were all conspiring to make an admittedly awkward task even more difficult.

Cole got the window and the shutter beyond it open, which immediately let in the bone-chilling wind. On the positive side, the rain wasn't much more than a mist at the moment. Lara decided to let herself be thankful for that as she tugged on the middle of the long, amazingly heavy roll.

She'd learned long ago to appreciate the little things. The big breaks were too few and far between.

Cole lifted most of the weight and had the front end of the roll balanced on the edge of the sill. Glancing back over his shoulder, he saw Lara wince as she tried to move it forward. It was easy enough to see that she was tired. Easier still to see that she wasn't going to give up. What little she accomplished now wasn't worth her considerable efforts.

"Let it go."

"It'll fall."

"No, it won't."

"Cole."

"I've got it." Impatience laced his tone. "Let go."

She didn't have any choice. With the roll draping out the window, he took her by the shoulders, set her back by about a foot and with a surge of lean, powerful muscle, he pushed the carpet out. A heavy thud marked its connection with the ground. Seconds later, Cole had pulled down windows and whipped the curtain back over the glass. "Come on."

"What now?"

"Just come on, damn it. It's freezing up here."

She'd wondered if he'd noticed. The droll glance she shot toward his head was completely wasted. He picked up the lantern from the floor, apparently forgetting that they'd planned to wipe up whatever water they could from the boards, and reached for her hand.

The sound she made when his fingers squeezed around hers was little more than a moan, but it was enough to slow him down.

"God," he mumbled, easing his grip. "Your hand's like ice."

That was why it had hurt when he'd grabbed it.

"They'll thaw," she gamely replied and looked up. What she saw stunned her. She'd thought him abrupt because he was anxious to be finished—with the task and with her. It wasn't impatience driving him, though. It was concern.

They stood awkwardly, their eyes locked, until he realized what she could see. Concern was quickly covered by the hardening of his jaw as he released her hand. He headed downstairs. Since she didn't want to be left in the dark, Lara followed.

She expected him to leave. After all, it was nearly one in the morning. Certain he was preparing to go, she planned to thank him for his help as soon as she closed the stairwell door. The latch caught with a solid click, closing out most of the draft, but her thanks died on her lips. He'd headed to her kitchen.

There was no particular reason she should have thought of it now. But as her glance settled on his broad shoulders, she realized that Cole was still doing what he had been all evening. Taking charge. No superfluous discussion. No indecision. No gratuitous seeking of opinion. Just doing what needed to be done. All evening, his manner had been that of quiet authority; a man in charge of men accustomed to being in charge of themselves.

It was true that everyone had worked together, but it had been Cole who'd called the shots. People seemed to turn to him naturally. Maybe that was why the community relied on him to keep its peace. That wasn't part of his job. Not officially, anyway, according to Sally. The days of the forest ranger who was part sheriff were long gone. Resource management and its red tape were what occupied forest service personnel now. But Cole had the respect of the people of Mist and that was saying a lot. The wilderness wasn't like the city where a uniform or a position often allowed a kind of obedience a person couldn't have commanded without it.

Lara wondered if Cole even owned a uniform. She knew the Forest Service had them, but she'd never seen him in one. All she'd seen him wearing were jeans and flannel shirts or a heavy sweater like the black one he wore now.

Having taken a cup from the cupboard he'd seen her take cups from before, he'd filled it with coffee from the large thermos Rosie had sent over. "Wrap your hands around this," he told her and crossed the room to build a fire.

An old brass coal scuttle held kindling. Logs, which she'd brought in from the dry locker beneath her porch, were stacked in a niche built into the wall of the stone fireplace. In half the time it would have taken her, he had a tepee of kindling formed around a little pile of sticks and splinters he'd dumped from the bottom of the container. Taking the smallest of the logs from the niche, he added it and struck a match he'd pulled from his pocket.

Sparks drifted upward as the kindling caught. Within moments flames licked the log.

Lara frowned at the traitorous fireplace. It took her forever to get a fire started.

"You're out of kindling."

"I know." It had taken her an hour to make enough to fill the coal scuttle. She wasn't looking forward to making more. "I'll split some more tomorrow."

"You might want to split this wood while you're at it. The log I put on is small enough to burn, but the rest of what you've got here will just sit and smolder." He pulled the screen closed, then frowned at the large chunks of wood in the niche. The sides were ragged rather than smooth.

"You're using an ax?"

Lara had sat on the edge of the raised hearth, anticipating the heat the fire would provide. Already she could feel that welcome heat creeping through her jeans. She also felt a not-so-welcome warning. Cole was only three feet away, still on his haunches, and looking as if he were about to deliver one of his lectures.

Now that she was sitting down, she realized she was too tired to feel the satisfaction she was due. No lecture was necessary.

"Yes, but I've ordered a chain saw." She knew he'd found her knowledge of what it took to live in the wilderness abysmally lacking. She was learning, though. It might take a few blisters and unbelievably sore muscles to have figured it out, but she was learning. She'd never had to chop wood in San Diego. "There's a back order on the model I want." A little gas-powered red one that the catalog called "ultralite." "In the meantime, I have no choice if I want firewood. Which," she said with a sigh, "I'm going to need even more of since I can't use the generator until I get the wiring upstairs repaired."

Cole shook his head. The thought of her swinging an ax filled him with an odd blend of amusement and admiration. She wasn't a big woman by any means. How she could heft an ax and get any power behind it was beyond him.

"I'm sure someone around here has a chain saw you could borrow. There is a timber operation up the road, you know."

"I've seen those saws." She'd heard them, too, the sound a distant drone carried on the wind. She hadn't paid any attention to that sound until she'd heard it one afternoon while attacking the woodpile. It had occurred to her then, that what she needed was a chain saw, too. "I know I'm no expert, but I doubt that you use a monster that cuts through five-foot trunks to make firewood. Even if you do, I know I couldn't handle one."

"I meant a utility saw."

"Oh."

He smiled. Almost. Whatever energy had kept her going seemed to be draining out of her. He kind of liked her like this. A little compliant. Less guarded. "How are your hands?"

She thought he was referring to whether or not they'd warmed up. Since they were beginning to, she said, "Fine." But what he did made the word come out in a whisper.

Chapter Six

Cole took Lara's cup from her and set it down on the hearth. To her quiet surprise, he then picked up her right hand. His expression was oddly grim when he saw her broken blisters.

She started to pull her hands back. She knew she shouldn't feel awkward about what a little hard work had done, she just felt strangely self-conscious that he should see how difficult some of that work was for her. It was important somehow that he didn't think her any more incompetent than he already did. She *was* managing after all. But more pressing than the need to let him know she was handling her new life adequately, if not well, was the need to protect herself. The gentleness in his touch made her feel too vulnerable. With everything that had happened tonight, that was not a feeling she trusted.

Though his hold tightened only slightly when he felt her resist, his quietly spoken ''No,'' effectively stilled her. He picked up her other hand, folding it into his. "They're cold."

"Only a little."

Her voice wasn't as strong as she'd have liked it to be. But then, not much about the evening was at an optimum anyway. She glanced down at their hands. Small and pale, hers looked like a child's cradled in his darker, broader ones. He had good hands. Big, strong, a little rough. It felt nice to have such capable hands holding hers. Comforting. A little unnerving, too.

He brushed his thumbs lightly over her palms. The skin at the base of her fingers looked as sore as it was.

"You should wear gloves to chop wood."

"I did. For a while." She hadn't had the right kind of glove, though. The leather ones she sold in the store were all too big. "I couldn't get a good grip on the ax. It was easier bare-handed."

He looked up from the delicate veins on the inside of her wrist. It didn't surprise him that she'd kept at her task through the discomfort. He'd seen her stubborn determination to finish what she started. He had a feeling that she'd worked through pain before. Real pain. She wasn't the type to give up. Not easily.

The line of her profile drew him. What was it that pushed her? What kept her going when her luck went from bad to worse? She was a strong woman; stronger than she probably even realized. But he was beginning to think that it wasn't strength that drove her. Her drive seemed powered more by denial. Like a logger Cole had known who'd lost his leg, but the nerves hadn't atrophied and he could still "feel" the limb, so he exercised anyway. The motion itself became the goal, because as long as he was moving he didn't have to admit the leg was gone.

He felt her fingers flex in his, holding on just a little tighter. Nagging at the back of his mind was the thought that somehow, she had done what he wouldn't have thought her capable of doing. In some way he couldn't yet define, she *had* given up.

"How are your hands now? Warmer?"

She nodded, certain he was about to let go.

"How about your leg?"

Hesitation crossed her fragile features. "What about it?"

"You've been rubbing it." His frown settled on her left thigh. "Is that the one you broke?"

When he saw her nod, his frown intensified.

"Did you hurt it while we were moving the stuff around upstairs?"

"Not really." Why did he want to know? she wondered. And why was he looking so disgusted with her. "It's fine. Or it will be when I warm up."

He didn't seem to believe her. Probably because she winced when she moved just then. He left her sitting to one side of the crackling fire on the foot-high hearth and sat down, Indian-style, on the rug in front of her. A moment later, he reached for her ankle.

"Lift it. Come on," he coaxed when she hesitated. Carefully he stretched her leg out so her heel rested on the floor by his hip and her calf was supported by his thigh. "Show me where it was broken."

It didn't occur to her to question what he was doing. Somewhere along the line she'd developed an implicit trust in Cole's judgment. What she did question was how she had let that happen. She pointed to a place about six inches above her knee—and drew a deep breath when he covered the spot with his large hand and squeezed.

She thought the pressure would hurt. It didn't. The compression felt good. Surprisingly so. He didn't move his hand at all. He just kept the same steady pressure on her leg. And waited.

She could feel the warmth from his palm and his fingers seeping through her jeans, warming the skin beneath. Easing the ache. He said nothing and she sat spellbound, concentrating as much on her fading discomfort as the man taking that discomfort away. Cole didn't move until he felt the muscles in her leg begin to relax. When he felt the tension ease, he cupped his hand around the back of her leg and did the same thing.

"How did you do that?"

"Does it feel better?"

She told him it did, as puzzled by that phenomenon as she was relieved. "It still aches a little, but not nearly as much as before."

"Good."

The power of the human touch. Babies failed to thrive without it. Children craved it. It could soothe, even heal. That a man such as Cole should understand such power only made her realize how little she knew of him.

He must have seen her questions forming.

"An old native used this on me. I'd wrenched my shoulder and he fixed me up. He said it was the energy of the spirits traveling through him that healed me. I told him I didn't believe in spirits. He said I didn't have to believe, I only had to hold still. What made you feel better just now wasn't so mysterious. It was just pressure and heat."

He moved his hand to the top of her thigh again. "Be thankful he was Tlinget and not from one of the more Northern tribes. If he'd been Gwich'in, he'd have pinched your skin between two willow sticks and slashed it with a boiled knife."

He didn't look serious. At least not about personally performing the bloodletting. But she didn't doubt the existence of the remedy he'd described. The man seemed part of the land. She didn't question that he would know its customs.

"What's a treatment like that supposed to do?"

"Gets rid of the bad blood in the affected area. Don't look so skeptical. Some of the old Natives still swear by their old methods."

"What about the younger ones?"

The light of a smile touched his eyes. "They don't."

She smiled back. "How had you hurt your shoulder?"

For a moment she feared the brief, companionable moment was lost. He suddenly looked much as he had when she'd asked about his wife, as if she were treading in an area he'd long ago closed off and would just as soon leave boarded up. To her surprise, the shuttered look didn't last.

"I was thrown into a wall," he told her, his tone sober. "I'd gotten the hell beaten out of me in a fight."

Lara hesitated. "What were you fighting about?"

"I don't even remember. I was only about sixteen. Maybe seventeen." He didn't remember that for sure, either. That period of his life just sort of blurred together. The years and the places he'd been all seemed the same. One odd job after the other; competing with men who didn't want some young punk horning in on their territory. It had been hard to get a break. Until Jud had found him.

"The old Native," he heard Lara say. "Was he the friend who gave you the Chilkat blanket?

"He was," he said and wondered why he was remembering any of this—let alone talking about it.

The memories usually brought back his old defensiveness. But oddly the old angers and frustrations didn't want to be felt. Not now. Sitting with this woman in front of her fire, touching her, made him feel less restless than he'd felt in a long time. There was a gentleness about her that calmed the agitation; a quiet acceptance that allowed him to be a little less guarded.

Jud had always told him that his anger would build many walls. Maybe he'd built more walls than he'd realized. Maybe, too, that was why he couldn't hear the Chilkat. Jud had told him he would never be alone as long as he listened to the Chilkat blanket, for those who knew how to listen could hear it speak. Cole had never believed the weaving could talk, but lately it seemed he'd spent a lot of time staring at its totemlike designs and wondering what it would say.

His hand still rested on the top of her leg. He exerted no pressure now but the relaxed weight of it felt good to Lara. So did the way he rubbed his thumb back and forth over the worn fabric. His head was bent as if he were watching the motion, yet the slight movement seemed almost absent-minded, as if he weren't even aware he was doing it.

The light from the fire played over the hard angles and planes of his face, warming them with the glow of yellow flame and red embers. He was a beautiful man, really. The thought struck her as odd, considering how totally masculine he was. But she didn't disallow the conclusion. She hadn't seen him like this before, so deep in thought that he didn't bother to guard his expression. She had the feeling that few people ever saw him this way.

His dark hair fell over his forehead. The temptation to push it back was strong. But she didn't want to move for fear that he would. He was thinking about his friend. She was sure of that. Maybe, someday, he would feel comfortable enough with her to tell her about him. Cole was not a man to be pushed. Nor was he a man who trusted easily. If at all.

One of the burning logs broke apart, sending a shower of sparks up the flue. The sizzle and snap of freshly exposed pitch underscored the quiet. Neither had said a word for the past couple of minutes. Neither had moved. Because of that, the intimacy of their positions had become more pronounced. A moment ago, Lara had thought it silly to feel shaky now that she was warmer. When she felt his hand inch up, she thought maybe the tremor did make a little sense.

He had his thumb on the inside seam of her jeans. He was rubbing it back and forth, the motion relaxed and easy. The movement slowed, though, almost stopping, and he rested his free hand over her other leg.

With both hands splayed over her thighs, his thumbs began riding the seams, moving together now. Not back and forth. Only upward, toward where the seams met. Slowly, his fingers flexing against her firm flesh, his hands crept up until, just as his thumbs threatened to touch, the mesmerizing movement stopped.

He raised his head to meet her eyes.

Lara sat utterly still. Expectation warred with anxiety, awareness with apprehension. Scarcely breathing, she searched his face as if something there would tell her what he was about to do.

His face was completely devoid of expression as his glance dropped from her mouth to his hands. He moved them apart, his palms skimming upward to her stomach. After a few jerky heartbeats, she felt his fingers splay to curve around her hips. It was as if he were measuring her, perhaps imagining how she would fit against him. How she would move. At the thought, Lara felt a liquid heat flowing through her limbs. In the space of seconds the feeling intensified. With his thumbs on her hipbones, his fingers flexed against her back pockets. They dug into her tender flesh, urging her forward.

"Cole?"

The sound of his name on her lips was little more than a ragged whisper. To Cole, she sounded out of breath. He felt as if he'd just run a marathon himself.

He brought his hands back down to the tops of her thighs. Feeling the smooth muscles in her legs tense, he dragged his hands back toward her knees. A moment later he was on his feet, sucking in a deep breath as he turned away from her.

Lara stared at his broad back. What he'd done and the intensity in his expression as he'd met her eyes had nearly turned her inside out. Heat burned low in her stomach. She wanted him to come back. She wanted him to leave. Not knowing which she wanted more, she decided to see what he would do.

His hand was clamped over the back of his neck when he faced her again. The look in his eyes was so bleak it almost broke her heart to look at him.

"It's late."

"I know," was all she said.

"I should be going."

She said nothing.

Cole wished she would. Hell, Lara, he thought. Tell me to get out of here. Don't just sit there looking as though you wouldn't stop me if I touched you again. Don't you realize how complicated this could get?

He wanted her. He wanted her mouth open under his; he wanted her long, incredibly firm legs wrapped around him. He wanted her beautiful skin beaded with perspiration and slick from sex. He wanted her in bed, plain and simple. Only there wasn't anything simple about it. What he wanted was all knotted up with some crazy need he had to be there for her and he didn't want that at all.

"Where's your ax?"

Was that disappointment in her eyes? "On the service porch. Why?"

He didn't answer. Putting all of his considerable frustration into movement, he picked up the two smallest logs from the fireplace niche. On his way to the service porch, he picked up the lantern he'd left on the counter. No sense cutting off a foot in the dark.

Bear didn't seem to mind having his sleep interrupted. Thinking he looked far too knowing for a stupid animal, Cole did the best he could to split the wood without room to get a good swing on the ax. The porch was wide enough. There just wasn't any real height, so he had to chop rather than do the job with one clean cut.

Two minutes later, he was back.

"This should keep the fire going tonight."

"You didn't have to cut wood for me."

"I know I didn't. You'd have done it with a paring knife if you'd had to. I wanted to cut it. Okay?"

She met his completely unreasonable tone with maddening calm. "Okay. Thank you."

"You're welcome." He dumped the split logs on the far end of the hearth. "Mind if I put some in? The fire's burning down."

She raised her hand to the fireplace. "Go ahead."

"Thanks."

He whipped open the screen.

"Cole?"

"Yeah?"

"Did I do something to upset you?"

He was acting like a fool. He knew it. She suspected it. And he didn't care. "Not a thing," he muttered. *Other than moving here,* he mentally amended. Even that wouldn't be a problem if she hadn't planned on staying. If she had only come for the summer, he wouldn't have thought twice about keeping his hands off of her. But since she planned on digging in, he'd have to keep his hands in his pockets and his thoughts off her very appealing body. He might want to consider dropping a few ice cubes in his pants, too. Mist was too small a place for ex-lovers.

Lara watched his agitated motions as he stuffed logs into the fire. He looked frustrated. If he felt what she did, she could well understand the basis for the feeling. When he'd touched her, when she'd seen the raw hunger in his eyes, the heat had penetrated clear to her soul. As compelling as that awakening was, she wasn't ready for what he'd made her feel. Not that the thought of sleeping with him was so shocking. What was shocking was how enticing she found the thought.

If Cole's manner was any indication, he was no more prepared for an alteration in their relationship than she was. So what was important now was that she make sure he wasn't upset with her. She didn't want anything to harm the odd friendship that had begun to develop between them. That he was becoming important to her was something she didn't care to examine too closely at the moment.

When Cole straightened, his hands were in his pockets. "That hole in your roof is going to need attention fairly soon."

She glanced toward the closed stairwell door. Even though they faced each other as if a bomb were on the floor between them, she was grateful for his attempt to take the focus away from the past few minutes. "I guess I'd better hire someone to fix it."

"I don't know who that would be. We don't have any roofers in Mist."

Her quiet, "Oh," was little more than a moan. Until that moment, she hadn't considered how the hole would get repaired. She'd only known that the repair was necessary. But getting a new roof, or even part of one, wasn't simply a matter of opening the Yellow Pages. Mist didn't have Yellow Pages. With only one telephone in town, it didn't even have a phone book.

"You're going to need to order insulation and lumber. The lumber will have to come by boat, so it could be a week or more before it gets here."

"Insulation and lumber," she repeated.

"Nails and metal braces. Shingles, tar paper, wood sealer. Paint."

"I have paint."

"Outdoor?"

She frowned. "Indoor."

"You'd better make a list."

She was going to have to do it herself. Lara pushed her fingers through her hair and glanced back at the closed door. It was one thing to sand and paint a few shelves. She'd even fixed a broken shutter. She didn't know the first thing about putting up a roof.

Maybe there was a book somewhere, she thought just as she saw Cole shake his head at her.

"You're actually thinking about doing it yourself, aren't you?" The flatness in his tone removed any possibility of a question. "I don't know if you're the most determined woman I've met, or the dumbest. You couldn't possibly do that job alone."

She'd just been thinking the same thing. That didn't, however, stop her from taking offense at his phrasing. "Why not?"

"Do you know anything about construction?"

Construction paper. Yes. Construction as in buildings? No.

She said nothing.

"I didn't think so," he told her, correctly interpreting her silence. "Even if you did, you're not physically strong enough to haul lumber up to the roof. I don't doubt that you

NO RISK, NO OBLIGATION TO BUY... NOW OR EVER!

GUARANTEED

PLAY "ROLL A DOUBLE" AND GET AS MANY AS SIX GIFTS!

HERE'S HOW TO PLAY:

1. Peel off label from front cover. Place it in space provided at right. With a coin, carefully scratch off the silver dice. This makes you eligible to receive one or more free books, and possibly other gifts, depending on what is revealed beneath the scratch-off area.

2. You'll receive brand-new Silhouette Special Edition® novels. When you return this card, we'll rush you the books and gifts you qualify for ABSOLUTELY FREE!

3. Then, if we don't hear from you, every month we'll send you 6 additional novels to read and enjoy. You can return them and owe nothing, but if you decide to keep them, you'll pay only $2.92 per book—a savings of 33¢ each off the cover price.

4. When you subscribe to the Silhouette Reader Service™, you'll also get our newsletter, as well as additional free gifts from time to time.

5. You must be completely satisfied. You may cancel at any time simply by sending us a note or a shipping statement marked "cancel" or by returning any shipment to us at our expense.

You'll look like a million dollars when you wear this elegant necklace! It's a generous 20 inches long and each link is double-soldered for strength and durability.

DETACH AND MAIL CARD TODAY!

BUSINESS REPLY MAIL

FIRST CLASS MAIL   PERMIT NO. 717   BUFFALO, NY

POSTAGE WILL BE PAID BY ADDRESSEE

SILHOUETTE READER SERVICE
3010 WALDEN AVE
PO BOX 1867
BUFFALO NY 14240-9952

NO POSTAGE
NECESSARY
IF MAILED
IN THE
UNITED STATES

could eventually get the job done by pulling it up there one piece at a time. But summers are only about three months long here and that's all the time you'll have before you'll be buried in snow.''

She wanted to sound irritated, but fatigue took the edge from her tone. ''Do you have any other suggestions, then?''

Resignation marked his expression. That was why his muttered ''I'll do it,'' didn't sit too well with Lara. Part of the reason, anyway.

She felt her back stiffen. ''I couldn't ask you to take on a job like that. You've done enough already.''

''You didn't ask. I offered. I'll stop by sometime tomorrow when I can see just what all's wrong up there. Then I can figure out what all we're going to need. You'd better talk to Ron at the marina about the wiring. I only know enough about that to blow the place up.''

''Cole, I can't accept your help. It's my problem. I'll figure out how to deal with it.''

She might as well have been talking to a tree. He completely ignored what she said.

Cole picked up his jacket from the back of the love seat. He was too tired to tackle her unreasonable stubbornness tonight. He'd planned on helping her all along. It hadn't occurred to him not to. Now that she knew it, he only had one other concern to put to rest for the night.

''You might want to think about bunking somewhere until you get your power back. With the draft coming down the stairs, it could get awfully cold in here. Even with a fire. I imagine Sally wouldn't mind if you stayed at her place.''

Lara didn't trust the way he'd changed the subject. Preparing to make sure he'd understood her, it took a second for what he was suggesting to register.

''No,'' she cut in the moment it did and knew the minute she'd said it that she'd been too abrupt. ''I mean, I wouldn't want to impose on her. She's got a family and with the kids, having a stranger around could be a real hassle.''

She knew the words sounded like an excuse. Probably because they were. But short of saying that being around Sally was difficult for her because she reminded Lara so often of what she couldn't have, it was the best she could come up with.

She rubbed the bridge of her nose. There were so many things she didn't want to think about. Tonight, it seemed she was facing them all.

Cole saw the odd bleakness in her eyes. He thought it was fatigue. ''What about Rosie, then? I heard her offer you a bed.''

''I'll be fine. I'll put a towel under the door to stop the draft and just sleep right here. There's plenty of room.''

Cole looked at the love seat facing the fireplace. The thing wasn't five feet long. Lara wasn't tall, but even at about five foot-three, it wouldn't be long enough for her to sleep on. Or so he thought until he remembered how he'd seen her sleeping on his cot. She'd been curled up in a ball tight enough to bounce.

He looked back to her. She had her arms hugged around her middle as she usually did when she wasn't doing something. The stance looked protective and, now that he thought about it, distinctly insecure. Maybe that same insecurity followed her into her sleep.

Since where she slept, much less her sleeping habits, were really none of his business, Cole abandoned the matter in favor of heading to his own bed. He was as beat as she suddenly looked. After saying that he'd see her in the morning, he left her standing by the fire he'd built and went out by way of the service porch. That he worried about her was a peculiarity he'd just as soon ignore.

* * *

He was still trying to ignore that concern when he found Lara out in back of her place the next morning. She was burning the debris they'd collected last night in an old thirty-gallon oil drum. The drum had been positioned well away from the buildings, in a clearing of mostly dirt, small stones and a few scraggly tufts of grass. Just in case the grass wasn't wet enough to deter a flying spark, she had a bucket of water from the rain barrel standing by.

Bear was tethered by a rope to her belt. Taking advantage of the ten-foot lead, the little animal was rolling around in the tall grasses edging the clearing. The grass was wet and to keep Bear's bandages from getting soaked she'd fashioned a raincoat of sorts out of a plastic bag by cutting a hole for his head and one forepaw. A band of some kind of bright pink fabric was tied where he assumed a bear's waist would be.

Cole shook his head at the garment and looked back to the smoke drifting through the screen on the burning barrel.

"Do you have a permit for that?"

Lara was rubbing her nose with the back of her hand. When she heard Cole, her hand froze. Slowly she lowered it. "I didn't know I needed one."

"You don't."

He smiled. It wasn't much of a smile. Just enough to let her know he was only teasing, which wasn't something he did often. The few times he'd done it to her, though, he'd liked the way her eyes narrowed with the exasperated look she'd given him.

She didn't disappoint him. Seeing the faint exasperation, he glanced around at the empty bags. "You don't waste any time, do you?"

"I needed to clean up the service porch. I've been doing my sanding out there and I need the space."

"Sanding?"

"On my shelves."

She saw him tip his chin as if to say, *Oh, yeah,* then watched as his glance moved on up. The sun was actually shining this morning. Between the clouds, anyway. The sky was a beautiful blue, the deep blue of cold, clean air. But he wasn't looking at the sky. He was looking at the roof. From where he stood he could clearly see where it sagged to one side. A section of the shingles on the far end had also blown off.

When he mentioned that, Lara said she'd noticed that herself first thing this morning.

"I think I'm going to have to replace the whole thing."

Cole agreed. "Looks that way." Gravel crunched beneath his boots as he turned back to her and stepped closer. "I won't be able to do anything about it today, though. Now that the rain's slowed up, there's something I've got to do first."

"I said last night that you don't have to fix my roof. I'll take care of it."

"I know I don't have to, Lara." Annoyance flashed in his eyes. "But I said I'd help."

"And I said I couldn't let you do that."

"Why are you being so stubborn about this?"

Even if she could have told him, she was sure he would think her reason foolish. She didn't want his help because she didn't want to need it. That she did need it, that she seemed to be needing *him,* was a very basic threat to the sense of control she was trying so desperately to attain. It was important that she make it on her own because that was what she was—on her own. She couldn't let herself forget that. And when she was with Cole, almost invariably, she did.

She tossed another piece of ceiling into the fire, immediately replacing the screen so the sparks wouldn't escape. "I'm not being stubborn. I'm being practical."

"How can tackling a job you know nothing about be practical?"

"I didn't say I was going to do it myself. I'll hire someone to work for me."

"Who?"

"One of Jack's men. Or one of Gus's."

"Jack's men are already working nine hours a day. When the days get a little longer, they'll be working twelve. Gus's men are out to sea six days out of seven. The day they're in, they're working on nets and gearing up to go back out. In case you haven't noticed, no one here has the time."

That was true. With few exceptions, everyone of employable age in Mist had a job. Those who didn't—a couple of old-timers on pensions and the unskilled labor waiting for work at the ice house—weren't what she was looking for.

"I could get someone from Sitka."

"I'm sure you could. And you can pay his transportation here and back and put him up in your spare room while he's here working for you. In case you haven't noticed, Mist doesn't have a hotel."

She didn't have a spare room, either, and he knew it. Not that the idea of having a stranger in her home for the duration of the repairs held any appeal to begin with.

Seeing her options shrink, she went on the offense. "What about you? You wouldn't have the time, either. You said yourself that it'll take another three weeks to get the campgrounds ready to open. You also said that once they are open, you'll never get to the reports that are already overdue because summers are so busy."

"I'd have made time," he cut in, not needing the reminders.

"When?"

"Whenever the material got here."

"Why?"

"You know Lara," he said, looking as if he'd just posed that question to himself. "It really beats the hell out of me."

With that, he turned on his heel, his long strides carrying him back the way he'd come. In less than thirty seconds he'd disappeared around the side of the building.

Lara, only now realizing that she'd had her hands on her hips, pulled her arms around herself.

"That has got to be the stupidest argument I've ever heard. Believe me, I've heard some doozies, too." The boards of Rosie's porch creaked in protest as she moved to the railing from where she'd stood by her back door. Smoke trailed upward as she exhaled. "The man wants to give you a hand and you're doing everything short of telling him to go to hell to keep him from doing it. I'd be careful of making him defend why it is he wants to do that for you, though. A man like Cole isn't likely to put it into words."

The fact that Rosie had overheard her discussion with Cole wasn't anywhere near as disconcerting as the woman's advice. Or her implication. "Put what into words?"

"How he feels," Rosie said as if Lara couldn't possibly be that dense. "It's clear as a bell to me, honey. Our ranger's got a thing for you."

That the feeling was mutual didn't help at all.

Lara looked away, feeling suddenly anxious and more than a little guilty. Sam would tell her that feeling guilty was stupid. Steve was gone and Lara should be relieved that she'd finally found herself attracted to another man. Another man. It even sounded wrong. She'd only been with one man in her whole life. Steve. Her husband. She hadn't been a virgin when they'd married, but Steve had been the first. The only.

"I don't want to be anything more than friends with Cole, Rosie."

Rosie seemed to consider that as she squinted at her cigarette. "If that's true, I'd make sure I wasn't sending him any mixed signals then. I like you, Lara. From what I've seen so far, you're pulling your own weight. Trying to anyway, and that's all a person can ask. But I've known Cole for a long time. I wouldn't want to see him hurt."

The cigarette sizzled as it hit the water in the coffee can by the railing. A moment later, batting at the red curls coming loose from her upsweep, Rosie went back into her bar.

Lara stayed where she was, tending her fire. Bear had become tired of rolling in the grass, so she held him in one arm until he fell asleep. A task he accomplished with remarkable ease. How she envied him that ability.

Absently stroking his soft head, taking comfort from the feel of his warm little body, she pondered Rosie's words.

It might be true that Rosie had known Cole for longer than Lara, but Lara knew something Rosie apparently didn't. He wouldn't let himself get hurt. He guarded himself too well to let that happen. As for Rosie's other observation, Lara was inclined to give that one a little more weight.

The argument she'd had with Cole *had* been pretty dumb.

She considered that as she carried Bear to his little den on the service porch. Short of twitching her nose and having a new roof appear—which some might think a possibility considering how she'd acted earlier—she needed Cole's help, whether she wanted it or not.

How to ask for that help now was the problem she pondered as she left a note on the store's front door that she'd be back in half an hour and headed down the boardwalk to the marina. Cole had said he'd be busy today so she could postpone facing him until later. Right now, she'd just ask Ron about the wiring. She needed the use of her generator back.

The marina was little more than an extension of the town's short boardwalk. Where the land ended, a series of long wooden piers jutted out into the water. The longer inner ones served Gus's trawlers and the odd lot of boats owned by locals for fishing and transportation. The outermost pier served the pontoon planes that flew supplies and mail in and fresh fish out. A twin-engine Cessna was presently secured there. To the land end of the nearest pier sat a squat, gray weathered building with a tarnished brass captain's bell over the door.

The bell didn't work; hadn't for quite a while from the looks of the rust freezing the striker in place. The marina office was a workshop, too, and that was where she found Ron Vorak up to his elbows in motor parts.

The smell of gasoline from the pump outside mingled with the smells of engine oil and salt air. Opening the window over his workbench wider, Ron shifted the cigar in his mouth from one side to the other. The stocky ex-engineer was amiable enough, despite the permanent grimace holding the cigar in place produced. Lara had never seen him without a cigar. He never lit the thing. At least Lara hadn't seen it lit. With all the fumes, the place would probably explode if he did.

"Morning," he mumbled, holding a screwdriver in his oily hand as he wiped his forehead with his sleeve. "Heard about your roof. Too bad, but heard it could've been worse."

One of the first things Lara had noticed about the wilderness was how quickly the people in it put matters into perspective. The other thing was how quickly word traveled.

"You probably heard I need some wiring redone, too. I was wondering if you could do it. And how much you'd charge," she added, though he knew full well he could name his price. Competition for his skills was virtually nonexistent.

Having once designed electrical systems for everything from trucks to tankers, there wasn't much of anything electrical he couldn't fix. Stating that he figured he could handle her request, he added that he'd give her a firm price once he saw what all he'd have to do. He'd also appreciate it kindly if she'd order him some stogies.

She was about to ask what kind when the door swung open. The smile on her face froze, then faded.

Cole stood in the doorway, his large frame blocking the weak sunlight. He'd been about to speak. When he saw her, his expression went from preoccupied to unreadable.

It was Ron who kept the sudden silence from becoming embarrassing. "Been wondering when you were going to show up," he said to Cole. Wiping his hands off on a greasy rag, he nodded to a clipboard lying on a surprisingly neat desk. "She's all gassed and ready to go. Just sign for your fuel. You've got a southeasterly blowing at ten to fifteen knots. Light showers off and on this afternoon. High of fifty-two, low of thirty-six and freezing above four thousand feet. Everything I'm getting here says that's going to be status quo for the day."

"Beach weather," Cole muttered and picked up the pad. The conditions Ron had described matched the aviation weather report he'd obtained himself less than half an hour ago.

He glanced back at Lara. He hadn't known she was here.
If he had, he'd have waited until she'd left to pick up the
plane. "Did you talk to Ron about your wiring?"

She nodded. "He just agreed to do it."

"Good," Cole said, and laid the clipboard back down.

Ron, moving his cigar from one side of his mouth to the
other, glanced from Cole to Lara and back again. Cole just
kept looking at Lara.

Having no reason to stay, and feeling more uncomfortable by the second, Lara turned to the door. Telling Ron
she'd see him later, not saying anything to Cole because he
didn't look at all receptive, she stepped out onto the dock
and pulled the door shut behind her.

"I'm planning on being back before nightfall," she heard
Cole mention before she could take another step.

"You're just over and back to Gelding Lake. Right? Oh,
before you go," Ron cut in. "Evie wants to know if you'll
come to the meeting at Rosie's tonight."

Evie, Lara knew, was Ron's wife.

"I don't think so. They don't need me there."

She couldn't hear Ron's reply, but a moment later, the
door to the shacklike shop rattled open. Ron's "Fly safe,"
followed Cole out onto the dock.

Lara hadn't meant to eavesdrop. And though she was
mildly curious about the meeting Ron had mentioned, her
sole purpose for waiting outside the door had been to talk
to Cole. Now that he was standing less than two feet from
her, looking very much as if he wished she weren't there, she
wasn't so sure what she'd wanted to say.

She started with, "I'm sorry."

He wasn't at all cooperative. "For what?"

"For the way I acted this morning. For being..."

"So obstinate?" he suggested.

"I was going to say unreasonable."

"I prefer obstinate. But you can have unreasonable, too."

"Are you going to accept my apology or not?"

"Does it matter?"

"Yes."

"Why?"

She focused on the third button on his blue denim jacket. "Because I need your help."

It had cost her to say that. He didn't know why and he didn't know how much. He just knew that she hadn't wanted to admit needing his help. He knew, too, that he was inordinately pleased that she did.

She'd have never known that by looking at him. "With the roof," he said flatly.

She nodded, then pushed back the hair the breeze kept blowing across her face. "If you wouldn't mind."

He wouldn't make her ask again. "Like I said before, I can't do anything about it today."

He couldn't help but notice that she was as careful as he to hide her relief. He didn't like them like this. But he didn't know any other way to be.

She looked toward the boxes sitting on the dock by the plane. A coil of copper tubing stuck out the top of one. It was the tubing she'd obtained for his friend Asa. "You're going to see the old bootlegger?"

"I think he'd prefer to be thought of as a miner."

A hint of a smile danced in her eyes. It reminded Cole very much of the delight he'd seen in her face when they'd spoken about Asa just last night. Cole found himself very much wanting to see that unrestrained smile again.

The question was out before he could think better of it. "Would you like to see where he lives?"

There it was. *God, Lara. Do you know what you do to a man when you smile like that?*

"Now?"

"Why not?" he said with a shrug and felt the knots inside him grow tighter when her smile answered yes.

Chapter Seven

When Lara was a little girl, her father would sometimes come in after doing yard work on a Saturday morning and tell her and her sister that it was time for an adventure. That meant he and their mom were taking them somewhere, but the destination wouldn't be revealed until they arrived. Sometimes they went to Sea World or the zoo, often to a museum or an outdoor concert. Lara never did care where they wound up. What she liked best was the anticipation.

Cole's invitation had brought with it a hint of that childlike feeling. It was so unfamiliar that she almost didn't recognize it. What she felt most was gratitude to Cole for not making it overly difficult to ask for his help, and relief that he wasn't upset with her. She didn't think he'd have invited her along if he had been, and she was very glad that he had. The idea of seeing where the eccentric old miner lived was very appealing. There was a certain appeal to being with Cole, too, but she already knew she couldn't indulge herself in the sense of security his presence provided. He wasn't offering her security. All he was offering was his help with matters she couldn't handle alone.

That point was driven home as soon as he asked if she'd read the booklet on gun safety he'd given her. As long as they'd be out and the weather was good, he'd show her how to shoot. She knew she looked less than thrilled with the prospect, but she'd had to learn how to live with a bear and she hadn't been too crazy about that, either.

Since they would have to hike to get to Asa's cabin after they reached the lake, Lara had to change from tennis shoes to boots. She also had to arrange with Sally to keep an eye on Bear and the store. She accomplished both in record time. Still, Cole had the plane loaded and the engine running when she returned to the dock. No sooner had she climbed in and closed the door, than, without a word, he reached across her.

His shoulder pushed into hers as he leaned forward. His face came within inches of hers, his body so close she could feel its heat through her heavy sweater. She had no idea what he was doing until his hand closed around the handle.

"It isn't tight."

The door might not have been, but her throat certainly was. Inhaling the clean smell of soap and fresh air clinging to his hair, she could do little more than sit there while he relatched the door. The contact wasn't deliberate. It was simply necessary.

"Better," he said and went still when he turned his head toward her.

His glance settled on her mouth.

Lara swallowed. "I could have done that."

"It's kind of temperamental."

A temperamental door on a plane? "It's not going to come open while we're flying, is it?"

"I wouldn't take anyone up in an unsafe plane. Don't you feel safe with me?"

Blessedly, he didn't wait for an answer.

He pulled back, his manner brusque as he told her to fasten her seat belt and reached for his own. He knew he'd rattled her. She was sure of it. After watching her fumble with the clasp to lock it in place, he pulled the plane away from the pier. The whir of the propellers changed pitch as he headed them into the wind and, within seconds, they were racing across the water.

Lara gripped her hands in her lap. If Cole noticed, she hoped he'd think her nerves were from flying. Suddenly she wasn't so sure coming along was such a good idea.

It didn't take but a minute for her to change her mind.

The plane lifted off from the inlet and Cole banked right. Out her window, the wilderness expanded from the isolated little settlement of Mist into a vast and wild land of incredible contrasts. She could see the ocean beyond the peninsula. At the mouth of the inlet, dozens of tiny, tree-covered islands dotted the gray-blue water. Cole banked farther and she forgot all about being anxious. Incredible jagged-peaked mountains loomed ahead. And mile after mile of spruce and hemlock and cedar.

"What do you think?" she heard Cole ask over the low drone of the engines.

She shook her head, her senses bemused. "I don't know how to describe it. I thought it was beautiful coming in on the ferry. All the green and the glaciers... But from up here..."

She couldn't find the words. As they skimmed the treetops and flew over tiny blue lakes so numerous they didn't even have names, Cole thought he might have been disappointed if she had been able to describe what she saw. He'd never been able to put his feelings for the utter vastness and beauty of Southeast into words. Therefore, he understood her silence; appreciated it far more than any verbal adjectives she could have supplied. If for no other reason than she shared his awe, he was glad he'd asked her to come.

"It's hard for a person to imagine just how big all this is until they've flown over it. You can fly for hours and see nothing but trees and rivers. Let me know if you want to know what you're looking at."

Lara was so intent on what lay below that she didn't respond. Words weren't necessary anyway. Cole seemed to know how overwhelmed she was by the lush land and he seemed unwilling to interfere with the experience. Lara didn't know of many people willing to allow that kind of privacy. Most would be pointing out spots they wanted her to see; giving names of mountains or streams that she wouldn't remember anyway because there were so many of them. Cole was very different in that respect. He didn't pull her attention from what she was looking at to have her look at something else. He simply let her drink it all in, absorb it, if that were possible. He didn't intrude, but if she wanted to know something he easily obliged.

As they flew on, they came upon and passed a couple of large areas barren of trees. Dense green carpeted those spaces, only an occasional scrub pine breaking the terrain. Approaching a third, she became curious. "Is that a clearcut from a logging operation?"

"It's a muskeg," he told her, not surprised by her question. It was a common misconception of people unfamiliar with Southeast's topography. "I know it looks like a clearcut, but loggers have nothing to do with them. They're holes left by glaciers that filled with water and moss. Over the centuries, the moss and lighter plant growth filled the hole in. It looks like solid ground, but it isn't solid at all. Step on it and you could be in anywhere from up to your ankles to over your head. Some of these go down hundreds of feet. A person can literally vanish in a second if he doesn't know where to step. As a rule, the greener and finer it looks, the more dangerous it is. If you come up on one, stick to the edges by the trees."

"Do people vanish like that often?"

"It happens," was all he said.

She remembered the night she'd first met him and the lecture he'd given her about the local wildlife. She remembered, too, that she'd thought him impatient and unsympathetic with her ignorance at the time. Now she was beginning to understand why he might have little patience with people who hadn't bothered to familiarize themselves with the area. In his position, he'd probably been called upon more than once to rescue a hunter or hiker who hadn't known of a muskeg's hidden danger. It was bad enough that a person endangered his or her own life. Worse, a person might endanger the lives of those required to save him from his experience. Accidents happened. But many could be prevented with a little knowledge.

The more she learned from Cole, the more she realized she didn't know.

Less than twenty minutes after they'd taken off, Cole landed the plane with what was more of a plunge-and-splashdown than anything resembling a gradual descent. No other type of landing was possible. Surrounded completely by skyscraping trees, Gelding Lake was barely half a mile wide and its narrow end could be measured in yards. Lara could tell by Cole's bland expression as he cut the engine to idle that he'd thought his laconic "Hang on" plenty of warning for the unorthodox landing.

Maybe, here, it wasn't all that extraordinary. Accepting that as probable, she realized she might just be getting a feel for this decidedly untamed place.

Cole glanced along the shallow shoreline as he guided the plane around. "I don't see him," he muttered, letting the plane float backward to the shore. "I'm sure he heard us. Hand me that pack behind you."

Unfastening her seat belt, she twisted around and reached for a bright orange pack as he opened his door. The thing felt as if it was full of rocks, and it took both hands for her to lift. By the time she'd hauled it over the seat back, Cole had stepped out onto the left pontoon, so she let it fall into the seat he'd just vacated.

With a mumbled, "Thanks," he picked the pack up in one hand, slung it around and slipped it onto his back. He then reached behind his seat and slid out a rifle.

"Can you handle that other one?" he asked, indicating a second pack with the nod of his head.

Gamely, she reached for it. Orange like his, it didn't weigh nearly as much. It wasn't light, though, and she hoped that they weren't headed very far away.

He stuck his head back into the cabin. The breeze had already rearranged his perpetually wind-blown hair. "You're going to have to walk the pontoon to shore. Stay put until I tie us up, though. Okay?"

Staying put was not a problem. While Cole headed down the pontoon as if it were a sidewalk, she opened her door to look out. The flat part atop the silver float was about six inches wide. The rest of it was round, like a long sausage. The water lapping against those curved sides looked very, very cold.

She glanced back toward Cole. From her position in the plane, she couldn't see him. She could see his pack and the rifle, though. The pack was on the ground and the rifle was propped, barrel-up, against a tree. Leaning out to check from the pilot's side, she saw him pulling on a rope he had apparently secured to the plane's frame. Once that was tied off, he disappeared around the other side where he tied another rope to another tree. The plane was now secured by the ropes in a tight V.

"Come on," she heard him call.

Trying not to think of why she'd always hated gymnastics in grade school, she slipped on the pack and made her way down the pontoon, holding on to the side of the plane as she went. Balancing wasn't nearly as difficult as she'd thought it would be even with the gentle roll and sway of the water and when she reached the end, she figured the worst was over.

Three feet of water separated the plane from the shore. She looked over at the rocky ground. Cole had jumped. She'd have to jump, too.

His sharp, "Wait a minute," came a second too late.

Three feet didn't look all that far. Springing forward, her left foot hit the water with a little splash and with the weight of the pack carrying her, her other foot hit solid ground. Her body, though, hit Cole.

He'd stepped forward just as she'd jumped and she landed right in his arms.

Solid. The man was as solid as the rock faces of the cliffs she'd seen along the sea. She felt his chest push the breath from her, and the strength in his arms as he caught her to him. Her head bumped his shoulder and she felt him shift backward, securing their footing. A moment later, she felt the rasp of his sweater against her cheek and the touch of his hand to the back of her head. His hand in her hair felt like assurance, assuring her that she was all right and himself of that same thing.

For the space of a few frantic heartbeats he held her that way, the seconds passing slowly enough to cement impressions but so quickly that it took a moment for their sudden stillness to register. When it did, his hand was suddenly gone, his chest no longer compressed hers and she was again able to breathe.

She'd rather have stayed right where she was.

He held her at arm's length. "Are you okay?"

The best she could manage was a nod.

"Knocked the wind out of you, huh? Sorry," he muttered. Letting go of one arm, he pushed the hair back from her face.

Realizing what he was doing, looking a little self-conscious about it, he let his hand fall.

"I didn't think you'd make it with the pack. I was going to have you toss it to me."

She couldn't seem to meet his eyes. It was silly, she knew, because he couldn't possibly appreciate the jolt he'd given her when she'd felt his arms go around her. And she'd only been in his arms for seconds. Thirty at the most. But that was all the time it had taken for her to know that she very much wanted to feel his solid strength again. To have him hold her and make her feel safe. For safe was how she'd felt when his hand had covered the back of her head and he'd pressed her to his chest.

Dear God. To be held like that again. It had been so long.

She took a step back, catching herself when she realized she'd be stepping into the water, and moved to one side. She couldn't think rationally when he was so close.

Her tone as casual as she could make it, she glanced around her. There was nothing to see but trees. "Now what?"

Cole was frowning. She could feel his narrow-eyed displeasure on her back.

She didn't know what to make of his silence. He watched her, his stillness making her uneasy. She looked down at the ground, but there was nothing among the pebbles and dirt to hold her attention, so she glanced toward the sky.

"We can wait here for Asa," he finally said, his tone oddly subdued. "Or we can start out for his place and meet him along the way."

The walk sounded like the best idea. "Let's go to his place."

"Fine. I'll get his supplies."

Asa's supplies were the two boxes of canned goods and assorted odds and ends that had been on his grocery list. Both boxes were full. Both were also heavy. And while Cole had no apparent difficulty with them—he merely stepped off the end of the pontoon, his long stride covering the distance to the shore—they'd be too awkward for her to manage for any appreciable distance.

She didn't see how Cole could manage them, either. He obviously couldn't carry both. "How do you get this much stuff to him?"

"I usually wait for him to show up with his sled."

"Why didn't you say so?"

"Because you seemed pretty definite about what you wanted to do."

With her arms crossed, she tipped her head to one side. Sunlight caught her sable curls, making the ends sparkle with burnished highlights. "Since when has that mattered?"

Cole set the second box down by the first. "Since you looked so frightened of me. I wasn't going to do anything to you."

She hadn't considered what he would think when she'd pulled away so abruptly a few moments ago. And though she certainly knew he was capable of being blunt, his words caught her completely off guard. She wanted to deny that she'd been frightened, but the denial wouldn't come. It would be a lie, after all. She *was* frightened of him. Of what he made her feel. She wasn't up to that bit of honesty, though. Short of that, she could at least relieve him of responsibility for the way she'd acted. If she could only think how to do that.

For several seconds, she stood wishing she knew what *he* was thinking. His expression, as it was so often, was completely unreadable. He didn't give much and she thought that terribly unfair. Especially when he expected so much from her.

"*Are* you afraid of me, Lara?"

"Please, Cole. I didn't mean..."

"It's a simple enough question." And he needed the answer. He wasn't sure what he wanted from this woman. The one thing he knew he didn't want was for her to fear him. "There's nothing very complicated about a simple yes or no."

It seemed to Lara that there was nothing "simple" about whatever it was happening between them. Cole wasn't giving her time to think of how to explain that without sounding irrational, though. He took a step forward. A branch snapped beneath his boot, seeming to echo in the eerie quiet of the forest. Lara scarcely noticed.

There was nothing particularly menacing about his approach. His arms hung loosely at his sides, his gait easy and loose-limbed. He just walked over to her as if they were discussing nothing more personal than the weather and planted his hands on his hips.

"Answer me."

She'd stood a better chance of doing that before he'd come closer. The man could intimidate without even trying.

"Let's just leave it. Okay?"

Something flashed in his eyes. Not impatience. That she could have dealt with. What she saw was more like inevitability.

"I don't think I can do that."

She was still wearing the backpack. Slipping his hands under the straps, he lifted it up and off and it fell to the ground with a solid thud. His hands came back up and before she could blink he'd taken her face between his hands and his mouth covered hers.

She was too stunned to move. Then, when she did, it was to bring her hands to his chest. She thought she sighed. She knew she leaned into him.

His lips were cool, his tongue hot. She felt the contrast immediately and opened to him because she couldn't do otherwise.

He groaned when she did that, the sound seeming torn from deep inside, and he pushed his hands into her hair. She felt his fingers splay over her skull as he angled her head to deepen the kiss. She let him. Not encouraging, so much as allowing. He tasted warm and sweet and the kiss he worked over her mouth was filled with dark, sensual promise. It wasn't only her senses he assaulted. It was the protective lock she'd kept on her emotions. Suddenly she felt that lock break and his heat seeping into the void. She'd felt so empty. So cold. So lost.

It was easier when she hadn't faced that.

He must have felt her tense.

He lifted his mouth, easing the pressure to let his lips graze hers. Teasing the corners of her lips, his arm circled her back. He drew her closer, his hand skimming her side and shaping the swell of her breast.

He kissed her again, gentler this time and was breathing hard when he finally drew back. The glimmer of heat was in his eyes; the hunger raw and real. But as his arms fell away, what she was aware of most was his confusion. It was as if he'd intended to prove something and in the process, had found something he hadn't expected. Or, maybe, hadn't wanted. Whatever it was, he didn't look overly pleased with himself. Or with her.

His expression was distant, his voice rough. "I'll see if Asa's coming."

Not trusting what she felt any more than he did, Lara watched Cole turn to a break in the vegetation just beyond where the plane bobbed near the shore. As he reached the break he stopped, then started forward more slowly.

He vanished into the trees. Seconds later, he came back out, dragging something long and narrow behind him. "Asa's not coming," he said as he drew nearer.

Lowering her hand from where it had been pressed to her mouth, she started toward him. "Is he all right?"

"I'm sure he's fine. He's probably out tending his traps or playing around in his mine. If he doesn't feel like talking, he leaves the sled here for me and I take the supplies to his cabin."

He dragged the sled to the boxes. When he let go of it and stepped aside, Lara continued to stare at the primitive contraption. The sled was made of two long branches laced together with strips of hide. Threaded between the handles, dangling from a stick was a large silver fish.

"What's that for?" she asked, wondering if the salmon served as some kind of talisman or something.

"It's Asa's way of saying thanks. He probably caught it this morning. Looks like a nice one, too."

Cole unhooked the stick from the handle. Leaving the fish on it, he stepped up onto the plane's pontoon and opened the pilot's door. A minute later, he'd taken a small cooler, filled the bottom with the icy lake water, put the fish in it and set the cooler back inside the plane.

"The cabin's about half a mile in," he said, jumping back to shore. He picked up his backpack and set it on the sled. One of the boxes followed. "He'll have left the money for the supplies there." The other box went on next and the backpack she'd carried. After slinging the rifle over his shoulder, he put his back to the sled and picked up the handles. "You lead."

"Where am I going?"

"Right through there." He nodded toward the break in the trees. "You'll see a path."

She didn't tell him that she didn't think much of his path when she saw it. For a moment she wasn't even sure she was on the right track as she started through the trees. But since Cole didn't say anything, she figured the openings between the vegetation must be the route he was talking about. The growth was unbelievably thick. Huckleberry, fern and shrubs with wicked-looking thorns shared space with blueberry bushes, moss and lichen. The trees themselves, fallen alder and standing spruce were so dense that, in spots, it had been centuries since sunlight had shown on the forest floor. Someday, inevitably, the spruce would fall, too, and hemlock would grow in its place.

That was what Cole told her when she asked why all the leaning, dead trees seemed to be a different type from those standing. It was simply because they *were* different, he told her and seemed to relax with her fascination at a forest's natural progression of change.

Lara was enraptured by the forest. The fact that it lived while its components eventually died out and other species took their places, affirmed that life did, indeed, go on. Not in exactly the same way, but in one that was just as vital. As she listened to Cole's smoky voice while he spoke of the continuity of the forest, she had the feeling that he was talking about more than the natural phenomenon. He was speaking of hope, for that was what he said lay in a dormant seedling. It was what pushed tender shoots from the darkness of decay toward the light. It was what fueled a sapling's struggle to reach the heights of what surrounded it.

Though he didn't say as much, Lara realized that hope was also what Cole found for himself in his forest. And, maybe, peace. That realization made her even more aware of him, of who he was. He was a man with an enormous respect for nature. A man who saw the land as he might see mankind. Struggling, thriving, surviving. She felt certain that was why he seemed such a part of it.

Cole fell silent long before they reached the perimeter of Asa's "property." Lara found that conversation wasn't really possible anyway when one was trying to avoid the nasty thorns of Devil's Club while traversing a not-so-gently sloping mountain. If Asa wanted privacy, the spot he'd chosen for his cabin virtually guaranteed it.

To call the place where Asa lived a cabin was to be most generous. The square little building was a shack built of odd scraps of wood nailed together patchwork fashion. A galvanized metal chimney stuck out the top, the thread of smoke drifting out of it indicating that a stove of some sort provided heat inside. It had windows, too. One on either side of a narrow front door. They weren't glass, though. They were made of treated animal hide, stretched thin enough to let in light.

Some light anyway. Following Cole inside after he'd received no response to his calls, she found the cramped interior depressingly dim. It was probably just as well. The lack of good illumination made it difficult to see the years' accumulation of dirt and soot. The place had a decidedly dank odor to it, too, which made her doubly appreciative of the fresh air when she got back outside. She'd stayed only long enough to carry in the books Cole had asked her to take from his backpack. Cole took the boxes in himself.

She was standing by Asa's woodpile watching a bug paddle around in his rain barrel when Cole came out and closed the rickety door.

"This is yours."

He held out several bills and a handful of coins, payment for the supplies from her store. Taking it, she pushed it into the back pocket of her jeans.

"Where does he get money if he stays up here?"

"He's been known to get a fee for taking a hunter down to where moose or deer are feeding." He looked up to the sky, still blue and studded with white clouds. "And I give him a few dollars for keeping an eye on things up here for me. If he spots trouble, he radios in."

"Do you run into problems up here often?"

"Had a couple of poachers here in '79. And a plane that went down this side of the ridge in '88."

"Busy, huh?"

"If it were any busier, Asa wouldn't do it. He really prefers to be alone."

Obviously Asa's duties were unofficial. Just as obvious were Cole's motives. The old man had no one. If Cole didn't keep an eye on him, no one would know if anything happened to him.

Lara thought she was also beginning to understand what Rosie had meant when she'd said that Cole and Asa were so much alike. Asa put physical distance between himself and others. The distance Cole chose was emotional. In its own way, it was just as effective.

"How did you meet him?"

Their backpacks lay on a clump of grass below one of the animal-skin windows. Handing her the one she'd emptied of books, he picked up the other and slung it over his back.

"Someone from Mist?" she pressed, not seeing the tightness in his expression.

"Someone I knew a long time ago."

He started across the clearing toward the path. The clearing wasn't very large and the slant of the sun covered the edges of it in shadow. She fell into step beside him. If his stride were any longer she would have to do double time.

"The old Native," she decided.

She wasn't exactly sure how she had guessed. But there was no doubt in her mind that she was right when Cole's next step fell short. He looked a little surprised at her perception and awfully reluctant to acknowledge it.

"Why don't you want to talk about him?"

"Because he's dead."

She saw the anger beneath the brusqueness. She recognized it because, for a while, and as illogical as it seemed, she'd been just as angry at Steve for leaving her. "That doesn't mean he didn't exist," she said quietly. "I understand what it's like to care about someone and have them die, Cole. Not talking about him won't make it not hurt."

"I didn't say it hurt."

"You didn't have to."

He'd known the first night he saw her that she was dangerous. She made him remember and it was painful to recall what he'd known so briefly. Cole wouldn't have traded the few years he'd known Jud Walker for anything, but in many ways those good years had taught him more than the skills he'd needed to survive. They'd taught him what he'd be missing for the rest of his life.

Somehow, looking into Lara's solemn blue eyes, he knew she understood how empty that feeling could be.

"Asa brought Jud an eaglet," he said, answering the question she'd first asked. "Jud was a shaman, a medicine man, and it was said that he could heal anything. Asa's still had blown up and knocked the bird out of its nest. The old-timers believed that harming an eagle would bring a curse to their mine, so he walked all the way to the Tlinget settlement to get it help. The bird had a broken wing, and Jud showed me how to fix it.''

It had been so long ago, nearly twenty years now, and he'd forgotten how grateful Asa had been to Jud and how he'd promised to nurse the eaglet back to health. The sight of the scruffy old man carefully holding that tiny bird in his hands would have brought a smile to Cole's face, if Lara's next question hadn't pushed his memories back even farther.

''What were you doing at the settlement?'' she asked.

The backpack slid from his shoulders. Cole sat down on it and stared at the rifle stretched across his knees. Jud had found him hiding in the woods, he told her, after he'd run away from the state-run boarding school. They hadn't been able to place him in foster homes anymore. Not that it mattered. He'd run away from them, too.

Cole wasn't sure how it happened, but with Lara's gentle prodding, he found himself telling her about Jud and how he'd taken him in and taught him how to love the land and its beasts. The land never betrayed you and an animal could never use you, the wise old man had told him. And Cole supposed he had felt used, though he'd never thought of it exactly that way.

He'd been six when his mother had left him. She'd promised to come back, but she'd never returned—even though he'd insisted to those with authority over him that she would. She'd *said* she'd come back, after all. And he'd believed her. For a very long time, he'd gone to bed each night, knowing that the next day she'd be there. But she never was, and one day, after she'd been gone for about a year, he realized that she didn't care enough to come back for him.

He didn't mention that part to Lara, or tell her that it was about that time, when he was seven, that he started growing up. He only said that a couple of the foster homes he'd been in hadn't been bad, but it was pretty clear the families only wanted him for the government support checks that came with him. By the time he was fourteen, he'd been labeled "hard to place" and had been relegated to a boys' home. He'd run away twice. The last time, he'd lied about his age and gotten a job on a fishing boat. He'd done all right, he supposed, until he'd been rolled for his paycheck and dumped in the woods, which was where Jud had found him.

Despite Cole's basic sense of distrust, Jud had treated him like a human being instead of chattel. Eventually, he'd treated him like a son. Cole would have done anything for him.

"Was it his idea for you to go back to school?" he heard her ask, her voice hushed like the wind through the trees.

Cole gave a hard chuckle. "Yeah it was. I fought him tooth and nail, too. He told me that if I wanted to stay with him in his settlement, I had to go to school. I wanted to stay, so I went."

In a voice curiously lacking in emotion, he also told her that when he'd finished high school, he'd done well enough to earn a college scholarship. Jud had been encouraging because he'd known that, while no one knew their land better than the people of the Tongass, education was necessary to educate others as to its intricacies. Cole truly believed in Jud's ideals; they had become his own. But Jud had died only days before Cole was to graduate. Cole hadn't attended the ceremony to pick up his diploma. Without Jud, the celebration meant nothing.

As they sat in the quiet of the forest, Lara was aware of much that Cole didn't say. Jud's death had taken away the only stability he'd had and, as when his mother had left, he'd felt abandoned. Cole's marriage would have fallen apart around then, too, and he had once again been left alone. Except for Jud, no one had ever really cared about Cole; no one had ever wanted or needed him for himself. As a result, he'd made sure he didn't want or need anyone else, either.

So he'd come to live in the forest.

Just as she had done.

Dear heaven, she thought. They were quite a pair.

Lara didn't question what she was about to do. She simply did it because she felt it was what he needed to hear. She laid her hand over Cole's.

"I think your Jud would have been very proud of you."

Her words seemed to reach into him, toward something deep in his soul that had never before been touched. His eyes searching hers, he lifted his hand to her cheek.

The sound of rustling leaves and snapping twigs made him drop it. His head jerked to the side, and a moment later, he was on his feet.

Chapter Eight

Lara didn't know when she'd ever seen anyone move so fast. One second Cole had been seated in front of her, the look in his eyes one of pain and thanks. The next, in a movement so smooth and silent she could have imagined it, he was on his feet, primed and alert. His glance focused in the direction of the commotion, his powerful body so still that she was afraid to move herself. Yet, he didn't look all that concerned about what it was that crashed through the trees on the other side of the clearing. He simply looked . . . ready.

The bushes parted. Instead of a charging moose or bear, what emerged from the trees was a grizzled old man, stick-straight and with a beard the color of dingy cotton. On his head was a wide-brimmed leather hat with a feather in its hide band. The elbows of his dark olive shirt were as holey as the knees of his baggy dungarees. He held a shotgun hip-high and pointed straight ahead.

Apparently, his eyesight wasn't all that keen. Halting just clear of the trees, he squinted across the open space. There wasn't a shred of welcome in his rusty voice. "That you, MacInnes?"

Without taking his eyes off the old man, Cole held out his hand for Lara. When she was on her feet, he held his hand up to indicate she should stay there, and stepped out of the shadows. "It's me, Asa. Just brought your supplies. Thanks for the fish."

Asa moved no closer. He'd seen that there were two of them. Even from the distance of a dozen yards, Lara could tell that he was skeptical of her presence. He also seemed skeptical of her gender.

"That a woman?"

"Her name's Lara. She owns the store in Mist now."

"She yours?"

A moment's hesitation preceded Cole's flat, "She's a friend."

That seemed to appease the man. A little. "Why'd you bring her?"

"Nice day for a ride," Cole returned, making the flight sound equivalent to a drive in the country. "Thought we'd get in a little target practice. If you hear shots, it's only us."

Asa gave a curt nod. "You best be gettin' then. Obliged for the supplies."

The conversation was apparently over. Shotgun over his shoulder, scratching at his ribs, the terse old man headed toward his cabin.

Cole stepped back into the shadows. Picking up their gear, he seemed to think little of the man's inhospitable manner. "Let's go," he said and started off. Lara was right on his heels, glancing backward. Asa was watching them from his door.

"Is he always like that?"

"Nah. Sometimes he's not so talkative."

She thought Cole might be joking. When he did nothing more than shrug, she knew he wasn't.

"Is he upset with you for bringing me?"

"It's hard to tell with Asa. That's the way he always is."

"I got the distinct feeling that he didn't like my being here."

The trees had closed them in, cutting them off from the eccentric old man as they went deeper into the daylight dimness of the forest. She felt Cole right behind her, and the brush of his sleeve to her shoulder when he reached past to push a low hanging branch out of the way.

"He probably didn't." The branch snapped back into place as they moved on. "But I do."

Lara's step threatened to falter when she heard his admission. With a nudge, Cole kept her headed along the route they'd taken earlier, saying they needed to watch for the two boulders with the tree growing between them; that was their cutoff.

He had no idea how remarkable Lara found his attitude. She'd been almost certain that after what he'd told her about his past he would pull back again. She could easily see him feeling that he'd exposed too much of himself already. He was such an intensely private man that it couldn't have been easy for him to allow her in as he had. It hadn't been comfortable for Lara to hear what he'd said, either. It took no effort to empathize with him. True, her background had been just the opposite of his—she'd had the loving family he'd never known, the closeness of a good marriage—but she understood loss and she knew how it felt to live with loneliness. But she could only imagine his sense of isolation.

He'd been used. In some ways by the families who'd taken him in as much for the money as any desire to help a child, and in the most blatant sense by his ex-wife. Now Lara felt compelled to make sure he never felt she was doing such a thing to him.

They were about halfway to the plane when Cole veered off course. When they'd passed through this spot before, Lara had noticed the sound of rushing water. Following him down a slight slope, occasionally grabbing at a moss-covered branch to keep balance, she saw where the sound was coming from. A swiftly moving stream wound its way down the hill toward the lake, the sunlight creating little diamonds on the water as it flowed past the embankment on the opposite side.

Cole turned when the land leveled. Removing his pack, he took out a box of shells and thick sheet of folded paper. "Your target," he said, pulling off one of the sheets.

A log had fallen across the stream here. The nearest end was a tangle of roots and dirt and the starts of tiny ferns. Its other end had landed on an outcropping of rock suspending the log a couple of feet above the water. Cole stepped up onto it and walked across, completely unconcerned with the water churning below him. On the other side, he tacked the target to the face of the ten-foot-high earthen ledge by pushing two thin twigs through the paper and into the dirt.

When he got back, he picked up the rifle.

He knew Lara wasn't crazy about learning how to use a gun. Every time he mentioned it, she'd looked a little less than enthusiastic at the prospect. She flat-out balked at the idea now.

"I don't think I could kill anything even if I did know how to use a gun, Cole. We really don't have to do this."

"You won't know what you'll do until you're faced with the situation. With any luck, that'll never happen. But you can't rely on luck. All you can rely on is yourself. We *do* have to do this,'' he said, probably a little more tersely than he should. "And you know it."

She reached for the gun, looking partly defiant but mostly uncertain as her slender fingers wrapped around the stock. It was heavier than she'd anticipated. Feeling its weight, she quickly grasped it with her other hand, too.

"The safety is off," he warned her.

She acknowledged the warning with a glance as cool as the water rushing in front of her. Her concern for him had obviously been misplaced. While she had instinctively felt his pain, she hadn't taken into consideration that he'd had years to develop a hide tough enough to stop a tank. Cole wouldn't allow himself to be used again. Ever. It had been amazingly naive of her to think that something like having him teach her how to shoot a gun could be misconstrued. It was, after all, his idea. "What am I supposed to do?"

"For starters, you could back up a few dozen feet. As close as you are, you could forget about firing. If that target were an animal, you could just knock it over the head."

The look she sent him said she wasn't in the mood to be teased.

You won't know what you'll do until you're faced with the situation, he'd said. She didn't appreciate that he felt she didn't know her own mind. She supposed she should appreciate his other reminder, though. When she was with him, she tended to forget how alone she was—she really did have only herself to rely upon.

She walked back about thirty feet from the target. Then continued for another ten or so at Cole's urging.

He snagged her arm to stop her and turned her around. For about two seconds, he thought about asking her what was wrong. She'd all but closed down on him in the past couple of minutes. Having already stepped beyond the parameters he'd laid for himself, he decided he didn't want to know.

He told her to raise the rifle. The barrel gleamed blue when he reached over and tipped it toward the target. "Hold it snug into your shoulder. Closer. You're going to get some recoil and if it's not tight enough you'll bruise yourself when the stock kicks back. You want to absorb the shock with your shoulder and arms."

To show her the proper position, he stood behind her. With his arm over her left shoulder, he lifted the stock higher, pushed it tighter into her shoulder and told her to line up the bull's-eye through the sight. As close as he was, every breath he drew brought with it the scent of the fragrant powder she wore. To see if she could line up the sight, he had to hunch down to make sure the rifle was high enough. When he did, he found it necessary to brush her hair back from her neck. The curling tendrils felt like silk against his rough hands and when he moved to look over her shoulder, the tops of his thighs brushed the curve of her bottom.

He felt her stiffen.

He was already a little stiff himself.

He backed up just enough to break that nerve-stretching contact. A woman had no right to smell as good as she did. To feel as good, either, he thought, remembering how she'd molded to him when he'd kissed her.

She had her finger on the trigger. "Squeeze easy," he said, and swallowed against the dryness in his throat.

The crack of the shot coincided with the jolt. As he'd thought might happen, the recoil was more than she'd anticipated. A .375 Magnum was not a light weapon—its bullet could rip a hole the size of a softball in a man—and the discharging force pushed her right into him. She almost dropped the rifle as she grabbed for her shoulder. He caught the weapon in his left hand and her with his right.

His arm was hard around her waist, her back flat against his chest. Still holding the rifle in front of her, he put his mouth near her temple and asked if she was all right.

Her hair fluttered with his breath and his lips touched her skin when she moved to nod. She was stunned, he was sure of it. He was just as sure she could feel the heavy thud of his heart, braced against him as she was.

"How about your shoulder?" Wishing he didn't have to release her, relinquishing his hold anyway, he eased his arm from her waist.

She seemed a little stunned. "It's okay. I think."

"Want to try it again?"

She didn't look at him, but gamely, she nodded. "Did I hit anything?"

He glanced at the target. "Afraid not."

"Then I guess I'll have to."

Lara wasn't surprised she'd completely missed the target. Feeling Cole behind her had made concentrating on anything but his hard body difficult.

It wasn't so easy now, either. But she knew how to make herself focus on what needed to be done. Coping with only one moment at a time was how she had learned to survive. And without her dreams, survival had somehow become what her life was now all about. She had no plans beyond repairing her roof—and that was hardly a solid basis for a future. She'd stopped thinking in terms of a future long ago. Her goal was simply to get from one day to the next and not to think of anything much beyond that. Cole said she had to be able to handle a gun. If that was part of what it took to survive here, then that's what she'd do. She wouldn't like it. But she'd do it.

She had to learn to live with a lot that she didn't like.

By the time she'd gone through two boxes of shells, her shoulder felt as if she'd been dropping linebackers with it all day. She'd finally gotten the hang of using her arms like shock absorbers after about the sixth time the butt had slammed into her. After her first try, Cole had her pad her shoulder with the denim jacket he'd worn over a cotton undershirt.

It had helped, but the weight of the gun still had both of her arms aching. She had, however, hit the target—every single one of the last ten times she'd fired.

She hadn't gotten a bull's-eye, though—something Cole had done when she'd handed him the rifle to see how he held it. He'd looked almost apologetic for the feat when he'd handed the firearm back to her.

Remembering the strength of his reflexes, how quickly he'd been at the ready when he'd heard the rustling bushes at Asa's, she had the feeling he was always that good.

She was rubbing her arms, wondering if she'd be so sore in the morning that she wouldn't feel like sanding, when Cole came back across the log. He'd crossed the stream to get the target.

"Not bad for someone who'd never held a gun before."

She smiled, looking pleased, and sank onto the mossy ground to take a swallow of water from his canteen.

He'd have bet anyone in Rosie's a month's pay that she'd have called it quits after the first five minutes. At least, he would have until he'd caught the abject determination in her face. It didn't matter that her shoulder hurt—and he was sure it must the way the rifle had bucked into her—or her arms ached. As he put the mutilated target and spent shells in the backpack, he couldn't help feeling that Lara was trying to prove something. Not to him so much. To herself.

"What can I do to repay you?"

Her question was asked with a smile as she held out the canteen. After taking a swallow himself, he added it to the pack. "Repay me for what?"

"The lesson," she said, trying not to think of how intimate it was to have been drinking from the same canteen.

"How about dinner?"

He couldn't believe he'd asked that. He didn't want repayment. But now that the offer was out, he knew that was what he wanted. To sit at her table as he had once before—even if spending more time with her probably wasn't the wisest thing to do.

She seemed to consider the exchange fair enough. "Sure. When we get back I'll fix whatever you want. As long as it's something I know how to make. What would you like?"

That, Mrs. Grant, he thought, is one loaded question.

It was one, however, that he was saved considering when he remembered that spending time with her this evening wouldn't be possible. He had a report to finish. It was already overdue. If he didn't make himself do it tonight, his supervisor was really going to get his jock in a knot. Again.

"I'd like anything that doesn't come out of a can. But let's make it tomorrow. I have something I have to do tonight."

He saw disappointment in her face and felt a twinge of satisfaction when he realized that she'd really wanted his company. Then he saw the light of recollection as she smiled. "Did you change your mind about going to the meeting at Rosie's tonight? Do the people around here do that often? Have meetings there I mean?"

"Once in a while," he returned, evasively. "But I'm not going. I'm typing up a report tonight." Wanting the subject dropped, he picked up the pack. "Ready?"

"Is it a community thing?"

He really wished this hadn't come up. "Uh . . . yeah. As a matter of fact, it is." His brow furrowed. "How'd you hear about it?"

"Actually, I overheard it." She stood up, brushing the moss from the back of her jeans. "Ron was asking you about it just as I was leaving his shop. If it's a community meeting, should I go?"

"I don't think you'll want to."

"Why wouldn't I?"

She didn't like his tone. Granted, she'd only been in Mist for a couple of weeks, and she knew she had a ways to go before people really accepted her, but she felt she had a right to know what concerned the town. How else could she become part of it?

"Cole?" she prompted when he didn't answer.

"You don't want to go because the meeting is about you. About your taking on the teaching position," he clarified when his response left her staring at him. "I assume you haven't changed your mind about taking it. Have you?"

Her quiet, "No, I haven't," didn't seem to surprise him at all.

After the way she avoided the issue last night, he didn't think she had. "That's why I wouldn't recommend your going. The meeting is to decide who will approach you and what kind of offer to make. You might find it embarrassing to be put in the position of turning down a room full of people."

She now knew why no one had yet come to her. The citizens of Mist obviously appreciated that it took awhile to get acclimated and were giving her a chance to settle in before bringing it up. The little "discussion" about it at Rosie's last night was just a test to see if she was approachable. Apparently someone had decided she was.

She should have felt pleased with that tacit acceptance. She could think only of how fleeting that acceptance might be. After the help everyone had given her when her roof caved in, she would appear awfully ungrateful turning them down. She really didn't have a choice, though. Taking the job would be a disservice to their children. And that was what she needed for someone to understand.

She hated that she couldn't just let the matter go. "They wouldn't want me, Cole. I've heard them, and what they want is what's best for their children. I'm not a good teacher anymore. The kids deserve better than what I could give them." She paused, her voice growing quieter. "That's why I left the job I had."

She looked out across the water, focusing on a spot far off in the distance. In some ways, it had been hard to let go. In others, far too easy. But what had been important was that the children had truly deserved more than what she'd been capable of giving.

She had wandered around in the state of shock for months after Steve's death. The accident had happened the first of December, the holidays having passed without her even being aware of them, and by the time she had healed from her own injuries and was physically able to go back to work, school was out. So she focused on September, thinking she could get her life back on track once classes got started. It had been hard enough getting through the days and nights without Steve at home, but the devastation hit all over again when she went back to school.

She had known it would be difficult to walk the familiar halls without him. After a couple of months, she had accepted that she wasn't going to enter the teachers' lounge and see him joking with one of the staff. She'd even reached the point where she didn't break down in tears when she drove past the coffee shop they'd stopped at every morning on their way to school.

What she hadn't been able to do was recover her enthusiasm, her ability to really care about what happened to each of those precious kids. She didn't have the energy to help Billy Beaumont with his math after school, or Sasha Thomas with her reading. She couldn't make her mind focus on creative ideas for the science fair, or art day, or even just to come up with a simple bulletin board display. She dreaded getting up each morning because the demands of the kids were sucking at stores of energy she didn't have, and she hated going to bed at night because she'd lie awake and think of how badly she was failing them—and of how terribly she missed her husband. She would lie curled up, hugging the emptiness inside her and waiting for morning to come. And then she hated morning because the cycle would start all over again.

She sighed heavily, and rubbed at a spot above the bridge of her nose.

Cole watched as she stood massaging her forehead, drawn as much by the sorrow in her expression as the dull certainty he'd heard in her voice. It was clear enough that it had been difficult for her to admit what she saw as a failure on her part. He wanted to ask what made her think she wasn't a good teacher, but the reasons didn't matter. How a person perceived herself wasn't an arguable point. She'd cared about the children she'd taught. He was sure of that. Her nurturing tendencies were so deeply ingrained that she couldn't deny them even if she tried. He had a feeling that she did try to deny them, though. He'd seen her try with Bear.

The decision she'd reached hadn't been made lightly. It couldn't have been. Not for Lara.

He moved toward her, touching her arm to draw her attention. "We'd better get going. We don't want to be wandering around in the dark."

She barely met his eyes. But the tiny smile she managed before she slipped the pack over her shoulder and headed up the hill spoke volumes. Thank you for not arguing with me, that smile had said. Thank you for accepting what I told you without making me explain.

She wasn't his responsibility, yet he couldn't seem to fight his compulsion to protect her. He found himself wanting to protect her now. He couldn't stop anyone from approaching her about the job, but he might be able to make it easier for her if he handled it himself.

"I'll go to the meeting and tell them I've already talked to you about it," he said. "But I'll tell them I think you're suffering burnout or something and that they should keep looking for someone else. How does that sound?"

It sounded too easy. And nothing had been easy for her lately. "I couldn't ask you to do that, Cole."

"You didn't ask, Lara. I offered."

It didn't occur to Cole that his offer was as much for himself as for Lara. It felt good to be able to make her situation easier, and when he felt good about helping her, he felt better about himself. During the days that followed their trip to Asa's, though, he began to think that what he'd done might not have been the best for her. Not that he felt that he had any right or obligation regarding how she chose to live her life—she was a grown woman and perfectly capable of those decisions. He just had the feeling that, having guided the parents' interest away from her as a potential teacher, he had also made it possible for her to crawl into the little niche she was carefully carving for herself. He knew what it meant to hold one's self back. But where he was comfortable remaining on the periphery of the others' lives—preferred it, in fact—that detachment seemed alien to her.

He noticed it most whenever anyone else was around.

Cole began having dinner at Lara's on the days he worked on her roof. Though they never specifically spoke of it, they accepted each other's presence with a certain inevitability. At least, that was how it seemed to him. They would talk and argue, as usual, and though he never did anything about it, she would make him crazy with thoughts of her slender body and unbelievably soft skin. He was very careful not to touch her. Since she avoided him whenever possible, he was sure she preferred it that way. But even though he was sure she preferred it, he couldn't help remembering how she'd responded when he'd kissed her. As incredible as it had seemed at the time, she had wanted that kiss as much as he had. The memory of how she'd leaned into him, of how she had opened to him, taunted him mercilessly.

He was wondering if she ever remembered that as, coming in the back way, he walked past her kitchen, his stomach responding to the appetizing aroma of whatever she had simmering on the stove. He'd been out back, nailing the new trusses for her roof, and broken a splinter off in his finger. He'd tried to dig the thing out with his pocketknife. Now it was bleeding and he couldn't hammer with his handkerchief wound around it. As a last resort, he was considering an adhesive strip.

He found Lara in the store. She was busy with a customer—a young man waiting for work at the ice house—so he stayed back, not wanting to interrupt.

He liked watching her anyway, especially when she wasn't aware of him. She looked a little different today; softer possibly. Her curling hair was drawn up with barrettes on either side of her face, the style making her look younger somehow. And she was smiling; Cole thought she always looked a little younger when she did that.

"Thanks, Bernie," he heard her say as she handed over the groceries she'd bagged. Cole had never known her to encourage conversation with her customers, though she was always unfailingly polite. "I'll see you later."

A moment later the young man was heading out the door, exchanging a greeting with Sally who was on her way in with the youngest of her two towheaded boys. Matt, if Cole remembered correctly. Matt gave Lara a grin that said he knew he was welcome and headed straight for the comics on the magazine rack. Sally, holding her back as her stomach preceded her into the store, grimaced a little and leaned against the counter.

The woman looked as big as a house to Cole and damned uncomfortable.

"Are you all right?" he heard Lara ask.

Sally waved off her concern. "I'm fine. Nothing wrong with me that giving birth won't cure. Did your fresh produce come in?"

"Just this morning." Lara skirted the counter, brushing at the red flannel shirt she wore open over a white cotton turtleneck and shape-hugging jeans. Cole's glance automatically slid down her figure. He liked knowing how slender she was beneath the long shirts and sweaters she wore so much. "Tell me what you want and I'll get it for you."

Again, Sally's hand lifted dismissively. "You don't need to do that. I've got three more weeks to go and other than maneuvering with the grace of a beached whale, I'm perfectly capable of doing what I need to do." She pushed herself from the counter, her rubber boots making squeaking noises on the wooden floor as she walked away.

She stopped short of the produce section. "Well, hello, Cole," she said, her grumbling replaced by her ever-present nosiness. "You working on Lara's roof? Or," she added, speculating, "just visiting?"

At the sound of Cole's name, Lara's glance swung from where Matt sat on the floor to where Cole was propped against the doorjamb at the back of the store. Judging from his relaxed stance, he'd been there for more than a few moments. Odd that she hadn't known he was there. She usually had a sixth sense about his presence.

"Working on the roof," Lara heard him say, his tone utterly nonchalant.

Sally didn't even bother to cover her disappointment. She'd wanted something newsy to relate. Everyone already knew Cole was fixing Lara's roof and Ron was doing her wiring. "How's it coming?" she asked, compelled to get some information anyway.

"We might get it raised next week. If the weather holds."

Curiosity was replaced with concern. "From what I hear, we're about to see the last of the sun for a while. When I talked to Tom on the radio awhile ago, he said he'd just picked up the marine station out of Anchorage. According to him, there's a front coming in from the northwest." Pushing back a strand of blond hair that had loosened from her ponytail, her thoughts wandered more in that direction. "If it comes this way, I just hope they make it back before it hits. Like I told Carolyn when she dropped her sons off to play with Tommy, I'm not in any mood to have to worry."

With that, she moved on past the boxed pastries and started squeezing tomatoes.

Lara didn't notice what Sally was doing to her produce. Cole was coming toward her, his eyes steady on hers in a way she always found unnerving. She hated the anticipation she felt whenever she saw him. She'd tried very hard not to feel it, but she was beginning to think the attempt a monumen-

tal waste of energy. She hadn't been able to stop the anticipation, but keeping her distance from him helped. That was
why she usually found something to do elsewhere when he
was around; unless he needed her help.

He seemed to need her help now.

She looked from his predictably unreadable expression to
the red handkerchief coiled around his ring finger. "What
did you do to yourself?"

With a shrug to indicate how inconsequential it was, he
muttered, "Got a splinter. Do you have any of those plastic
adhesive things?"

"Did you get it out?"

"Most of it."

She frowned at the dark blotches on the cloth. Because of
the handkerchief's color she hadn't first noticed the blood.
"Why is it bleeding so much?"

"I tried to get it out."

"With what?"

"My pocketknife."

"You're kidding."

"What would you have used?"

"A needle and tweezers."

"Well, I don't happen to carry a needle and tweezers in
my pocket. The knife works fine."

"Obviously," she drawled and held out her hand. "Let
me see it."

"I just want something to put on it."

"You might need more than just a little bandage."

"No, I won't."

Sally set down her purchases. "Do you two always bicker
like this?"

"Yes," said Cole, exasperated.

"No," came the countering reply.

"We do, too, Lara."

The only way she could prove her side was to say nothing. Holding his glance until she saw the devilment move into his eyes, Lara reached for a bag under the counter. She could have sworn he was about to smile. If he had, she would have, too, and then the world would know how much she enjoyed his company. It wasn't something she even cared to admit to herself.

She added a sack of apples to the lettuce and onions already in the bag. "Will this do it for you, Sally?"

Sally was apparently too preoccupied with her aching back to play guessing games about what might be going on between the store's new owner and the local ranger. Putting away the comic book that had occupied her son, she told Lara she had everything she needed and within the minute she was out the door. Her voice drifted back, carrying weariness as she hollered at little Matt to come back and carry the bag for her.

Poor Sally, Lara thought, then made a mental change of subject before she could start wishing the impossible again. It did no good to yearn for something she could never have. How long, she wondered, before the desire would diminish?

Her voice was strangely subdued when she turned back to Cole. "I'll get you a bandage," she said and left him staring after her when she disappeared through the doorway.

She had just closed the medicine cabinet and stepped out of the bathroom when she found him waiting for her.

She held out the strip, reluctant to offer an assist. He took it, seeming just as reluctant to ask for one and stuffed his handkerchief into his back pocket. He spoke even as she wound the adhesive around the small wound.

"If Sally heard we were getting a storm, I'd better finish up out there so I can get everything put away and the trusses covered with plastic. These storms can hit awfully fast sometimes.''

''I'll be out in a few minutes to help put the tools away.'' While she didn't know anything about construction, she did know how to straighten things up. That was an unspoken part of her job; an agreement that had been reached without ever discussing it. They seemed to have many of those. ''I've got to feed Bear right now. After we get the tools in, I'll put some corn bread in the oven to go with the stew. Think you'll be ready to eat in an hour or so?''

She liked it when he smiled at her as he did now. As if she should know better than to have to ask. She liked it far more than she should have. ''I'll be ready,'' he said and held out his hand. It was curled in a fist, facing down.

She put hers six inches below it, open and palm up.

The paper wrapper from the adhesive strip fell into her hand when he splayed his fingers. Another unspoken agreement. Don't touch.

Lara smiled. Somehow, they had come to accept each other—and each other's basic sense of loneliness. Its existence gave them something in common and since Cole wasn't making any attempt to be anything other than a friend, she wasn't forced to make any decisions about what their relationship was. Something she would have to do were either one of them to acknowledge the physical awareness between them. That awareness was there constantly. It seemed to shade every remark, every glance. It caused her to catch her breath when he would accidentally brush against her and it filled their silences with a kind of tension that was almost palpable. The way it was now.

It had been a mistake not to move away. Cole was watching her as he did so often, as if he was remembering the brief moments they had spent in each other's arms.

Her smile faded, her heart racing as she remembered, too. "I've got to go get Bear's bottle ready," she said, her voice strained. "He gets cranky when he's hungry."

Cole's eyes held hers, refusing to relinquish the only hold he had. "I appreciate the feeling," he said, and before he could do something he might later regret, he headed out back to pound a few nails.

There had been some debate as to whether or not the storm would stay on its earlier course. The debate ended when it hit just before nine that evening. The fishing boats hadn't made it back yet. The last word was that they were about a mile west of the inlet. That was what Rosie had told Lara when she showed up at her back door minutes after Lara had finished Bear's last feeding and tucked him in for the night. Cole had left over an hour ago.

Rosie wasn't alone. Sally's two boys were with her, both looking very frightened and, because they had been out in the rain, very wet. Rosie looked a little apprehensive, too, but Lara assumed it was because of the deep-throated growls Bear made the instant he saw her.

Rosie's unease had nothing to do with the slightly spoiled little animal.

"I think Sally's in labor," she said, making herself sound very calm as she hugged the boys to her side. "You and I had better get over there."

Chapter Nine

Sally was having her baby?

Lara stood frozen in the doorway, her fingers clutching her sweater at her throat. Rosie wanted her to go with her. To Sally's.

Every self-protective instinct Lara possessed screamed at her to back up and close the door. She had come thousands of miles for a chance to start over, to leave behind all that she'd lost. She'd wanted to forget—and babies were what she'd wanted to forget most of all.

"Lara?"

At the sound of Rosie's throaty voice, Lara relaxed her grip on her sweater. It would be best not to think about why she would rather be put to sea on a melting iceberg than go to Sally's. What she needed to do was focus on this particular minute. Even thinking about the next hour loomed too large at the moment.

What she focused on now was that Sally was about three weeks early.

"Do I need to bring anything?"

When Rosie said she didn't, mentioning only that they should hurry, Lara grabbed her jacket from its peg and followed Rosie and Sally's boys down the wooden steps. It was dark and the rain was steady. Not the fire-hose blast she'd been caught in her second day in Mist, but the rain fell hard enough to bounce back from the boardwalk and then turn the earth to mud once they were out on bare ground. Matt fell back to take Lara's hand. She gave his hand a squeeze and let herself concentrate only on *his* anxiety as they hurried toward the tidy little house nestled back in the trees.

Rosie called out the instant they burst through the door of the Cassidys' comfortable home. "Sally? Where are you? I'm here with Lara."

"She's in her bedroom," Tommy said, bolting ahead.

Rosie caught him by his jacket collar. "You stay here," she told him. "I know you're worried about your mom, but let me see her first."

Tommy didn't like that idea at all. He was the man of the house when his father was gone and it was his job to take care of his mom and little brother.

Lara saw his struggle with that responsibility, along with the sheen of tears he clearly thought too babyish for a nine-year-old. He jerked the backs of his hands across his eyes and stared toward the door Rosie closed behind her. Matt, his fair hair two shades lighter than his brother's and his brown eyes just as dark, stood at his shoulder, looking too bewildered to cry. It was easy enough to see that they were both frightened.

Feeling a little anxious herself, Lara coaxed the boys out of their jackets and boots, keeping one ear tuned to the bedroom door. She could hear Rosie's no-nonsense questioning and Sally's quieter voice answering. It wasn't possible to discern what was being said, but Lara felt it a positive sign that Sally sounded reasonably strong.

"She's not going to die, is she?"

Tommy's question pulled Lara up short. "Oh, no, honey," she said, sinking to her knees. The position was so familiar; crouching like that to bring herself to eye level with a child. "She'll be fine. She's just having a baby."

"But she hurts bad. She was making dinner and then she grabbed her tummy and got all funny looking and laid down on the floor."

"She wet," said Matt.

"She did not," Tommy quickly defended. He looked embarrassed. Not for himself. For his mother. "She had an accident."

Lara glanced from one to the other. She had the feeling she knew what had taken place. What she needed to do now was assure the boys that what they had witnessed was perfectly normal. Clearly their mother's atypical behavior caused them distress.

"I think what happened was that her water broke. That usually happens not too long before the baby is born," she explained—and saw the boys' eyes widen when Sally began a deep, painful moan.

Half a minute later, Rosie's head popped from the doorway. It was apparent from her expression that this wasn't a false alarm. "Where does your mom keep string and scissors? And I need some bleach. And towels. Lots of towels."

Lara and Rosie looked at each other. In silent acknowledgement of what was about to happen, each took a deep breath. Neither looked particularly comfortable with the situation, but neither was going to admit it.

Lara turned back to the boys and sent them off with the warning not to run with the scissors. As soon as they were out of earshot, she walked over to Rosie.

"She isn't due yet," Lara whispered.

"I know. She said she radioed in to her doctor in Sitka before she sent the boys to me. With the weather as bad as it is, her doctor couldn't get here and we can't get her there."

"Do you know how to do this?"

"My first husband and I had a little spread outside of Cheyenne. Many a night I sat up waiting for a foal. I don't know if that counts or not, but I don't see where it much matters. That baby's coming whether we know anything about getting it here or not."

Lara took a calming breath. There were vast differences in the chances of survival for a baby born three weeks early and one born three months too soon. Reminding herself of that helped put the situation in perspective. What helped, too, was the numbness that began to diffuse her panic. The last thing in the world she wanted was for her concern to upset Sally.

She peeked past Rosie, into the room with Victorian curtains and walls filled with Sally's handicrafts. The woman on the bed was drenched in sweat, her blond hair tangled around her pale face. "Hi, Sally," Lara said, reluctant to disturb the few moments' peace she had between her pains. "Don't worry about the boys, I'll take care of them out here."

"They need their dinner." Sally pushed her hair back from her face. "I was fixing it when this started. I know the second and third ones don't take as much time as the first, but it feels like this kid's really going to hit the ground running." Her smile was pitifully weak. "I really wish Tom was here."

Lara heard the need in her voice. All too easily she could remember that same feeling, that need to have the father of your child with you to ease the hurt; to soothe the fear. And in Sally's case, Lara fervently hoped, to share the joy she would never know herself.

The boys both returned at the same time. Matt had his arms wrapped around a gallon bottle of bleach. Tommy had his mother's sewing scissors and a ball of kite string.

Matt looked up at Rosie. "What are you going to do with this stuff?"

He looked worried. His mother was in pain and a woman with painted eyebrows and red hair piled six inches high on her head was going to do something to her with scissors and string and bleach.

Rosie blinked at Lara, her expression utterly bland. "You were the teacher. You explain it to them."

"Gee, thanks," Lara muttered.

"Don't mention it."

Another pain grabbed Sally. Telling Rosie she'd take care of the sterilizing, Lara closed the door. The boys stood behind her, wide-eyed and worried. Turning them by the shoulders, she headed them into the large kitchen that opened out into the living area. It seemed that a project was in order.

While Rosie sat with Sally, Lara helped the boys pour bleach into a bowl, to which they added two lengths of string and the scissors. Water was put on to boil for the rinse. Tommy, naturally, wanted to know why they were doing all this, so Lara explained about bleach being a powerful disinfectant and how it was necessary to remove bacteria and other organisms that might make their mother or the new baby sick. She then had to answer Matt's original question about what the string and scissors were for.

She had never taught a class on reproduction, but she'd once read everything she could get her hands on concerning childbirth. Dealing only with the process and not what started it—which was strictly up to Sally and Tom to explain—she drew what looked like an incomplete lightbulb on a sheet of paper.

Tommy leaned across the table with his chin propped on his fists and scowled down at the page as she drew. She wasn't an artist by any means, but something resembling a human began to take form inside the odd oval shape.

"That looks kinda like the picture in Mom's book," Sally's oldest son observed.

Lara stopped drawing. Professional illustrations would be perfect. "She has a book on this? Where?"

Tommy pointed to the closed door. No sound had come from behind it for the past several minutes. "In Mom and Dad's room. In their nightstand. We're not supposed to go in there."

"I see," Lara mumbled.

Matt piped up. "She showed it to us, though. It has a picture of a baby inside a mommy. It was all folded up like this." He slid back from the table and dropped back into his chair. Scrunching up his eyes, he twisted himself up like a pretzel.

Tommy slugged his brother in the arm. "It wasn't like that, you dork. You're so dumb."

"Am not."

"Are too."

"Boys?" Lara said, thinking she and Cole had sounded a little like that at times.

The thought of Cole made her restive. In some ways she wished very much that he was here. But mostly, she was very glad he wasn't. She didn't think she could cope with what he would make her feel. He always seemed to make her face what she didn't want to think about, and she was trying very hard not to think about too much right now.

Tommy punched Matt once more, just to let him know that being older had its privileges, and turned his attention back to Lara. Rubbing his arm, Matt did the same.

It didn't take long to explain that once the baby was born, it had to be separated from its mother. The boys didn't have any problem with that idea, fortunately, and she went on to tell them how that separation was accomplished by tying the umbilical cord off in two places a couple of inches apart and cutting in between. That was what the string and scissors were for.

Tommy and Matt both seemed quite satisfied with her explanation. Their only comment was how gross it was that a cord had once stuck out of their own belly buttons.

Matt was inspecting his and Tommy looked like he was about to punch him again when they heard their mother's faint moan. Matt pulled his striped shirt down and belly buttons were forgotten as they stared at the door. Lara's own glance darted in the same direction. Sally, bless her, was being pretty quiet about the whole thing.

The scissors and string were ready now. Taking them to Rosie, Lara had Matt gather clean towels and a blanket and sent Tommy off to find one of the new kimonos she knew Sally had made for the baby. Then, once Rosie had everything she thought she and Sally would need, Lara started on the boys' dinner.

Sally had started a salad. From the ingredients sitting on the counter she had also apparently planned to make something with potatoes. As late as it was getting, Lara opted for simple—hot dogs. The boys had said hot dogs were their favorite, but they weren't much interested in their food. Tommy ate his, but left his bread, and little Matt did nothing but play. He had the kite string wrapped around his hot

dog the way Lara had explained Rosie would tie the cord
and had taken his mother's pinking sheers to cut in between.

At least he had the right idea, Lara thought with a sigh
and gently took the scissors away to wash.

The boys finally wound down and fell asleep on the couch
shortly before midnight.

Lara stood in the middle of the room, looking at the two
exhausted little boys. She wished they'd stayed awake. She'd
delayed putting them to bed for nearly half an hour. Once
she'd got them there she'd have nothing to do but pace—
which she did until a knock at the door interrupted.

Her first thought was that it might be Tom. For Sally's
sake, she hoped it was, but he wouldn't knock on his own
door. Unwrapping her arms from around herself, pushing
back the curls from her face, she reached for the handle.

It was Cole. A dull heaviness centered in her chest. She
wished with all her heart that it had been anyone else.

She assumed that his frown meant he was surprised to see
her. But he didn't say a word until he'd stepped inside and
closed the door on the rain and the wind.

He took off his hat and pushed his fingers through his
hair. "Tom's been trying to get through on the radio. He's
worried about Sally." He glanced at the boys sleeping on the
couch in the comfortable, family-oriented room, looking a
little concerned himself. A cry of pain, low and distinct underscored the beat of the rain. "Where is she?"

Lara's arms found their way back around her waist. The
nod of her head indicated the room the sound had come
from. "She's in labor. It shouldn't be too long. The pains
sound awfully close."

"Is she all right?"

"So far. Is Tom coming in?"

Cole glanced uncertainly toward the closed door. "They had just passed the mouth of the inlet when he called. They should make better time now that they're not fighting waves as much. He thought they should get here in about an hour."

"I'll go tell her."

"Wait a minute," he said, stopping her as she turned. He glanced back to the boys, their blond heads visible above the blankets she'd laid over them. "Do you want me to put them in their beds?"

Thinking that probably wouldn't be a bad idea, she asked him if he would. A moment later, they both heard the distinctive cry of a newborn baby.

Lara went still. She knew Cole's glance had jerked to her, but she couldn't look at him. She couldn't seem to do anything but stare at the panels on the closed door.

"Lara?" called Rosie. "We need you."

Concentrating only on putting one foot in front of the other, Lara left Cole staring after her and went inside Sally's bedroom.

It was a boy. "Just what I wanted," a tearful Sally said, forgetting about all the tiny pink clothes she'd made. "Is Tom here, Lara? I thought I heard him."

Lara shook her head. Telling her it was Cole, she relayed Tom's message then told her the boys were sleeping.

Sally's attention turned completely to her newest son. Her eyes were filled with wonder and no small amount of relief as she gazed at the tiny, towel-draped infant. The baby was covered with streaks of blood and shiny mucus, but he was a pretty good size—about six or seven pounds, was Rosie's guess. From the tears on the new mother's cheeks, he was the most beautiful sight Sally had seen. Since her last child, anyway.

It was easier for Lara to focus on Rosie. She sat at the side of the bed, gently kneading Sally's stomach. The sheets were bunched up over Sally's legs, the blankets and bedspread on the chair by the dresser. Lara bent to pick up the bloody towels dropped by the foot of the bed.

"I'll put these in the wash to soak," she said to Rosie, "and bring you some clean ones."

"Would you clean up the baby, then? We're not quite through yet."

Lara didn't look up. Her heart snagged painfully. "Sure. I'll be right back."

She didn't want to go back in there. She wanted to go home, back to her cabinlike shelter with its hole for a roof and sit huddled in the corner of her love seat and stare at the fire until somehow she fell asleep. It would be better in the morning. Since she had moved here, it had always been better in the morning.

You can do this, she told herself and, after putting the towels in cold water in the utility sink, went back to get the baby. She would pretend it was a rubber doll.

When she returned with the tiny bundle, Cole had put the boys to bed and was in the kitchen, looking down at the table. He seemed a little hesitant when he saw her. Even more so when he noticed the movement from the thick blue towel. But he wanted to know if everything was going as it should. When she assured him that it all appeared to be, he held up the illustration she'd drawn. "Looks like it's been an interesting night."

Hellish was how she would describe it, but she chose to merely nod in agreement. One thing at a time, she told herself and stiffened her shoulders as she walked past him. Cole didn't budge from his spot by the table. He took further possession of it by leaning against the edge and crossing his arms to watch.

If she'd had any nerve she'd have asked him to leave. She hated it when he followed her every move. It was as if he could see through to her very soul. And her soul was feeling a little raw at the moment.

After laying the baby on a blanket by the sink, she unwrapped him only part way so he wouldn't get chilled, and set to work. He might have made his appearance a little ahead of schedule, but Sally's baby was robust, pink and, as far as Lara could tell, perfect. He was also pretty unhappy. His little limbs jerked and flailed as he cried, and Lara was as gentle and quick as she could safely be as she carefully washed and diapered him.

Cole kept his distance, seeming interested but not especially anxious to get too close. The little half-beat cries seemed to disturb him. "Should he be crying like that?"

"He needs to cry. Babies need to expand their lungs when they're first born."

There were other things babies needed, too. Drops for their eyes to prevent blindness; physical evaluations to make sure everything was normal. But thankfully this baby didn't need oxygen to help him breathe, or fluids to keep his tiny body from dehydrating because it hadn't developed the instinct to suck. The way this little guy's fist kept popping to his mouth, Sally wasn't going to have any trouble with feeding.

"Why is he jerking like that?"

"He's used to being curled up tight and surrounded by warmth. Without anything around him, he feels like he's falling. He'll stop once he's bundled up."

He watched as she gathered the kimono up and slipped it over the baby's head. Miniature arms and hands were guided into sleeves. A moment later, she'd folded the baby snugly in a soft cotton blanket and drawn the top over the fuzz on his little head. Immediately, he quieted.

Cole was impressed. "For someone who's never had kids, you seem to know a lot about them."

Cole had already thought Lara looked rather pale. At his words, what little color she had seemed to drain below the collar of her white turtleneck. When he'd first seen her, he'd thought she might just be tired. Considering her almost detached manner, he no longer thought it was just fatigue. Something else was wrong.

She'd yet to look at him. Ever since he'd arrived, she'd avoided meeting his eyes. That made it as plain as the mud on his boots that there *was* something wrong. It also made it obvious that she didn't want him around.

That was too bad. He'd told Tom he would stay until he got home.

Sally took the baby over by the wood stove where it was warmer. Cole followed her and on his way he passed the closed door to Sally's room. He could hear Rosie and Sally talking, their conversation too muffled to be heard well, but they sounded busy. Maybe that was why Lara hadn't taken the baby in to his mother.

She cradled the baby close. Its tiny head was tucked under her chin and she swayed gently with it, the motion seeming automatic as she gently rubbed its back.

Cole had never been around babies and he found himself studying this one as if it were something decidedly alien. All he could see of it was the small face. It was kind of wrinkled and reddish and the eyes were puffy, but Lara held it as if it were the most precious thing in the world.

That was what touched him. Though he had to admit it was kind of neat to see what people looked like when they started out, what drew him to Lara was the way she soothed the newborn, cradled it as if to protect it from a hostile world. But it was the look on her face when he glanced from the baby that caught him like a blow to the gut.

Her eyes were closed, her lashes a dark, silky curve against her cheeks. From beneath those lashes, tears streamed silently down her face.

"Lara?"

At the sound of her name, her eyes opened. To his amazement, she smiled, a sad smile that made her look incredibly fragile.

Her voice was as soft as the baby's breath. "I'd give anything for one of these." She gave a quiet little laugh, trying to make light of her yearning. "Absolutely anything."

If the sight of her holding the baby touched him, the pain in her admission was more than he wanted to hear. It frightened him to feel what he did for her. It frightened him more that he'd gone so long without that feeling.

"You'll probably have all the babies you want someday."

"No." The word came with a quiet finality. "No, I won't." The smile faded, leaving only the sadness. "I can't have any more children."

"Never?" he asked, not knowing why it mattered.

She met his eyes then. She looked so vulnerable.

"Never," she repeated, waiting to see if he thought any less of her for her admission. She'd needed to make it clear that "never" was an absolute. She couldn't bear to hear any assurances about nebulous possibilities. There were no possibilities for her.

Assurances hadn't occurred to him. "What do you mean by any more?" He looked hesitant. "Did you have a child?"

She held the baby closer, willing strength into her voice. Dear God, wasn't it ever going to get easier? "A little boy. He'd be over a year old now."

Cole wanted to touch her, to draw her against him and absorb the hurt. He wanted to know, too, what had happened. But that could wait. Holding her would have to wait, too. If she'd even let him.

The front door slammed open, startling Lara so badly that she jumped.

Easy, honey, Cole silently soothed and squeezed her shoulder as Tom barreled into the room.

Tom, his face creased with worry, peeled off his yellow rubber jacket as he tracked a path of water to his bedroom. He barely glanced at Cole and Lara and with Lara turned as she was and Cole at her shoulder, he didn't see the baby.

"Is she all right?" he wanted to know and probably caught less than half of Cole's nod and none of what Cole said as he barged into the bedroom.

"Oh, my God," was Tom's only comment before Cole heard Rosie chuckle.

The next half hour was a little hectic. Once Tom realized he had another son, he came out to retrieve Daniel Cassidy from Lara. Rosie emerged next, looking very proud of herself, and then Sally wanted to see Lara, who'd headed for the kitchen to fix Tom something to eat. Everyone's mood was expansive—everyone's except Lara's. Her smile was there, gentle and quiet, but the look in her eyes was haunted.

Cole didn't trust her paleness, or believe for a minute that the smile on her lips was one of pleasure. He'd seen her before when she seemed to be going through the motions, recognized the protective numbness he'd once mistaken for indifference. He knew that what had her holding herself in so tightly was rooted in what she'd told him just before Tom had come in. It was hard for Cole to imagine the importance of not having children. Simply because it wasn't something he'd ever felt very strongly about. If anything, after the way his wife had used pregnancy to snare him, he'd done his best to prevent the possibility of his ever becoming a father.

He didn't have to understand it to see how much having a child meant to Lara. But because he was coming to recognize a little of himself in her, he knew she kept what hurt her the most buried the deepest—the pain she'd felt at the loss of her child.

He wished they could get out of there.

"Listen, Rosie," he said when it looked as if everything was calming down. "I'm going to take Lara home."

Rosie was just finishing the mug of coffee Lara had given her. Taking the last swallow, she glanced to where Lara stood at the sink finishing up the dishes. She hadn't missed the disquiet in Cole's eyes.

"Something wrong?" she asked, her voice low.

"I just think it's been a rough night for her. She looks tired."

"Been a rough night for everybody," Rosie muttered, curious about his concern but too tired herself to do much more than note it. She rolled her shoulders to ease the stiffness. "Lara had the easy part. All she had to do was explain the facts of life to the boys. But now that everything seems to be under control, we should probably all get out of here and leave the family to themselves." She handed Cole her mug. "I'll tell Sally we're leaving."

Cole took the mug to the sink. On his way there, he picked up Lara's jacket, along with his own. He'd have given a month's pay to have seen Lara telling Big Tom's boys about the birds and the bees. He'd have to remember to ask her about that later. Right now, he just wanted to get her out of here. She obviously hadn't said anything to Rosie about what she'd told him. Rosie might not be the most sympathetic woman in the world, but she wasn't insensitive. Had she known what Lara had been dealing with all evening, she wouldn't have been so quick to dismiss his concern. He didn't know what difference it would have made, but he'd wished he'd known sooner himself.

Lara didn't appear to have heard anything he and Rosie had said. Lost in thought, she was rubbing the bottom out of a saucepan when he set the mug down. He took the pan and dish towel out of her hands. "Come on. You're going home."

She looked puzzled, a clear indication that, mentally, she was a thousand light years away. "I need to finish drying the dishes."

"Leave them. I know from personal experience that they'll dry all by themselves. Rosie's in telling Tom and Sally we're going."

Moving behind her, he held her heavy jacket for her. Lara didn't let herself feel relief to be leaving. Not yet. She concentrated only on what she was doing—putting her arms into the sleeves and shrugging her jacket up over her shoulders.

She felt Cole's fingers at her nape as he lifted her hair from her neck and pulled it from beneath the collar. She'd been about to do that herself. She was also about to zip her jacket up when he turned her by the shoulders and did it himself.

"Do you have gloves or anything?"

She shook her head to indicate that she didn't and watched the shadowy line of his jaw flex as he pulled her collar up. Had she allowed herself to respond, she might have been amused by what he was doing. He looked very much like a protective parent, checking to be sure his offspring was properly bundled before facing the elements. It wasn't odd that he was doing something for her. It was the nature of what he was doing that struck her.

He was taking care of her.

A knot formed in her throat and she turned away. She wasn't sure she could handle much more tonight.

She felt even less stable ten minutes later. Rosie had talked all the way back to the boardwalk, which was fine with Lara because by listening to her she hadn't had to wonder what was going through Cole's mind. He hadn't touched her since he'd helped her put on her jacket. In fact, he had kept his hands in his pockets, his head ducked against the rain the whole way back. He had, however, kept glancing over at her as if to make sure she wasn't going to veer off into the woods or something.

They said good-night to Rosie at the bar's front door and moved down the darkened boardwalk to the store. Lara had the door open when she turned to thank Cole for the escort.

"I'm coming in," he told her. Before she could agree or protest, he nudged her inside and closed the door on the drizzle.

The only illumination came from the fluorescent tube in the refrigerator case on the opposite wall. That dim light seemed to magnify the shadows stretching down the aisles. Mostly it enhanced the shadows marking Cole's expression.

She didn't want him here. He was too close. Too accessible. "What do you want?"

"We'll talk about it inside."

"I don't feel like talking tonight, Cole."

"Then we don't have to talk. Just make me some coffee."

She knew she should ask him to leave. If for no other reason than because she wanted so desperately for him to stay. Lacking the energy to argue with him, much less with herself, she said nothing as she let them into her living area.

In her hurry to get to Sally's, she'd left on the lamp by the love seat. The room was bathed in pale light, but the air was cool. The fire had died down to a glowing pile of coals. As if on autopilot, she slowly unfastened the jacket Cole had zipped for her awhile ago and started toward the hearth. She'd get the fire going first.

"I'll put on the coffee in a minute," she said, when what she really wanted was to feel the strength of his arms; to know, if just for a while, that she wasn't as alone as she felt.

She shouldn't let herself think like that. It only made her feel worse.

The touch of Cole's hand to her shoulder stopped her just as she reached for a log.

"I'll do that."

"It's okay," she said, fearing what he'd see if she were to look at him. She needed to keep busy. As long as she was occupied she'd be fine. "I've almost got this fire-building thing nailed. It's pretty easy when the coals are this good."

"Lara."

"I don't even have to use kindling."

"Lara. Look at me."

She couldn't do that. It made no sense at all because she wasn't thinking about anything other than the stupid fire, but she was desperately afraid there were tears in her eyes.

"Look at me." He sounded remarkably patient. Mostly, he sounded determined.

Her hand stilled on the screen, then fell. With a hard blink, she straightened, took a deep breath and turned around.

Cole's eyes locked on hers. He'd suspected what he might see. He just hadn't realized how deeply he could be affected by someone else's struggle.

Chapter Ten

Lara felt as if Cole so much as touched her, she would shatter into a million tiny pieces. All she had left was the little self-control she could manage. If she let that go, she wouldn't have anything.

She handed him a log. In a ragged whisper, she said, "I need to put on the coffee," and slipped past him.

She wasn't in the kitchen thirty seconds when she dropped the metal lid of the coffeepot. The thing clattered over the floor and she snatched it up, anxious to still the nerve-jarring noise. Gripping it in her hand, she stood at the sink, trying to remember what she meant to do next; dump the old grounds, or rinse the pot.

All she could think of was her son.

She hadn't shuttered the window over the sink. Rain streaked down the outside in erratic paths. On the inside, with the night behind it, the glass caught her own reflection. She didn't notice. She didn't notice Cole's reflection, either, as he stood back. Watching. She saw nothing. She only remembered. Remembering is what she'd tried very hard not to do. Yet, the memories were there, so clear she could almost hear the tiny, feeble cry her son had made. He only made the sound once, the sound so weak it had barely been audible over the quiet hum of monitors and nurses' voices.

"I'd wanted to see him, but they took him away so fast."

Cole heard her, but he didn't move. He was reluctant to do anything that might make her close up on him. In some way he couldn't define, it was necessary for him to truly know this woman, to understand what kept her from him. That need felt as essential to him as his next breath.

His own voice was as hushed as hers. "Who took him, Lara?" he asked, wondering if she was talking about Steve.

She didn't question his presence.

"The nurses. The doctor." She shook her head as if trying to clear it. "I don't know exactly. Everything was so confusing. I didn't know that Steve...hadn't made it. They wouldn't tell me anything." Her shoulders rose, then lowered again as she released a shaky breath. "I just wanted to hold our baby. But they said he was too small."

Her thoughts were disjointed. At least they seemed so to Cole. He wasn't at all sure that he understood—until he saw her push back her bangs and he noticed the scar.

A sense of foreboding filled him. He'd seen her like this once before; the night she'd brought Bear to him. At the time, he'd thought she might be in shock. He realized now that, having hit the cub with her truck, she'd probably been remembering the accident that had taken her husband's life. As regrettable as that loss had been, Cole had the horrid feeling that the accident had taken much more.

With a kind of caution that wasn't at all familiar, he closed half of the space he'd allowed her. He stopped by the stove, close enough for him to see her profile and far enough not to pose a threat.

"We had so many plans, Cole. So many dreams. And suddenly they were all..." Her hand rose, then fell. In her quiet voice he heard the desolation. "They were all just...gone."

He knew nothing of dreams. "What kind of plans?"

"Just ordinary things," she said as if seeking some understanding of her own in the rain-streaked window. "That's what I've never figured out about any of this. We didn't want anything unusual or outrageous. We just wanted each other and a family. I keep wondering what I did to deserve having everything taken away. All I'd ever wanted was Steve and babies. Then one night, everything was taken away so fast that it still seems like some horrible nightmare. I keep thinking I'll wake up and everything will be as it was. That Steve will be there and we'll be painting the baby's room and I'll still be pregnant—"

Her voice caught.

For several seconds, she said nothing. Then, sounding very far away, she whispered, "We were going to teach him how to build sand castles."

He didn't want her to dwell on lost dreams. Or maybe he just didn't want to hear them. "Tell me what happened, Lara."

It was the flatness in his voice that drew her. That rock-solid steadiness that was as much insistence as concern.

"Tell me all of it. What happened that night? What happened that you lost your baby?"

The rain picked up. The sound of it filled the room. As she stood clutching the ache inside her, she truly didn't believe she could tell him. But the thoughts had been there all night and they were there now. In some ways it felt that by keeping them in, she didn't have to face them. Yet, by keeping them in, she'd never be free of them, either.

Cole was asking to share what hurt her. He would never think to tell her that because he wasn't that kind of man. But his presence was steadying; his caring real. Only because of that was she able to find the words.

They didn't come easily. It took her awhile to piece the fragments together. She'd been in and out of consciousness, so there were pieces forever missing, but she told him what she remembered. The impact of the crash had pushed the dashboard into her lap. She'd tried to push it away, to get to Steve because he was slumped over the wheel, but when she'd tried to move she must have blacked out. She remembered only pain. Pain in her leg where it had been broken, and a more ominous pain low in her abdomen.

Lara didn't tell Cole how frightened she'd been, or how she'd begged the nurses to let her see her husband. She told Cole only that they had tried to stop her contractions when they started, but the baby had been born anyway—three months too soon. Incongruously, she remembered how sympathetic the nurses were because she was so scared and how awkward it had been giving birth with her leg in a brace. She remembered her mother crying before they had taken her in and Steve's mother looking absolutely lost. But mostly she remembered wanting to see the baby.

He had been taken away so quickly that she'd caught only a glimpse of his tiny face. She had ached to hold her child; the child she and Steve had created. But the baby had weighed less than three pounds and the tubes and electrodes attached to him hadn't allowed her to do that. So Lara had sat in a wheelchair for the fifteen minutes each morning and evening her own doctors would allow and held her son's tiny hand through the portholes of the incubator.

She would have kept up that vigil forever if she'd had to. She only kept it for six days. On the seventh, she finally held the tiny child. *He's not going to make it,* she remembered someone saying. *Do you want to hold him while he's alive?*

Lara didn't recall what she'd said. She remembered only feeling the incredible lightness, little more than the weight of the blanket itself when the nurse put him in her arms. They'd taken away the tubes and the tape and she'd stroked her finger over his perfectly rounded little head and along his downy little cheek. His skin was so soft it felt like air, and he'd seemed to respond to her touch; to know that she was the one who'd held his little hand. He was so weak he could scarcely move, but he'd turned his head toward her and then he'd gone utterly still.

For a long time after Lara stopped talking, she stood staring at the scuff marks on her floor. She wasn't even sure what she'd last said to Cole when she heard him coming toward her.

His boots covered the scuffs, and she looked up.

Tears shimmered in her eyes. "It still hurts so much."

She wasn't given a choice. As Cole reached for her, it was no longer up to her to be stoic or strong or all the things she'd needed to be for so long.

"I imagine it does," she heard him say.

She'd known it would happen. But it didn't help that she'd been right. The instant he folded her into his arms, a sob broke loose. It was muffled by his sweater and she did her best to hold back the one building behind it. But when she felt his hand at the back of her head, the hiccuping sound escaped anyway.

She sank against him, needing very much what he was offering. She was tired of fighting it. Tired of dealing with it alone. So she gave in and let the tears flow. She didn't want to be brave like she'd had to be for her family. She didn't want to pretend that she had healed when she felt so raw inside. It hurt them to know that she hurt, so covering her pain had made it easier for them to be around her. There was no one here she had to protect. If anything, here in Cole's arms, she was the one being protected. For the moment, because that's all she could face, she lost herself in the feeling.

Cole knew the instant she caved in. Her slender shoulders sagged, and she turned her face into his sweater, weeping. Beneath his hands he felt the shudders shivering through her. He held her closer. She felt so fragile in his arms; her trembling like a small, frightened bird. He had no idea what to say to make her feel better. So, when a full minute passed and she still wept, he simply scooped her up in his arms and sat down with her on the love seat. He kept her in his lap, cradling her like a child and rocking her a little like he'd seen her do with Sally's baby. She curled up into him, almost as if by making herself small enough, she could disappear into his chest. He sat with her for a long time that way, watching the flames consume the log he'd shoved into the fire earlier and quietly stroking her hair.

It occurred to him as he sat there listening to the rain as she spent her tears that he was feeling a little guilty. He hated what she'd been through, but he very much liked comforting her. He liked being there for her. It wasn't right that he should feel good about something when she felt so miserable.

The moment he'd met her, he'd been struck with an inexplicable need to protect her. At the time, he'd had no idea that what he might need to protect her from the most was himself.

The end of a log broke off in a spray of sparks. Cole shifted his glance from the fireplace to the woman in his arms. He couldn't see her face, but that was okay. It was enough just to hold her.

She'd relaxed a little as her quiet sobbing gave way to long, ragged breaths. She wasn't curled against him now, so much as she was curled around him. Her head was on his shoulder, tucked just under his chin. She was angled sideways so that her shoulder fit under his arm and her knees were pulled toward his side. In between, her firm little hip nestled sweetly in his lap.

He realized that his hand had strayed off course from her back. He was now rubbing the back of her thigh. Over the past several minutes, there wasn't a nerve in his body that hadn't become achingly aware of how incredibly female she was. Pulling his hand away, he settled for touching her hair.

With his thumb and index finger, he drew out one of her long, spiraling curls and let it pop back into place. "How you doing down there?" he asked, ducking his head a little so he could see her face. It was still buried in his chest, her hand hiding most of it.

A shuddering sigh preceded a muffled, "Don't know."

"Sure you do. Tell me what you're thinking about." He pulled on the curl again, this time letting it wrap itself around his finger. "Tell me what you're thinking right now."

He felt the tension in her neck as she started to lift her head. Those taut muscles relaxed when she decided to stay right where she was.

"I was thinking about my mother."

"Your mother?"

The curls at the top of her head tickled his chin as she nodded. "When I was in the hospital, I'd sometimes wish she'd hold me like this. Pretty dumb thing for a grown woman to want, wasn't it?"

"Oh, I don't know. There've been times when I've wanted something like that myself."

Cole once couldn't have imagined himself ever saying such a thing to anyone. He didn't even question it now. Lara made it easy for him to admit things like that.

"There's something nice about being held," she said.

"There's something nice about holding."

She looked up at him then and gave him a shaky smile.

He smiled back, the movement a little rusty. "Your nose is red."

Her hand immediately covered it.

"Don't." Pulling her fingers away, he curled them in his and nudged her chin up. "It's kind of..."

"Don't you dare say cute."

"I wasn't going to. I was going to say colorful. Goes well with your shirt."

He obviously meant the red flannel. Lara swallowed. He was going to make her laugh and if she did that she'd start crying again.

"You might want to blow it, though." Leaning forward and to the side, his arm tightening around her shoulder to keep her from sliding, he pulled his handkerchief from his back pocket. "Your vowels are all sounding the same.

"Better," he said, when she had rather inelegantly done what he'd suggested. He reached out to push the hair back from her eyes.

"Thank you, Cole."

"It was only a handkerchief."

"That's not what I mean."

Damn it, Lara, he silently swore. Don't look so sad. "I know. But there's nothing for you to thank me for."

She opened her mouth to protest his conclusion. The touch of his hands stopped her. He cradled her face between his palms. "I wanted to be here."

"You've done so much for me already."

"Don't worry about it. Nobody's keeping score."

He hadn't planned on kissing her. It just sort of happened. His lips feathered over hers, a tender kiss of compassion. He heard her breath catch and touched his lips to hers again to still the tiny sound. She didn't move; she didn't even seem to breathe as he tipped her face to kiss her temple, the base of the scar above her eyebrow, her tearstained cheek. He'd never kissed a woman that way before, as if she were someone very precious. As if she mattered.

He wondered if she even realized what she was teaching him.

That thought flitted vaguely through his consciousness. But his thoughts were turning in other directions. When his lips brushed hers a third time, they held a gentle promise. A promise that he would do no more than she would allow, and absolutely anything that she would.

Oh, Cole, Lara sighed to herself. Please don't do this to me. Please don't make me want you.

It was too late for such a plea. She already wanted him; wanted what he could make her feel in his arms. And when she leaned toward him, she knew she would take whatever he would give her.

"That's it, honey," he breathed into her mouth. "Kiss me back."

She did. A little desperately. Tongues touched and tangled, bodies shifted to get closer. She hated feeling so greedy, but she very much needed to lose herself in him. It didn't make a lot of sense, but then so little had lately.

She skimmed her hands through his hair, loving the silky feel of it. His whiskers felt rough against the tender skin of her face, his tongue incredibly smooth. She welcomed the sensations, even if she did wince a little when his jaw grazed hers.

He must have heard her quiet intake of breath. His fingertips touched her cheek. "I hurt you."

"No," she said, catching his hand. "You didn't."

"You're going to have a whisker burn."

She didn't care. All she cared about was that he was kissing her again. Gently at first, until gentle no longer satisfied. Then with a hunger that would have been a little frightening had she not felt it herself.

"I want to touch you, Lara."

"You are touching me."

"Without this." His hands slid down her sides until he reached her waist. Tugging at her shirt, he freed the hem of the turtleneck from her jeans and pushed his hands back under the cotton fabric.

"This way," he said, his voice ragged when his hands came in contact with bare flesh.

A shiver shimmered through her.

The heat of his palms caused echoes of that tremor everywhere he touched. Along her sides, over her back, around to cup her breasts.

His mouth came down on hers again.

The sensations were exquisite. Nearly drowning in them, Lara gave herself up to the feelings. Everywhere Cole touched, she burned. And where she burned, she felt alive.

She felt like heaven in his hands. She was all soft curves and silky flesh and he was as hard as a post. He'd touched her breast and her nipple had bloomed in his palm. He wanted to taste that pebbled bud, to sit her astride him and bring her up to his mouth. He wanted a hell of a lot more than that. But what he wanted and what he would do were entirely different things. He'd probably hurt all the way home, but he couldn't take her now. Not tonight.

The word noble came to mind, and he almost laughed at the absurdity of it. While there probably was a certain honorability to not taking advantage of a distraught woman, Cole couldn't claim it. His intentions were purely selfish. There was tomorrow to consider and the day after that. He and Lara had something going between them. He didn't doubt that. He also didn't want to analyze it too closely. All he cared about was that if matters kept progressing as they were at the moment, she might very well hate herself, and him, in the morning. If and when the time came that they wound up in bed together—and he'd already ruled out the love seat as holding any potential—she would be there because she wanted him. Not because she was grieving. And not because he'd caught her in a weak moment.

He pulled his hands out from under her shirts, stroking them down her back to soothe her. To soothe himself. "I thought you were going to make coffee." He didn't need coffee. He needed to dive in the inlet. The water ought to be around thirty-five degrees by now.

He felt her go still—and made her look at him because he needed to make her understand. There were tears in her eyes. New ones.

"Oh, Lara."

"I can't seem to stop," she said, trying to smile, unable to manage it. "I'm sorry."

"Did what I was doing make you cry?"

She couldn't tell him that it had, because he might not understand that she'd wanted his kisses anyway. The holding, the touching, brought out feelings that were good and whole and human and those were things she'd wondered if she would ever feel again.

If he would just keep holding her. "Do you really want coffee?"

He looked uneasy, but his answer was honest. "No. I just thought we'd better slow down."

"Can we just sit here for a while, then?"

With the pad of his thumb, he caught the tear that slipped down her cheek.

"Sure," he said, and pressed her head back to his shoulder.

She didn't want him to leave. He didn't want to go, either. So he held her, soothing her, until, not long before the fire died out, she drifted off.

Pulling the heavy quilt off the back of the love seat, he covered them both. Somehow he, too, fell asleep.

He had cramps in his legs. His arm was asleep. But it was the crash that woke him. "What in the hell...?"

Cole came to with a start, only to immediately freeze. Lara's head came up, almost nailing him in the chin. He grabbed her by the shoulders to keep her still. It wasn't his chin he was worried about. It was what her squirming around in his lap was doing to what strained against his zipper.

He growled down into her hair. "Do me a favor, would you?"

"What?" she asked, sounding a little flustered at having wakened in his arms.

"Either stay still, or stand up. Don't scoot around in my lap. You want up?"

"Please."

Spanning her waist, he lifted her easily. Her feet had just hit the floor when a sound like a battering ram hitting a wall came from behind him. It was the same sound he'd heard thirty seconds ago.

"What is that?"

Lara shoved her hair out of her eyes, certain she looked perfectly horrid. "Bear wants breakfast."

"What's he doing to make that noise?"

Cole was standing now, stretching his long limbs and making the small room seem even smaller. The shadow of his beard was darker than usual, making him appear rough and hard. It was difficult to believe that a man so rugged could be as gentle as he'd been with her last night. He had held her, caressed her. He had filled her with longing.

And he was watching her now as if he were remembering all that, too.

"Why don't you go see?" she suggested, and had the feeling she actually blushed when his glance had traveled the length of her body.

While Cole wandered out to the service porch to find Bear bumping one of the logs in his cage against the floor, Lara hurried into the bathroom to wash her face. Her eyes weren't as puffy as they could have been, but her lips felt tender and her cheeks were whisker-burned. She didn't know if she should be encouraged or distressed about how shamelessly she'd responded to Cole. She knew only that she was feeling awfully awkward about having poured her heart out to him last night.

She needed coffee.

Remembering that Cole had wanted some even last night, she was prepared to offer it to him when she went to the service porch. He wasn't there, though. Neither was Bear. From the doorway, she saw that they were both out back.

She pushed the screen open.

Cole caught the movement at the door. Lara still had on the red flannel shirt and white turtleneck she'd fallen asleep in last night, but she'd tied her tousled curls back with a length of ribbon.

"Coffee?" she called, her voice as soft as the morning mist.

He'd have loved some. "No time. I've got to get going in a minute."

He did have to leave. Now that the weather had cleared he could fly into Sitka for a meeting today. Not his favorite form of activity. And he'd yet to finish the report he was to turn in. He'd get on it as soon as he took Bear back inside.

Cole watched the inquisitive animal root around in the bushes. The little guy seemed to be healing nicely. As pleased as he was about that, he was now apprehensive, too. He had the feeling that Lara was more attached to Bear than she was prepared to admit. Letting it go wasn't going to be easy for her, especially after everything he'd learned last night.

The animal couldn't stay with her, though. For its sake as well as the town's. Its nature wouldn't allow it. And neither could he.

He decided not to say anything about it right now. He also didn't say anything about how she was spoiling the animal when Lara met them at the door with a bottle and a towel. Mist and damp grass did tend to make Bear pungent, so he said nothing as she dried off the baby grizzly before feeding him.

"Listen, Lara," he began, the aroma of perking coffee testing his willpower. "I'm going to be gone for a couple of days. Three at the most. If you need anything, you can reach me at the Chatham Area office in Sitka."

Bear was sitting in Lara's lap, his head tipped back as he rapidly drained the bottle. Cole looked from the cub to the quiet attention in Lara's eyes. She probably wondered why he was telling her this. He was kind of wondering that himself.

"Like with the roof or anything," he added, compelled to supply a reason. Ron would certainly be more accessible, but he didn't mention that. "Everything should be fine with it until I get back. I'll pick up the braces we've been needing while I'm gone. Once I have those, we should have the job finished within a week."

"Are you going for the cooperative projects meeting you told me about?"

He said he was and pushed away from where he'd leaned against the counter.

Lara wasn't sure what she'd expected Cole to do. She knew she did not expect him to tip her chin up and kiss her senseless. One moment he was standing in front of her, the next he'd bent and his mouth had taken possession of hers. The kiss was a slow, sweet seduction of the senses. Unhurried, thorough and unashamedly bold. Only his lips and tongue touched her and the tips of his fingers where the lightest of touches kept her head angled the way he wanted.

Not until Bear's bottle hit the floor did he raise his head. When he did, he smiled.

She looked beautiful when she was well kissed. She also looked as if she wanted more.

"Hold that thought," he told her.

Picking up Bear's bottle, he handed it to her and let himself out the back door.

Chapter Eleven

A vague restlessness haunted Lara, settling in within moments of Cole's departure, escalating insidiously as the day progressed. It wasn't long until the lethargy she'd once awakened with each morning became little more than a memory. An unsettled energy replaced it, making it difficult for her to focus. She'd start to read and find she couldn't concentrate. She'd start to work on the new curtains she was making for her bedroom and find she couldn't sit still. Mental tasks were constantly interrupted by undetermined longings, and pacing took up the time she'd once spent huddled on the love seat staring at the fire.

She decided she had cabin fever. So the next morning, taking Bear with her, she spent the day outside. She did the same the next day after that and managed to completely restock her woodpile. She cut an entire cord of wood with her new chain saw and when she finished stacking it, she attacked the winter-killed weeds growing along the back of her house. In the process, she uncovered an old cold frame.

She wasn't sure what the long, boxlike shape was at first—until she remembered the cold frame her maternal grandmother had in Michigan. The snow would have barely melted when Grandma Kate would put out her tomato starts. Now, having cleared away the overgrowth, Lara stood with her hands on her hips and thought she might try to grow tomatoes, too. Or lettuce. Or whatever it was that people planted in the protective boxes.

She'd never grown a vegetable in her life. She didn't even know if she wanted to take up gardening. She knew only that she was desperate to keep herself occupied. She wondered if she was supposed to stock seeds.

When was he going to get back?

With a groan, Lara pulled off her work gloves and slapped them against her thigh to get rid of the bits of dried leaves sticking to them. It didn't matter what else she thought about. The question of when Cole would return nagged with the consistency of a toothache and, being unable to shake it, she felt just as touchy as if she'd had one. She wasn't sure why she felt so anxious to see him again. Or if her anxiety was because she feared seeing him. She knew only that since he'd left, she'd slowly been going stir-crazy.

A light breeze was blowing as she squinted toward a yellow Cessna cutting a descending arc overhead. Planes had been coming and going all day. The mail plane had come and gone, as well as the one that flew the fish out from the ice house. An air taxi had delivered Tom, on his way back from the hospital in Sitka, awhile ago. He'd stopped by to tell Lara that Sally and the baby, both doing just fine, would be back Saturday. Just after that, another shuttle had

landed. With all the arrivals, it was entirely possible that
Cole was already back.

Because she couldn't stand the restlessness anymore, she
decided to walk past his cabin and see. She needed some
more exercise anyway.

Since she'd been outside most of the day, she had a note
stuck on the door of the store saying she was out back. Several of the locals had found her out there and depending on
what they needed, Lara had either accompanied them in or
continued working and let them help themselves. She knew
all the locals by now and the honor system the Stanleys had
used served her well, too. A customer simply took what he
or she needed, wrote down what it was on the pad Lara left
on the counter and she'd add it to their bill if they didn't
leave the money.

After checking on Bear in his "den"—she'd had him
outside with her most of the day—she left by way of the
front door, taking the note off and replacing it with the
closed sign. It was nearing six o'clock in the evening, yet the
sun was still high in the sky as she followed the boardwalk
past Rosie's to the dirt path paralleling the marina.

Her pace slowed to watch Ron. The sun shone down on
his balding head as he tied off the plane that had just come
in. She didn't recognize the two men who stepped from the
pontoons to the wooden pier, though. Photographers from
the looks of the equipment piled up on the dock.

Lara moved on, past the long piers jutting out into the
water and listened to the squawk of circling gulls as she cut
toward the trees. If Cole wasn't back, Ron would find out
where the men were going and how long they planned on
being there. It was information Cole would ask of anyone
setting out into the wilderness, so he'd know if and when he
had to go looking for the lost or injured. She glanced back

over her shoulder to see Ron point in the direction of the Forest Service cabin—and took that to mean they would find the ranger there.

Anxiety met anticipation. It was also possible, she reminded herself, that Ron was only showing the men how to get to the logging road. The cabin sat less than twenty feet off it. She could see it now. It could very well be that Cole was *not* there.

What are you *doing?* she asked herself, not sure whether to feel disgust or bewilderment. This was the kind of thing she'd done when she'd first had a crush on Steve in high school—pretended to have a purpose as she'd walked past his locker in the hopes that he'd be there. What if Cole was home? What was she going to do? To say?

She stopped twenty feet from the brown cabin with its beige trim and USFS shield to the left of the front door. The window beside the door was open. Through it she could see the Chilkat blanket hanging on the wall. And Cole's dark head as he rose from his desk.

He was home.

Another thought trampled that one.

If he'd wanted to see her, he'd have stopped by the store.

Feeling utterly foolish, she turned on her heel. Three steps later, her heart gave a painful thump.

"Lara?"

The air smelled of pine and the sea. She scarcely noticed as she drew a deep breath, prayed for the quick return of her sanity, and turned around again. Cole stood on the porch, his large frame filling the doorway.

He was in uniform; obviously, a concession to the formality of the meetings he'd attended. The impeccably pressed tan shirt with brown tabs on the shoulders and trim brown slacks looked good on him. Better than good. It made him look quite . . . physical.

"What are you doing?"

It didn't help that she'd asked herself that same question only moments ago. She still didn't have an answer. "I wasn't sure if you were back."

Even as she spoke, he descended the steps. His loose, easy gait concealed a wealth of leashed power; his expression, as usual, revealed little. He stopped an arm's length away. "I got in about an hour ago. Is something wrong? When I saw you from the window, I thought you were coming in."

"I was. But I changed my mind. Nothing's wrong," she went on, because he was frowning at her. Her voice grew quieter. "I just wanted to see if you were home."

"Why?"

Until that moment she hadn't been sure herself. Now, she knew exactly why she'd nearly paced up the walls since he'd left. I missed you, she silently admitted.

"I missed you," she said to him.

He didn't say a thing. For about three interminable seconds, he looked at her with his cool gray eyes reflecting nothing but her own image. Then something shifted in those indiscernible depths; a quick intensity that barely registered before voices behind her drew his attention.

"You the ranger?" one of the men she'd seen at the marina called.

Lara took a step back. It was impossible to know what Cole thought of her little admission. It might be best if she never did. Had she been thinking at all she'd have realized that the new arrivals would be coming here and that Cole would have to talk to them. Her timing was truly terrible.

Cole's hand on her arm canceled her next step. "Don't go," he said, ordered actually, and turned back to the two newcomers.

A brief exchange of pleasantries and Cole requested that the men go inside and show him on his map where they were headed. Telling him they'd be happy to, they left their gear at the base of the half-dozen steps and were already halfway in when Cole turned to Lara.

He looked as if he were about to say something else, then decided against it. Taking her by the hand, he led her up the steps behind them. Just inside the door, he muttered, "Give me a minute," and joined the men at the large map on the end wall.

It took less than five minutes to get the information he needed. The two men, amateur wildlife photographers, had planned their trip well and easily indicated the areas they were interested in on the map. Cole entered their names and the date they planned to return in a log, and after asking a couple of friendly questions about what kind of protection and supplies they had, wished them luck and a safe trip. They were anxious to be off. It was after suppertime, but they still had a good four hours of daylight left to reach their camp. Alaskan days were definitely longer this time of year than those down south.

Cole watched the men gather their gear from the foot of the steps and head down the narrow logging road. He wanted to make sure they hadn't forgotten something that might make them come back. Not wanting an interruption, he waited until they reached the bend and disappeared from sight before heading inside.

Lara was standing on the opposite side of the room when he finally closed the door. Her head was turned from him as she studied the map on the wall. She had her hair tied back with a blue ribbon and the blue-and-gold football jersey she wore with her jeans nearly swallowed her.

"So you're a San Diego fan," he said, referring to the jersey.

She glanced down at the big number 16 on the front of it. "My sister is," she said with a little shrug. "She gave me this for my birthday."

"That the same sister who gave you the hand weights when she started aerobics so she could borrow them?"

Lara smiled. Cole had come across the tiny barbells when they'd been cleaning out the upstairs. He'd never seen weights that small. Or that pink.

Her reply was philosophical. "It's the thought that counts."

Cole knew that he had no reason to feel what he did. It was petty, really. But he was kind of relieved that the jersey hadn't belonged to Steve.

Seeing her smile falter as he crossed the room, he had to admit that relief was actually the least of what he felt. He was edgy and uncertain, curious and frustrated. About the only thing he didn't feel was the ease he pretended as he leaned against the edge of the desk to face her.

He had to have this woman. It was as simple and as complicated as that. He'd thought of little else for days.

The room had become very quiet, the only sound the sigh of breeze-caressed cedars drifting through the window. Lara looked a little wary with the silence.

He let it stretch out for a few more moments, then crossed his arms to keep from reaching for her. He wanted her to make the first move. "Why did you want to see me, Lara?"

There was no demand in the question, but he thought she might have heard some. Her eyes widened in confusion. Folding her arms over the bottom of the numbers on her shirt, she focused on his pocket, clearly at a loss as to how to answer.

He knew he'd get nowhere if he let her crawl inside herself.

Snagging her by the hips, he pulled her forward. She was between his knees now, at eye level with him, but her eyes were still averted. He tipped her chin toward him. He needed that answer.

"I'm lousy at guessing games. I want to know why you're here."

Her voice was little more than a whisper. "I told you why."

"To tell me you missed me?"

She gave a small nod, looking reluctant now to admit even that much.

Cole felt his heart give a funny little flip. No one had ever missed him before.

He was almost afraid to touch her. With the back of his hand, he caressed her cheek. "I don't want you to say things like that unless you mean them. You be honest with me, and I'll be honest with you. Fair?"

Again, she nodded.

"Then why else are you here?"

"I'm not sure I understand what you mean. I had no other reason. I just wanted to see you."

His hand brushed her jaw. "You didn't want me to hold you?"

The breath she drew caught where his knuckles grazed her throat.

He touched one finger to her bottom lip. "Or kiss you?"

His glance moved from her mouth to where his hand slipped over the slope of her breast. His eyes lingered there for a moment before meeting hers. "If you didn't, then you didn't miss me half as much as I missed you."

The expression in her eyes nearly stole his breath. "You missed me?"

Ached for her was probably more like it. "Would you like me to show you how much?"

Her hand flattened on his bicep. Through his shirt, he felt her faint trembling. "Please."

He pulled her to him. How could a man feel good just looking at a woman? "Ah, Lara," he breathed and covered her mouth with his.

He could be tender. She knew because he had been tender with her before. But he could also demand. That was what he did now. He demanded that she not hold back, that she answer his need with her own. So she did and when he took her deeper, he made sure she was with him by pulling her arms around his neck and encouraging her to lean into him. And when he was no longer satisfied with touching her back, her breasts, he let her know he wanted more.

His hand molded her bottom, pulling her against him as his tongue sought hers. She felt his fingers flex against her soft flesh, and the hardness of him pressed against her stomach. He braced his legs wider to draw her even more intimately against him. What she felt in his body was raw desire. What she tasted in the bruising pressure of his kiss was hunger—the kind of elemental hunger that tore at the restraints of civility and demanded fulfillment.

His heart was beating like a trip-hammer when he eased her grip on his neck. She felt it when her hand slid over his chest.

A thrilling gleam turned his eyes nearly black. "We have a choice," she heard him say. Still holding her hips to him, he rested his forehead on hers. "You can walk out that door right now. Or I'm taking you down the hall."

Her tongue unconsciously touched her top lip, feeling the moisture he'd left there. "What's down the hall?"

The feral gleam darkened. "I'm not kidding, Lara."

Several strands of gray nestled at his temple. Raising her hand, she tested their texture against the surprising softness of his dark hair. "Neither am I," she said, and watched, fascinated, as his jaw tightened. He was such a beautiful man, she thought, needing to touch him as he touched her. She laid her palm against his face, feeling the shadowy roughness of his skin.

He turned his mouth into her palm. A moment later, he drew her arm back around his neck and her feet left the ground.

It didn't occur to Lara to question what she was doing as he lifted her in his arms. What lay beyond this moment didn't matter to her. All that mattered was that she do as Cole had asked, that she be honest with him, and with herself. She honestly needed Cole. Now. This moment. She had since she'd met him.

A suitcase lay open on the bed. Cole set her on her feet, keeping one hand on her waist as he flipped the top over and pushed it out of the way. A moment later, he'd sat down on the edge and brought her down with him. Her feet had barely left the rug when he pulled the ribbon from her hair and turned her onto her back.

He was astride her, rearing back to unbutton his shirt and work at the buckle of his belt.

"Let me," she said, needing to touch him.

He didn't try to mask his pleasure at her request. He moved his hands away. "Go ahead."

Her mouth felt dry and her fingers shook, but she got the buttons undone and the shirt off. The white undershirt he wore beneath it was gone in seconds. In one swift motion, he'd pulled it off and sent it to the floor. A beautiful impatience touched his expression as the rest of their clothing joined the heap.

She reached out to touch him, feeling almost shy. He was all hard muscles and sinew. So beautiful. So strong. He made her feel very soft and very feminine next to his coarser, rougher body and when she met his eyes, he made her feel just a little bit powerful, too. Almost as powerful as he looked when he pressed her back into the blankets and covered her body with his.

She wanted him, but more importantly, she needed to give him a part of herself for the escape he offered. He'd become a part of her, anyway. The part that was whole. What she wanted—needed—was to absorb his strength, because without him she didn't feel very strong at all. When she was with him, she didn't have to be the person she'd become. She could be who she once was: a woman who could give as well as take. A woman who could feel.

Cole felt the muscles in his stomach tense as her fingers skimmed over him. He knew she wanted him and that made him impatient. Yet, he needed to hold back. He didn't want to rush her, to frighten her. And he was afraid he might, given the immediate demands of his body. What she was doing didn't help his control at all. But he'd have cut out his own tongue before he'd ask her to stop. The softness of her bare hands on his skin was almost more than he could bear. No woman had ever inflamed him as this woman could. No woman had ever touched him as she did. Not just physically, though his body screamed for release as her fingers drew little lines of fire along his back and over his buttocks. She touched him inside, made him reach beyond himself. That was why he wanted to wait, to make it good for her.

His hands caressed her, soothed her. He wanted her to ache everywhere he touched, so that when he filled her he could drive away all thought of anything but him. His palm flattened over her breast, kneading as his tongue searched the smooth, secret surfaces of her mouth. He carried his touch to her stomach and along the insides of her thighs. For these isolated minutes he would be all she would think about, all she would need.

Sweet heaven, he was going to explode.

"Cole?"

His name was a plea. The same plea that was in her eyes.

"What, honey?" He shifted over her, stroking the damp hair from her forehead. "Tell me what you want."

"You." Her restless hands pressed along his sides. "Just you."

A growl of satisfaction flowed from deep in his chest when he felt her arch against him. She raised up to kiss him. He loved it when she kissed him, when she took any initiative at all. There was a seductive innocence about her that drove him crazy. It wasn't that she didn't know what to do. She was just so sweet about it. So tender.

He felt her arch again and slid his hand beneath her hip. Her legs wrapped around his rougher ones, the sensation of smoothness and supple strength compounding when he felt her heat. He thrust forward, dying by slow degrees as he lost out to the primitive urge to bury himself deeper. He'd tried not to move for a moment, to hold back and make it last, but she countered the effort. With her name on his lips he thought of nothing but driving them toward release.

* * *

Lara didn't realize she'd fallen asleep until she opened her eyes to the shadows. Even then, she wasn't fully awake and her eyes closed to block out the shifting shapes before consciousness fully returned. Flirting at the edges of her dream was the comfort of being wrapped in Cole's arms, his body fitted to her back. She had a fleeting impression of being protected, of feeling safe, before she stretched out and drifted off again.

The next time she awoke, the pale light of morning filled the room—and she smelled coffee.

She stretched, the movement long and languid, then froze when the soreness of certain muscles registered. Consciousness returned with almost physical force. It was morning. She was in Cole's bed.

Not quite sure why she felt such trepidation, her feet hit the floor as she whipped back the covers. She pulled them right back up.

"Looking for this?"

Cole stood in the doorway wearing a pair of jeans he hadn't bothered to snap and nothing else. He rubbed his beautifully muscled chest and held up her jersey by one finger.

"What time is it?"

"Almost six."

She couldn't believe she'd slept so soundly. She always woke up at night. Tossed and turned for hours, it seemed. Yet last night, when she'd needed to wake up so she could go home, she'd slept right through.

There was the intimacy about spending the night in his bed that she hadn't been prepared for. It reminded her too much of what had once been—of waking to the smell of coffee and the sounds of someone she cared about puttering in the next room. That wasn't her reality anymore.

Cole apparently sensed her consternation. Sitting down on the edge of the bed, he cupped his fingers around the back of her neck. Kneading the muscles knotted there, he drew her toward him. "Morning," he mumbled against her lips.

"Morning," she returned and felt his mouth curve in a little half smile.

He knew what got to her. Last night he'd discovered that she liked slow, deep kisses. The kind that tortured and teased. And by the time he pulled back, he'd made sure he'd resurrected several very explicit memories of what they'd done last night. Her breathing had altered substantially.

Satisfied that she'd forgotten whatever misgivings she'd suffered, he held up the jersey. He didn't want her wrestling with regrets. "The only reason I'm giving you this is that I have to leave here in about fifteen minutes. If I didn't have to meet Jack, believe me, I'd be in there with you." His mouth brushed hers again, warm, thrilling. "You make me hungry, Lara."

He wasn't talking about breakfast. As his lips worked their way from her neck to her breast, he made it very clear what kind of hunger he meant. The same kind he awakened in her.

He pushed her back to the pillow, his hand straying beneath the sheets. "I thought you had to be somewhere," she said, gasping at what he did to her.

"I do." Turning sideways, he moved his hand from her stomach to his zipper. "But I think I'm going to be late." His hand stilled. "Am I?"

Reality could wait. "I think so."

* * *

Cole was late. By about an hour. When he arrived at Lara's place that evening, he told her that it hadn't mattered anyway and wondered if her smile didn't seem awfully reserved when she told him she was glad she hadn't caused him any problems. She seemed quiet, as if there was something she wanted to say, but didn't know if she should. Or maybe, her reserve was just because there were others around.

Cole had picked up the metal braces for her roof and discussing how much he and Ron would get done that evening seemed to be the main topic of conversation. With Ron there, nothing more personal could be said. Or done.

Cole felt a certain, unfamiliar frustration at that, but the proximity of the others was why he didn't think anything of it when she chose to stay inside instead of being out back with him and Ron while they worked. Rosie was there, too, leaning over her rail to supervise while the two men raised the rafters.

Had there been any other able-bodied men around, Cole knew Rosie would have volunteered their services. But old Walt was her only customer at the moment. Summer was a time for work, so winter and the rainy season were when she was busiest. Just the opposite of everyone else.

Cole noticed that Lara had been busy, too. He'd seen the wood she'd cut and the cold frame that had once been hidden. In the back of his mind had played the thought that she might not actually stay. If she was laying in that much wood and thinking about putting in a garden, it seemed she still planned to remain. Of course, it was way too soon to know if she'd last—no matter that she was the most determined woman he'd ever met. A lot remained to be done before the snows came and she'd yet to go through a winter.

As he and Ron raised the first of the new trusses and nailed them into place, Cole realized that the idea of spending that long isolation with her held a definite appeal. What he found extraordinary, was that he found as much appeal in the idea of helping her prepare for those dark, snowy months they could spend together. The weather stripping needed to be replaced on her windows and the siding, like most every other building in town, could use a coat of paint. She'd need a lot more wood, and they could build a larger storage room so she'd have more space for the winter's supply of merchandise. If she wanted to do any canning, as some of the other women did with what they grew, she'd need shelves on the service porch . . .

Cole stopped short and swore to himself. Reaching for the rope to pull up a beam, he wondered what the hell he was doing thinking of such things. He was hardly in the habit of planning his own life, much less someone else's. He needed his own space. He always had. Lara seemed to prefer hers. And that was how he wanted it. Now and forever more. Amen.

As if to prove the point to himself, when he and Ron finished for the night, he didn't take the time to see why it was that Lara hadn't even come out to check on their progress as she usually did. Leaving the tools on the service porch, he made a mental note to have Lara take Bear off the bottle when he saw the animal curled up under the branches in his cage, stuck his head inside the door, yelled "See you later, Lara," and went home.

Ten minutes later, he was sitting on his desk staring at one of the stylized ravens on the Chilkat blanket when he heard the soft knock at his door. He knew it was Lara before he even opened it.

She stood with her fingers clasped tightly in front of her, much as she might in front of a classroom. "I've been thinking about it a lot today and I need you to know that nothing has to change because of what happened last night." And this morning, he thought she might add, but didn't. "I'm not going to make any demands on you. Or expect you to make any commitments or anything. I just need you to know that, in case that's why you didn't come in tonight. I don't want to regret what we did, but I will if it means we can't be friends."

He found the little speech monumentally irritating. "Friends?"

She nodded, looking far less sure of herself than she probably realized.

"I don't want to be 'friends,' Lara. I don't sleep with my 'friends.' Look," he muttered, exasperated as much with himself as with her. "Do we have to have this discussion in the doorway?"

She stepped inside. Only then did he notice that her eyes held the haunting vulnerability that left her so exposed. She was doing her best to keep him from seeing that, though. That irritated him, too. He wanted her to be honest with him, as she had been when she'd cried in his arms and when they'd made love. It seemed that when he held her, it was easier for her to open up, as if she found reassurance in the physical contact.

That was why, as he stood with his eyes locked on hers, he reached over and unfolded her hands. "Come here," he whispered and saw her eyes close in relief as he pulled her into his arms.

He felt a shuddering breath tremble through her body and held her just a little tighter. She felt good there, in his arms.

He'd been crazy to leave tonight without letting himself do this.

"I'd like to tell you that nothing's changed," he said, because that was what she'd seemed most worried about. "But I can't do that. I know what your skin feels like next to mine, how you taste. I can't look at you without thinking about that, without remembering. Something has changed, Lara. But we don't have to let it scare us." He slipped his hand under her chin, tipping her face toward him. "Right?"

She gave a little nod, apparently accepting that they were two adults who might have been just a little overwhelmed at the sudden shift in their relationship.

"Good." His fingers eased into her hair. "Now, how about a kiss good-night?"

Lara knew the instant his lips touched hers that he wanted more than a kiss. She wanted more, too, because he managed to banish all her insecurities with his possessive caresses. He was drawing her out, releasing her somehow. And when they came together this time, their touches were bolder, designed to learn and discover. To express. There were words that she couldn't say, thoughts she couldn't share. To say the words would mean admitting feelings that were only now solidifying, and what she felt was too fragile to survive such a test. Too filled with need to risk. So for now they would hold and savor and learn. And maybe, someday, they'd learn to trust themselves as much as they implicitly trusted each other. Lara had always trusted Cole. She'd never thought otherwise. It was the someday she couldn't get past. She'd become so accustomed to focusing on the immediate, that she'd forgotten how to think beyond tomorrow.

It was the need to avoid considering what lay beyond tomorrow that, long after midnight, drew Lara from Cole's arms. Leaning on her elbow, she studied his face. In the shadows, he looked peaceful, content. A smile touched her mouth. She'd never seen him that way before. "I have to go."

"No, you don't."

Her tone was light as she told him that she did, too, but she meant what she said. She didn't want to wake up in his bed again. It was too much like playing house and she couldn't handle that little game. "You know how Bear is if he has to wait for his breakfast."

"He should wait for it anyway."

It wasn't what he said, so much as how he said it that canceled Lara's departure. Aside from a quick and certain distance in Cole's voice, he'd sounded reluctant.

"Why?"

"Because he needs to be weaned." The sheets rustled as he sat up. The timing of this subject was really lousy. "You're going to have to let him go pretty soon. You know that don't you?"

Her silence wasn't unexpected.

He wished he could have seen her face. It was hidden in shadow. "Are you all right with that?"

"Yes," she said, and slid her bare leg from under the blanket.

His hand snagged her wrist. "Don't go."

"I have to."

"Why? You stayed last night."

She knew that. And she shouldn't have. "I really have to go, Cole. Please."

Without another word, Cole pulled back his hand.

He remained where he was, propped up against the headboard and watched the moonlight gleaming on her skin as she turned her back to him and picked up her shirt. He'd seen and touched and kissed every inch of her body, yet she was turning her back to him to dress.

"I'll see you tomorrow," she said, and bent to kiss him before she left.

There had been a time when he would have welcomed the emotional distance she was so quick to put between them. A purely physical relationship with no demands and no promises was exactly what he'd have once wanted, especially since the physical part was providing some incredible sex. It wasn't just that she was so responsive. There was more to it than that. When she lay beneath him, they were doing more than satisfying urges. They were sharing. Giving and taking and making something beautiful out of what they couldn't seem to express any other way—until it was over and she closed herself up again. She'd done it this morning. She'd done it just now.

Maybe, he thought as he heard the door close with a soft click, he should be protecting himself, too.

Chapter Twelve

The face of Mist changed almost overnight. Though Gus's fishing operation was the only one based there, dozens of commercial fishing boats used the ice house during the summer months. Within days of Cole's return, Bud's summer crew arrived en masse and the fish-packing operation turned full swing. The men and women hired to work there stayed in the big dorms behind the huge building and labored nearly around the clock to keep up with the hauls. Except for those brief stops to unload their catch, the fishermen were always at sea. The loggers were always gone, too. When summer came, Jack took full advantage of the good weather and his men rarely emerged from the woods.

To Lara, the community suddenly seemed deserted of locals. In addition to the summer employees at the ice house, the warmer weather brought campers and sportsmen anxious to experience the magnificent wilderness. A small but steady stream of them funnelled through the marina, arriving either by boat or by plane, and the inlet saw more boat traffic now than it had in months. The big luxury liners that cruised the inside passage, carrying their passengers past ancient glaciers to the towns of Juneau, Haines and Skagway, never came into Mist's inlet. But the "blue canoe," the ferry Lara had arrived on nearly two months ago, arrived twice a week now instead of only once. Summer was busy and bustling, and Lara loved it. Not quite as much as she had the quieter months, which surprised her a little, but the contrast was nice. She'd have liked it even more had Cole been around.

She'd only seen him twice since the night she'd left his bed; the day after when he'd come by to pick up some groceries and three days ago when he'd had a few hours to spare and he and Ron finally finished her roof. The week in between he'd spent in the woods with a resource management team and checking on the campgrounds. He'd almost kissed her right in front of Ron when she'd offered to type up the report he'd been grumbling about, so pleased was he at the thought of not having to do it himself.

When he had kissed her, much later that night, she'd nearly cried from the sweetness of it. The time they spent together was becoming unbearably precious to her. But she was afraid to want anything more than what they had. So she didn't think about tomorrows. They inevitably arrived, anyway.

One of the tomorrows she hadn't wanted to consider arrived on a Wednesday. The time had come to say goodbye to Bear.

It had been over three weeks since Bear had last had a bottle. Even while he'd been on it, Lara had supplemented his feedings with a disgusting combination of fish parts and something Cole said she didn't want identified. Now, the precocious little guy was teaching himself how to catch his own fish. He did best with spawned-out salmon, since they didn't put up a fight, but he was getting better at snagging the faster ones. Cole had assured her that between the forest's abundance of berries and plants and what the streams provided, Bear wasn't going to starve.

Lara stood by the rushing stream, mindless of the hair the breeze blew from her ribbon, her thoughts on the man beside her and her glance fixed on Bear. The animal was balanced on the rocks in the stream, swatting at the fish struggling against the current.

Lara felt a little like that struggling fish, battling to get an inch ahead. That was about how much progress she'd made in her attempt to figure out why Cole was acting so strangely. He'd been preoccupied ever since he'd picked her up a couple of hours ago. It wasn't his silence that bothered her, so much as the way he kept his distance in a physical sense. He was being very careful not to touch her.

She hated how insecure that detachment made her feel. Especially since she would very much have liked the comfort of his arm around her. She didn't really want to let Bear go. "You said a female usually watches over her cubs for a couple of years?"

He apparently knew what she was thinking.

"Orphaned cubs do survive, Lara. They've been doing it for centuries."

She was sure they had. She just hadn't known any of those cubs personally.

"He's perfectly healthy now," she heard him add, his deep voice muted by the rushing stream. "The longer you keep him, the harder it will be for him to adapt."

Lara lifted her chin, acknowledging that he was, of course, right. Bear was a wild animal. Not a pet. As Cole had pointed out, Bear had started bonding to her and that wasn't good. Another problem was that, while Bear clearly trusted her, he wasn't so accepting of others. It was easy enough to see that he was growing, and it wouldn't be long before childlike playfulness would give way to more adult behaviors. Bear belonged in the wild. So she wouldn't think of the nights he'd spent curled up behind her knees under the covers. Or the comfort she'd found holding his soft little body. He wasn't so soft anymore anyway. And, having doubled his weight, he couldn't be cuddled quite so easily.

"His only alternative is a cage."

Her quick, "No," left no doubt how she felt about that option. "Caging something meant to be free bothers me more than leaving him on his own. He might have a better chance of survival protected in a cage with humans looking after him. But he'd be miserable. He wouldn't really be living and I want that freedom for him."

At the conviction in her statement, Cole turned to study her delicate profile. The woman was a walking contradiction. It's too bad you don't want that for yourself, he thought, and wondered if she had any idea what kind of a cage she was building for herself. That he was standing by while she drove those nails into place bothered him. A lot.

"I guess I am going to miss him." Looking a bit like a parent putting a child on a bus for camp, she smiled uneasily. "I just hope he doesn't have any trouble adapting to the real world."

"I don't think you need to worry. Animals are probably more adaptable than some people when it comes to facing reality."

At his cryptic remark, Lara frowned. She watched as he turned away, her eyes sweeping over the tension in his powerful frame.

He bent to pick up a cedar cone, seeming intent on the concentric shape. "What time is the christening party at Tom and Sally's?"

"Eight, I think. I don't know for sure."

His jaw bunched as he turned. "Aren't you going?"

"I don't think so." Gulls were scavenging Bear's leftovers on the opposite bank. Pretending great interest in them, she kept her attention there. "Are you?"

"It would be kind of rude not to."

With a suddenness that startled her, he drew his arm back and sent the cone sailing. It disappeared with a faint skittering sound as it hit a long-needled branch.

Cole turned back around. He didn't look angry or irritated, which surprised her a little because he'd certainly sounded that way. What she saw in his eyes was a puzzling sadness.

"Answer something honestly for me, will you? I mean really think about this before you say anything." He took a step closer, his eyes searching her face. "Why don't you want to go to Sally's tonight?"

She didn't know what to make of the question. "I just have other things to do. That's all."

He looked very much as if he'd expected such an answer. "Then tell me this. Have you held the baby since she's been back?"

Confusion altered her expression. "I don't understand what that—"

"Just answer me. Please."

"No," she admitted, remembering how she'd told Sally she thought she might be coming down with a cold when she'd offered her the baby. "I haven't."

Without bothering to explain that odd line of questioning, Cole abruptly changed the subject. Or he seemed to, anyway.

"I was out at the logging camp the other day," he said as if she had made the strange mental leap with him. "Jack said Carolyn has enrolled their oldest boy in a boarding school in Anchorage. The Reiners are thinking about sending their oldest now, too."

He waited to see if she cared to comment. When she just stood there looking a little bewildered at his choice of topics, his eyes narrowed as if he were trying to comprehend something himself. "Did you ever reconsider taking on the teaching job?"

A knot of dread formed in the pit of Lara's stomach. Cole's voice was remarkably void of challenge. Yet the questions he asked, irrelevant as they seemed, pricked her defenses. "No, I didn't. Even if I'd wanted to, I wouldn't have had the time."

The excuse rang hollow. "I thought you said you didn't want to teach because you couldn't do a good job of it anymore."

There was still no challenge in his manner. No accusation. Lara would have felt better had there been. The need to defend herself was strong, but against what, she wasn't sure. "That is what I said. And I meant it. But as busy as I've been—"

"Winters aren't busy at all, Lara. That's when school would be in session. In the middle of winter here, you'll have maybe six hours of daylight and that leaves a lot of dark. What are you going to be doing then?"

Her hand fluttered in a gesture of futility. He looked very dangerous, suddenly, watching her as if he'd caught her in his sights. "I don't know. I haven't thought that far ahead."

"Then what about us?"

The heaviness centered in Lara's chest suddenly made it difficult to breathe. "What do you mean?"

The agitation that had been missing in his manner now became evident. Not in the level of his voice, which remained chillingly calm, but in his eyes. "Tell me what you want from me."

"I want just what we have," she said, afraid to ask for more.

"Except for some great sex, I'm not sure just what it is that we do have, Lara."

He'd needed to shake a reaction out of her, to get her to step out of that protective shell she was closing up in. He wanted the woman beneath all the control. His eyes narrowed on her pale features. "Is that what I am for you? Stud service?"

He got his reaction. Shock registered. She was too much of a lady to slap his face, but he considered that the thought could have crossed her mind. He might even have deserved it, but he was too frustrated to care.

Her voice was tight with hurt and disbelief. "Is that what you think of me? That I would use...? I *care* about you."

"That must be why you leave my bed after we make love."

Until he'd bitten out the sarcastic words, Cole hadn't realized how much her doing that had bothered him. Until now, he hadn't realized a lot of things.

Needing time, needing distance, he muttered, "I'll see you at the truck," and turned away.

His long strides were angry as he moved toward the meadow beyond the stream. The logging road ended a mile beyond that lovely, open space. That was where they'd left his pickup.

Lara watched him go, and felt the quiet desperation that comes when something essential slips from a person's grasp. Compounding that fearful ache was the knowledge that she had no choice now but to say goodbye to her furry little friend.

When she turned back, Bear had already wandered off.

The ride back into Mist was painfully silent. Hugging the door, Lara tried not to worry about Bear, or the brooding man beside her. Focusing on the never-ending forest, she tried to call up the numbness that had once protected her so well. There was no protection now. She hurt as badly as she ever had.

Or so she thought until Cole parked the pickup at the end of the boardwalk. The hard edge in his expression told her matters were about to get worse.

His hand clenched on the wheel. Turning to her, he questioned just how much he should mention of what had been eating at him for the past twenty minutes. He knew he couldn't leave matters as they were.

He decided to go for broke.

"When you first came here, you said you needed a change. I don't think that's the whole story, Lara. I don't think you came here to build a new life. I think you came here to hide from the old one."

"That's not true!"

He could have predicted her reaction. "No? Just think about it for a minute. You refuse to take risks, to really involve yourself. You're always holding something back. You do it with everybody.''

He felt himself falter, not sure how to continue.

"Take Sally's baby," he said, thinking that as good an example as any. "You won't even let yourself hold him again because you're afraid you'll start missing what you can't have. I saw how hard it was for you that night, and I understand all about wanting to protect yourself, but ignoring that baby isn't going to change the fact that you can't have one of your own. And the teaching position," he pointed out, now that he had a handle on it. "I think you're afraid to take that on because teaching was part of who you once were. You're so busy thinking about what you've lost and what your future *won't* hold that you can't see what's right in front of you anymore."

He hated what she was doing to herself. He hated what she was doing to him. If she'd just said she was going to Sally's, he'd have known she was trying and he probably wouldn't have said another word. He'd have waited to see if time was what she needed. He had the feeling now, that the more time she had, the more securely she'd lock herself away.

"You're needed here," he went on, hoping he sounded calmer than he felt. "The children need you. I need you. And just in case you've ever wondered about it, I don't care that you can't have children. That doesn't matter to me. What matters to me is you. I never thought I'd feel about a woman the way I feel about you, but I need more than you're giving. I want to wake up next to you in the morning. To sit with you in front of the fire at night and not have to worry about getting up if I fall asleep and going home. I want you across from me at my breakfast table."

He dragged his fingers through his hair, wishing she'd say something even as he hoped she wouldn't interrupt.

"We're good together, Lara," he told her as his hand fell. "At least we are when you're not so busy protecting yourself. I'll admit I'm not exactly lily white on that issue, but I've been trying and the closer I want to get the further you back way. I know you had a good marriage. I had a lousy one. But I think I'd be more willing than you would to give it another shot and frankly it would make a hell of a lot more sense to me if it was the other way around. I'm not Steve. I never can be. He's gone. And it's probably time you stopped punishing yourself for the fact that you survived."

The color had long since drained from Lara's face. Her eyes looked huge as she stared at him. Cole couldn't believe he'd laid himself open like that, but there wasn't a thing he'd said that he was willing to reconsider. He'd laid it all on the line. The ball was, so to speak, in her court.

"You're wrong," she whispered, her mind grappling with the enormity of all he'd said. "You don't understand any of it."

"Then make me understand."

"I can't."

"What you mean is you won't try."

The seconds ticked by as he waited for her to prove him wrong. Not knowing how to answer him, not knowing if she could, she reached for the door handle. The moment she did, he turned away and jammed the transmission into gear. She was out of the truck in seconds. Before she'd taken a half dozen steps, he'd pulled away with a spray of dirt and gravel.

"Is everything all right?" a familiar voice asked from just ahead of her.

Sally stood in the middle of the boardwalk. She had the baby in a blue canvas tummy-carrier and a thick sheaf of papers in one hand. Another of her father-in-law's boats had apparently come in for the christening party—the whole crew had been invited—and she was on her way home with its manifests.

Lara's first inclination was to say that everything was fine. But any idiot could see that it wasn't and Sally didn't deserve the insult. "We just took the cub back to the woods," she said, hoping it would sound as if she were upset only about that. "How's the baby?"

If there was anything that could sidetrack Sally, it was little Daniel and his progress. He was, according to his mother, just wonderful. Lara smiled at that and, swallowing the instinct to pull back, reached out to stroke the powder-soft cheek. If Sally saw the wistful longing in Lara's face, she was astute enough to let it pass without comment. She did want to know, however, what time Lara was coming to the party.

Because she refused to put any credence into Cole's accusations, Lara told her she'd stop by around eight—which she did. She left exactly an hour later, when she saw Cole walking up to Sally and Tom's house from his cabin. They passed each other on the path, but since several men were sitting on the porch—two of them offering Cole a beer even before he reached them—they said nothing to each other. Though Cole clearly hadn't expected to see her there, he'd apparently said all he'd had to say.

Lara tried not to think about that as, several hours later, unable to sleep, she paced a path between her kitchen and the fireplace.

Cole was wrong. She *had* come here to start over, to build a new life. And that was what she'd done. She'd even convinced her parents of that to the point where they'd booked a cruise up the inside passage next summer so they could come visit. She had new friends and a new means to support herself and what difference did it make that she hadn't decided what she was going to do next winter? She and Steve had once had everything planned right down to the timing of when they'd retire, and those plans hadn't materialized so why should it matter that she didn't have dreams anymore?

But it did matter. Because without dreams a person simply existed. Like an animal in a cage, she thought, and remembered what Cole had said about animals adapting to reality better than some humans. He wasn't right, was he? she asked, hugging her arms around herself. Was she hiding? Was she blaming herself?

She missed Bear. Had he still been here, she'd probably be pouring her heart out to him now. The poor little guy had certainly suffered through her sleepless nights before. Worried about him because he was still so little, she took another lap across the room.

The route took her past the windows. She'd closed the curtains when she'd gone to bed, so she'd at least have the illusion of night. Deciding it didn't matter that it was only four in the morning, she pulled the curtains back so the room wouldn't feel so gloomy.

It was raining. Lara thought nothing of that, but as the pale gray light filled the room, she caught a flurry of movement in the tall grass growing up to the trees. She looked closer through the soft mist wondering if it was a deer or a moose. Whatever it was, was brown. And small.

"Bear?"

The animal's head came up when he heard her on the porch. He started moving toward her, then stopped and his head went down.

Lara felt her heart catch. Something wasn't right.

Gathering her robe against the rain and the chill and wearing only her fuzzy slippers on her feet, Lara hurried down the steps. Bear looked up again, seeming quite sure of his welcome, and waited for her to drop to her knees in front of him before returning his attention to his back paw.

"What's the matter, fella?" she heard herself ask and gingerly reached out to see.

The pad of his back paw was swollen.

Brown eyes blinked back at blue ones. "What did you do to yourself?" she muttered, hugging him a little tighter than she should have when she picked him up and trudged back inside.

The problem was a thorn. And she couldn't get it out. Every time she tried, Bear would growl. By the time six o'clock rolled around, she was tempted to ask Rosie to help her. But for whatever reason, Rosie was not Bear's favorite person, and as cranky as Bear was getting, Lara didn't think seeking her assistance would be wise.

She needed Cole.

There was a certain inevitability to that conclusion.

It wasn't raining nearly as hard as it had been the first time she'd appeared on Cole's porch. But just like that first time, when the door opened, her first impression of him was that the man was definitely intimidating. Then, as now, his solid frame filled the doorway, dwarfing her. His face was as immobile as granite. The first time his gray eyes had held curiosity. Now, the expression there was as guarded as her own.

With her and Bear warily watching him, she wondered if he, too, was remembering the first time they'd met. If the way the muscle in his jaw jerked was any indication, he obviously didn't find the memory pleasant.

"I'm sorry to bother you so early," she said, truly wishing she didn't have to subject herself to his cool silence. "But Bear needs you."

His glance moved to where she had Bear balanced on her hip. Resignation marked his tone. "I was afraid he might come back." He motioned them inside. "What's wrong?"

She told him about the thorn and about how she'd tried to get it out herself. He seemed to be only half listening to her as he carefully picked up the little animal's back paw. Bear immediately pulled his paw back, protecting it.

With a muttered, "Hang on a minute," Cole left her standing by the desk. She watched him until he turned into the bathroom, not at all sure how a man could look so appealing with the tails of his flannel shirt hanging out of his jeans, then looked at the mess on his desk. From the looks of the wadded papers covering the surface and the surrounding floor, he was apparently working on another report. A manual typewriter, the same one she'd used to type his last report for him, sat in the middle of the little paper balls. Obviously the task wasn't going well.

He came back down the short hall carrying a pair of tweezers and a tube of ointment.

"You look tired," she said, her voice hushed.

"I didn't sleep much."

She hadn't slept at all.

"Hold him up here."

Lara did as he asked, holding Bear so Cole could get to the cub's back paw without the animal pulling it back again.

"It's really in there," she heard Cole mutter, and he tried for a better angle with more light.

It was difficult being so close, especially when it seemed to Lara that Cole was merely tolerating her presence while he worked on Bear. His concentration on his task was complete, his sole focus the hapless little animal. To keep the ache in her heart from getting worse, she decided to focus only on Bear.

"You said you thought he might come back?"

"What I said, was that I was afraid he would," came his cryptic clarification.

Had it not been for how ominous the words had sounded, she'd have dropped the matter. "Why did you put it like that?"

"Because his coming back isn't good for his health. Grizzlies that keep wandering into settlements usually wind up getting shot sooner or later." His eyes narrowed as he finally saw the end of the thorn and tried to grasp it with the tweezers. "I'll have to take him farther out."

"What if he comes back again?"

"Just hope that he doesn't."

Lara knew what Cole wasn't saying. Bear wasn't a problem now, but when he got bigger he could be. And bears that became pests would be destroyed if transporting them out of the area didn't work.

"What about Asa?"

At the hopeful note in her voice, Cole glanced up—and cursed when he realized he'd lost sight of the thorn in the cub's thick pad again.

Since he hadn't been swearing at her, Lara ignored the expletive. "You said he'd nursed an eagle once. And you mentioned that he used to keep a wolf for a pet. Maybe he'd want Bear."

Her stomach twisted as Cole's glance scanned her face. She had no idea what he was thinking until he told her he liked the idea. It would be good for Asa to have something to care about and it wasn't impossible that Bear would take to the old man. Stranger things had happened. And Asa's place was miles from anything remotely resembling civilization.

A moment later he'd turned back to his task.

Lara watched him run his thumb over Bear's paw again, his large hands so capable, so gentle. He was such a good man, though she knew he'd only frown at her if she told him that.

There were so many things she needed to tell him. And one, most important of all.

Last night, while she'd paced the polish off of her floor, she'd reached some rather uneasy conclusions. Though she had vehemently denied Cole's accusation about coming to Mist to hide, she had finally admitted that he may have had a better perspective of the matter than she had. One could see the forest a little better when not standing directly in front of a tree.

When she'd left California, she hadn't been able to imagine that her life would ever be complete again. Her relationship with her husband had been so good, as close to perfect as she could have wanted. They had planned everything together since college and their plans had fallen into place over the years just as they had expected. Then the plans, the family, the life they'd lived, everything they'd worked for and dreamed of, had all ended in the blink of an eye. She'd been utterly lost after that—until Cole had made her look at herself, at what she had, at who she was.

What she'd seen when she finally opened her eyes was that she and Cole shared something very special. Something just as compelling for her as what she'd shared with Steve, but in a completely different way. There was a solidity to Cole that Steve had lacked; a rocklike strength she hadn't realized she'd craved. But then, she hadn't needed strength before. From herself, or from anyone else. Her life was different now. She was different. And that meant her needs were different, too.

Cole had known exactly what she'd needed. He'd made her feel whole again and that process had began the day they'd met. Because of little things he'd done, she'd found that no matter how much she wanted it, she couldn't hide from caring. From living. And she couldn't keep herself from loving him any more than she could prevent drawing her next breath.

So she said the words, her quiet, "I love you," hushed, but as strong as the feeling itself.

She knew he heard her. Though his head was bent and he was concentrating on the cub, for the briefest moment, he went stock-still.

"I just needed you to know that," she said. "In case it mattered."

The thorn was out. Laying the tweezers and the inch-long barb on the desk, Cole picked up the tube of ointment.

Lara's heart felt as if it were beating in her throat when she saw that his hand wasn't quite steady.

"It matters." He met her eyes then. "I love you, too."

The overhead light caught the strands of silver at his temple when he turned his attention back to the cub's paw. Bear was getting restless. With the quick swipe of his finger, he smeared the ointment on the sore spot, then wiped his finger off on his jeans.

A moment later, he'd caught her chin, tipping her face back to him. "I've never said those words to another living soul, Lara. Not even Gina. But I need more than words. I'm sorry I came down on you like I did yesterday, but I told you then what I want." He'd spent half the night wishing he'd kept his mouth shut, the other half wishing he could make her see how good they were together. He never had been any good at expressing how he felt. Hell, he thought, he wasn't sure he'd ever even tried before. "I still want to marry you."

"You do?"

He frowned at her confusion. "That's what I asked yesterday."

"You didn't ask me to marry you." She would have recalled a proposal. That was not the sort of thing a woman overlooked.

"I did, too. Lara," he said, seeing that this had the potential for getting them nowhere, "I'm sure I mentioned marriage."

Bear squirmed in her arms, tired of being held. Lara ignored him. "You did mention it. But all you said was that you were more willing to try it than I was."

"Well?"

"Well, what?" she asked, almost afraid to breathe.

Exasperation met the quick intensity darkening his eyes. His hand snuck around her neck, drawing her forward. "Just how specific do I have to get?"

"A little more than you have been, I guess."

Even over the musky smell of Bear's damp fur, Cole caught the clean scent of Lara's soap. The breath he drew carried that essence to every cell of his body, making it a part of him—just as the woman herself had become a part of him.

Taking Bear from her, he set the animal on the floor. A quiet anxiety filled him as he touched her cheek. "I'll make this as specific as I can, then. Will you marry me?"

"Oh, Cole," she whispered, loving him. The thought of *not* marrying him was the more frightening possibility.

"Be more specific."

"Yes."

A sense of coming home filled Lara as he pulled her to him. Hunger, desire, need, were all contained in her kiss. But more than that was the hope she'd lived without for so long. Later she would tell him of another decision she'd made, to teach the children of Mist. She was sure he'd like that. Parts of it anyway. If she was going to be typing his reports, the least he could do was help her correct papers during those long winter nights.

Lara was suddenly looking forward to winter. And to spring and next fall. Yesterday was over. Living for the present wasn't necessary anymore. And because Cole had made her see, she now knew that the future could hold all manner of dreams.

* * * * *

Silhouette Special Edition

COMING NEXT MONTH

#697 NAVY BABY—Debbie Macomber
Hard-living sailor Riley never thought he'd settle down with a preacher's daughter. But he couldn't steer clear of Hannah and their navy baby, though it meant riding out the storm of his life.

#698 SLOW LARKIN'S REVENGE—Christine Rimmer
Local bad boy Winslow Larkin, was back in town . . . and out to seduce the one woman who'd almost tamed his heart years ago. But loving Violet Windemere proved much sweeter than revenge!

#699 TOP OF THE MOUNTAIN—Mary Curtis
The memory of Lili Jamison's high school passion lived on in her love child. Reuniting with Brad Hollingsworth rekindled the actual fire . . . and the guilt of her eleven-year-old secret.

#700 ROMANCING RACHEL—Natalie Bishop
Rachel Stone had her hands full raising her stepson on her own. When strong, stern Tyrrell Rafferty III entered the picture, he completed the family portrait . . . better than she knew!

#701 THE MAN SHE MARRIED—Tracy Sinclair
Teenager Dorian Merrill had fled her hometown and broken marriage to find her fortune. Now the *woman* was back, a penthouse success— but lured to the other side of town by the man she married.

#702 CHILD OF THE STORM—Diana Whitney
When Megan O'Connor lost her beloved sister, she vowed not to lose her seven-year-old nephew. Not even to his father, who resurfaced to claim him . . . and Megan's heart.

AVAILABLE THIS MONTH:

#691 OBSESSION
Lisa Jackson

#692 FAMILY FRIENDLY
Jo Ann Algermissen

#693 THE HEALING TOUCH
Christine Flynn

#694 A REAL CHARMER
Jennifer Mikels

#695 ANNIE IN THE MORNING
Curtiss Ann Matlock

#696 LONGER THAN . . .
Erica Spindler

Bestselling author **NORA ROBERTS** captures all the romance, adventure, passion and excitement of Silhouette in a special miniseries.

THE CALHOUN WOMEN

Four charming, beautiful and fiercely independent sisters set out on a search for a missing family heirloom—an emerald necklace—and each finds something even more precious... passionate romance.

Look for THE CALHOUN WOMEN miniseries starting in June.

COURTING CATHERINE
in Silhouette Romance #801 (June/$2.50)

A MAN FOR AMANDA
in Silhouette Desire #649 (July/$2.75)

FOR THE LOVE OF LILAH
in Silhouette Special Edition #685 (August/$3.25)

SUZANNA'S SURRENDER
in Silhouette Intimate Moments #397 (September/$3.29)

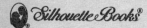